"Nice patch there, Major."

The words fell from her soft lips with a light Southern drawl, whiskey warm and just as potent.

Gray glanced down at his sleeve. *Anything. Anywhere. Anytime.*

The insinuation crackled along the humidity- and memory-laden air. Gray let his gaze slide back to her. "Wanna test the motto out?"

Lori laughed, husky, if a bit tight. "Same old Gray." Her chin tipped. "Been there. Done that. Lost the T-shirt."

His arms folded over his chest. "You left it at my place."

She laughed again, the great husky laugh of hers that rolled right into him. Just as fast, she had his hormones bombarding the defenses of his reason. Of course sex, great sex, incredible anything, anywhere, anytime sex, had never been their problem. But the minute they'd set their feet on the floor…

Dear Reader,

It's always cause for celebration when Sharon Sala writes a new book, so prepare to cheer for *The Way to Yesterday*. How many times have you wished for a chance to go back in time and get a second chance at something? Heroine Mary O'Rourke gets that chance, and you'll find yourself caught up in her story as she tries to make things right with the only man she'll ever love.

ROMANCING THE CROWN continues with Lyn Stone's *A Royal Murder*. The suspense—and passion—never flag in this exciting continuity series. Catherine Mann has only just begun her Intimate Moments career, but already she's created a page-turning military miniseries in WINGMEN WARRIORS. *Grayson's Surrender* is the first of three "don't miss" books. Look for the next, *Taking Cover,* in November.

The rest of the month unites two talented veterans—Beverly Bird, with *All the Way,* and Shelley Cooper, with *Laura and the Lawman*—with exciting newcomer Cindy Dees, who debuts with *Behind Enemy Lines*. Enjoy them all—and join us again next month, when we once again bring you an irresistible mix of excitement and romance in six new titles by the best authors in the business.

Leslie J. Wainger
Executive Senior Editor

Please address questions and book requests to:
Silhouette Reader Service
U.S.: 3010 Walden Ave., P.O. Box 1325, Buffalo, NY 14269
Canadian: P.O. Box 609, Fort Erie, Ont. L2A 5X3

Grayson's Surrender

CATHERINE
MANN

Silhouette®

INTIMATE MOMENTS™

Published by Silhouette Books
America's Publisher of Contemporary Romance

If you purchased this book without a cover you should be aware that this book is stolen property. It was reported as "unsold and destroyed" to the publisher, and neither the author nor the publisher has received any payment for this "stripped book."

SILHOUETTE BOOKS

ISBN 0-373-27245-6

GRAYSON'S SURRENDER

Copyright © 2002 by Catherine Mann

All rights reserved. Except for use in any review, the reproduction or utilization of this work in whole or in part in any form by any electronic, mechanical or other means, now known or hereafter invented, including xerography, photocopying and recording, or in any information storage or retrieval system, is forbidden without the written permission of the editorial office, Silhouette Books, 300 East 42nd Street, New York, NY 10017 U.S.A.

All characters in this book have no existence outside the imagination of the author and have no relation whatsoever to anyone bearing the same name or names. They are not even distantly inspired by any individual known or unknown to the author, and all incidents are pure invention.

This edition published by arrangement with Harlequin Books S.A.

® and TM are trademarks of Harlequin Books S.A., used under license. Trademarks indicated with ® are registered in the United States Patent and Trademark Office, the Canadian Trade Marks Office and in other countries.

Visit Silhouette at www.eHarlequin.com

Printed in U.S.A.

Books by Catherine Mann

Silhouette Intimate Moments

Wedding at White Sands #1158
**Grayson's Surrender* #1175

*Wingmen Warriors

CATHERINE MANN

began her career writing romance at twelve and recently uncovered that first effort while cleaning out her grandmother's garage. After working for a small-town newspaper, teaching at the university level and serving as a theater school director, she has returned to her original dream of writing romance. Now an award-winning author, Catherine is especially pleased to add a nomination for the prestigious Maggie Award to her contest credits. Following her air force aviator husband around the United States with four children and a beagle in tow gives Catherine a wealth of experiences from which to draw her plots. Catherine invites you to learn more about her work by visiting her Web site: http://catherinemann.com.

To my parents and my husband's parents.
Thank you for giving us both such a beautiful,
enduring example of happily-ever-after.

Acknowledgments:

Some books require an extra dose of research. This happened to be one of them. Many hands touched this story of my heart, and I thank every one of them for their generous and speedy help. Any inaccuracies are my own.

Joanne Rock, Deb Hale and Sue Morgan—endless thanks for the critiquing, mentoring and friendship!

Thanks also to:
Major Paul "Snoopy" Shultz,
Major James "Reggae" Regenor and, of course,
Major Robert "Wanna" Mann for sharing
their air force expertise.
Karen Tucker, RN, and Virginia Taylor, RN, RM,
for their medical insights.
Celeste Davis from My Child and Me for responding
to my numerous e-mails about sign language.
Sandra F. Woods, MEd, EdS (LPC, NACC)—
a.k.a. MOM—for the details on South Carolina's
DSS foster parenting and adoption procedures.
And my dear sisters, Julie Morrison and Beth Reaves,
for reminiscing with me about our C of C days
in historic Charleston.

Chapter 1

Anything Anywhere Anytime.

Major Grayson Clark whipped the crooked Velcro-backed patch free from his flight suit and slapped it on straight. The stitched squadron motto sure as hell applied today.

Muggy steam radiated from the cement, penetrating Gray's flight boots. Anticipation fired through him hotter than the stored heat from the tarmac.

Prepped and ready on the flight line, the Charleston-based C-17 glistened in the late-day sun. The mammoth aircraft frequently flew heavy-duty cargo around the world, and Gray had logged on for a number of missions. But carting a planeload of orphans out of their war-torn country across the Atlantic would be a first for him.

An incredible first. Talk about job satisfaction. And the military was his life.

"You ready to fly?"

The gravelly voice yanked Gray back to the flight line. He glanced at the seasoned loadmaster waiting beside him.

''Hell yeah, Tag. You know me, always ready to log more hours.''

''Shouldn't be much longer, Cutter.''

Hearing Tag use the call sign ''Cutter'' reminded Gray of his primary function on this mission. He was a doctor—a ''cutter''—first, flyer second. As a flight surgeon, he would assess the children before they left their Eastern European village for the States. He would only strap into the cockpit as a relief pilot.

Gray shrugged, as if that might loosen the T-shirt long since plastered to his body by sweat and restlessness. ''Five seconds. Five hours. Won't matter if we melt out here first waiting for the civilian relief team.''

''Bet that's them now.'' Tag nodded toward the Air Force bus lumbering across the ramp like a blue whale. ''Head on in while I load 'em up. The auxiliary power unit should be cranking the air by now.''

''In a minute.'' Gray hooked his hands on his hips. He shifted his weight from foot to foot, itchy to leave, ready to roll. But the aircraft commander and copilot wouldn't need him while they ran the checklists.

Gray peered through his aviator sunglasses at the setting sun, already soaring toward the Carolina sky in spirit. Doctor. Pilot. He'd met his every goal head-on and won.

Except one.

''Damn.'' Gray spit out the curse while sweat trickled down his spine. He'd gone five days without thinking about *her*. He had thought this would be it, a Lori-thought-free week.

His first in a year.

Now all the talk of the children's relief organization accompanying them had nudged her right back into his mind. Lori lived for that kind of thing, making contributions, volunteering on her days off to countless NGOs—nongovernmental organizations. Always trying to make a home for everyone, even a wanderer like him.

The bus rumbled to a stop. Gray shook off the past as easily as Lori had walked out of his life. Or so he tried to tell himself. He didn't need memories screwing with his concentration before a flight.

Gray backed a step. "I think I'll head in after all, Tag."

"Good idea. I'll just get our guests settled." The loadmaster paused as if waiting to make sure Gray would leave. Tag waved him away. "See you when we're airborne."

When Gray backed another step, the loadmaster sighed and scratched his salt-and-pepper buzz cut, then along his neck. Could even an experienced crew dog like Tag be uptight about the flight? Should be a simple in and out operation. Renegade guerrilla fighting in Sentavo's civil war had left the area. But it would sweep through again, soon, thus the orphanage's SOS plea that an NGO negotiate military evacuation for the children.

Men and women stood inside the bus, ten scheduled from the NGO, as well as additional military medical personnel and extra loadmasters. Gray pivoted on his boot heel just as a pair of long, khaki-encased feminine legs descended the bus steps. Great legs, like—

What a sap. Must be because he had Lori on the brain. No need to imagine those legs belonged to—

Her.

Lori Rutledge stepped from the bus. The woman who'd dumped him flat a year ago, which made her the smartest damn woman alive in his opinion.

The late-day sun caressed her face. She flipped her bourbon-brown braid over her shoulder. Khakis and a crisp white cotton shirt bearing her NGO's logo nipped and tucked along gentle curves, smoothly, without a wrinkle or mar of perspiration. Lori rarely lost her cool. Except for those moments when her incredible legs had been wrapped around his waist and—

Don't go there, pal.

She lowered a foot to the next step and paused. Her eyes

met his across the runway, then widened below the slash of her brows. The piercing brown of her eyes darkened in contrast with her ivory skin.

Air abandoned his lungs like an aircraft in a rapid decompression. He couldn't have looked away if a bomb detonated in the middle of the runway.

He shouldn't be surprised. He'd long ago given up trying to figure out what about this woman drew him. Chemistry was a damned unpredictable beast.

She certainly wasn't his type. Lori had one of those wholesome, pretty faces, minimal makeup, not like the Officer's Club babes who waited around for a chance at a flyboy. His mother had called Lori a classic beauty, like one of the princesses from his little sister's old storybooks.

Except princesses weren't usually drawn with full, pouty lips that made a man think thoughts far from princely.

His mouth quirked into a grin as it had when he'd seen those same lips for the first time over a year ago.

Lori blinked. Her face went blank, and she cleared the bus steps.

What did he expect? That she would blush flame red and run screaming back onto the bus? That wasn't Lori's style, and quite frankly there hadn't been enough between them to warrant such a strong reaction. They were just old lovers, after all. No big deal. Right?

You probably shouldn't go there, either, pal.

Lori glided toward him, an official-looking knapsack slung over her shoulder. Stopping in front of Gray, she smiled, a perfect smile if it weren't for the tiny strain lines in the corners of her eyes. No awkward looks or shuffling, just practical and open like the woman.

"Hello, Lori."

"Gray." His name fell from her soft lips with a light Southern drawl, whiskey warm and just as potent. She nodded toward his arm. "Nice patch there, Major."

He glanced down at his patch. Anything Anywhere Anytime.

The insinuation crackled along the humidity- and memory-laden air.

Gray let his gaze slide back to her, strapping bravado on like a parachute. "Wanna test the motto out?"

Her laugh was husky, if a bit tight. "Same old Gray."

"Guess that's a no."

Her chin tipped. "Been there. Done that. Lost the T-shirt."

His arms folded over his chest. "You left it at my place."

"I figured you could use it to shine your boots."

"Probably the safest bet."

She laughed again, the great husky laugh of hers that rolled right into him. Just as fast she had his hormones bombarding the defenses of his reason. Of course sex, great sex, incredible anything, anywhere, anytime sex had never been their problem. But the minute they'd set their feet on the floor…

He'd told her from the start he wasn't what she needed. It had taken her three months to agree with him and leave.

Yeah, damn smart woman. He wasn't what she needed now any more than he had been then. "Are you here as a volunteer?"

"I'm heading the team."

Gray straightened and reassessed her. Not that he was surprised. Imperturbable, competent Lori could manage a full-scale deployment without breaking a sweat. "Really?"

"I'm director for the southeast branch that just opened in Charleston." She hitched the canvas knapsack higher. "What about you?"

"Double duty. Doctor and flyer. Putting all that training to good use and making the taxpayers' money work for them." This wasn't so bad. Keeping it light. Shoot the breeze, catch up, move on. Gray settled back into his comfort zone.

"It's...nice seeing everyone again. But I thought Captain O'Connell was the flight surgeon tasked for this one. At least, she was the one who briefed us on the medical aspect."

"I'm filling in. O'Connell has the stomach flu. She went DNIF, uh, duties not including flying, at the last minute."

"Just our luck, huh?" Lori's gaze locked with his for three beats before skittering away to the others in her group. "I should listen to what Tag has to say. See you later."

Gray looked down the length of the 174-foot aircraft. "Not much chance of missing each other."

Her chuckle floated over her shoulder, dive bombing his senses with a final sucker punch as she strode up the metal ramp into the back of the plane. He watched the graceful sway of Lori's hips as she joined the group clustered around the loadmaster dispensing instructions and walk-around oxygen bottles.

"Yeah, dumb luck," Gray mumbled offhandedly.

Then it clicked, like a one-second grenade warning about to demolish his comfort zone.

Tag trying to hustle him on board until they were airborne.

Toe-the-line O'Connell bowing out of a primo assignment because of a lame stomach bug.

The copilot, Bronco, grinning like a kid with a secret all day.

Luck, his ass. He'd been set up, and he knew just who to hold responsible for slotting him into thirty hours straight with Lori Rutledge radiating her sweetness all over a plane full of orphans.

A year's worth of frustration, and even some unsuspected anger, upgraded from a simmer to a boil inside Gray with a ready target for once.

Not bothering to circle around to the front hatch steps,

Gray lumbered straight up the load ramp, past the small crowd, through the belly of the plane. His flight boots thudded, heavy, echoing the power and invincibility soldiers all needed in combat.

Bronco better have his boots strapped on tight, because there would be hell to pay when Gray got to the cockpit.

Lori watched Gray stride past her like a man on a mission. Of course he was. And she couldn't do anything except stare at his retreating broad shoulders and great butt, all the while praying her knees wouldn't fold.

A few hits off the oxygen bottle dangling from her hand might not be a bad idea, either.

It was just his flight suit turning her into some adolescent drool machine. Who wouldn't look awesome in that woodsy-green, military flight suit? Okay, so Tag didn't send her pulse pumping double time with *his* baggy uniform. But she and Gray had history, some good, some…really bad.

His coal-black hair glistened in the dim light, tapered up the back in a military cut revealing every inch of that powerful neck.

Her lungs constricted. She eyed the oxygen bottle with longing.

When she'd gone to the military briefing for her team, she'd been prepared for the possibility of seeing Gray again. No problem. They were both adults, after all. The crew members had filed in, faces still familiar from her summer spent with Gray. Bronco, Lancelot, Tag, they hadn't forgotten her, either. Then the flight surgeon had joined them—Kathleen O'Connell.

Relief had squashed the momentary flash of disappointment.

Seeing Gray on the flight line a few minutes ago had blindsided her. Hands hooked on his hips, boot propped on the load ramp, he'd stood—all six feet tall, toned muscle and too handsome, with his best bad-boy grin leaving her vulnerable in a way she hadn't felt since their last fight had stripped her soul bare.

Something she never intended to let happen again.

Grayson and that cute butt could just keep walking. She had her world right where she wanted it with a great job that let her travel yet provided the stability of one place to call home. Forever.

This rescue mission would establish her career and set her life on the right path. The mission definitely promised new lives for seventy-two homeless children.

No way would she let Grayson Clark distract her for one moment of the next thirty hours.

He turned sideways to slip past a portable kitchen locked down on a pallet in the middle of the plane. He whipped off his sunglasses. His jewel-green eyes glinted with determination, the playful major nowhere to be seen.

His strong, square jaw, set and thrust, already carried the black stubble of a five o'clock shadow, although they'd only just reported in. Of course Gray had always looked like he needed a shave ten minutes after he put down his razor.

An image of him leaning over the bathroom sink wearing nothing but a towel as he shaved flashed through her mind, drawing all the air right out of the cavernous aircraft.

Lori's hand clenched on the oxygen tank. "Hey, Tag. How long's this bottle good for?"

"You only need to carry it around in case there's a rapid decompression and you have to get back to your seat." Tag rapped his knuckles against the yellow canister. "So don't worry. This baby carries fifteen minutes worth."

"Fifteen minutes," Lori echoed, watching Gray disappear into the cockpit to prep the plane for their thirty-*hour* mission. Her lungs already burned.

* * *

Gray angled into the cockpit, frustration firing to life like a C-17's jet engines. Bronco and Lancelot bantered checklist call and responses into their headsets.

"Circuit breakers in," Bronco said into the microphone.

Lancelot ran his hands along the circuit breaker panel. "Checked in pilot."

Bronco mirrored the gesture with his panel. "Checked in co."

Gray grabbed Bronco's headset, snapped the earpieces and barked, "What the hell did you think you were doing?"

Bronco yanked around with a shout, eyes blazing, then relaxed into his seat, the blaze dimming to a mischievous sparkle. He swept a hand across the instruments. "Running the checklist, of course."

"Yeah, right. Try again."

"Running the checklist, *sir,*" he added, not in the least daunted.

Gray braced a hand across the bulkhead blocking any possible escape route for his so-called friend. "You'd better have a good explanation for this one, pal."

"For what?" Captain Tanner "Bronco" Bennett shrugged, his massive chest filling the seat. An Air Force Academy graduate and football tight end, Bronco was a big, blond poster boy for American patriotism. Rumor had it pro ball teams routinely tried to recruit him. Apparently, Bronco preferred to duke it out on battlefields rather than ball fields.

Bronco had picked one hell of a battle to start today. Gray reached to pop his headset again.

The copilot ducked and draped it around his neck. He plastered on a prim air at odds with his bulk and not quite suppressed laugh. "Please, I'm trying to maintain checklist discipline."

Gray yanked the checklist from his hands and slammed it on the console. "You set me up."

A grin twitched along his close-shaven mug. "Set you up?"

"Don't mess with me today."

"Wouldn't dream of it."

"You just forgot to mention her?"

"Her?"

Gray stepped forward.

Bronco raised his hands in surrender. "So Lori's on the flight. No big deal. You two are history. This shouldn't be a problem if she doesn't mean anything to you. Right?"

A chuckle sounded beside Gray. He pivoted toward the aircraft commander. Lance "Lancelot" Sinclair was stuffing cookies in his mouth, eyes twinkling as he chewed. Lance swallowed and held out a Ziploc bag full of chocolate chip cookies. "Want one? Julia made 'em fresh yesterday." He rattled the bag. "Good stuff, man."

The warm scent of chocolate wafted from the bag to fill the confined space. Just like the kitchen during one of Lori's cooking jags.

Gray suppressed the urge to tell pretty-boy Lancelot where to stuff his cookies.

Focus on one Judas at a time. Gray pinned Bronco with a glare. "What did you promise O'Connell to get her off this flight?"

"She's sick. Stomach flu. Probably puking her gorgeous guts out as we speak."

Gray almost bought it. Almost. Except he knew Bronco and O'Connell better than that. "What'd you guys promise her?" he pressed.

Bronco's gaze ping-ponged around the cockpit before he mumbled, "The Spain deployment."

"Geeez, Bronco!" Gray chewed on a number of curses swarming in his brain. He could have been sunning on the beach next week. What had he ever done to deserve this day?

Let Lori down.

The failure settled over him like a toxic fog fueling his anger. "Why didn't you just give O'Connell your car? Would have been less valuable. Damn it, I wanted that deployment. Instead I get—"

The copilot's eyes lost their humor. He jabbed a finger toward Gray. "You get to settle unfinished business and move on. We get the old Cutter back." His finger curled into a fist, and he slugged Gray on the arm. "We've missed you this year."

Bronco turning sentimental? That shut Gray up faster than any shouting match. The world had gone freaking nuts today. "What do you care? I'm transferring out at the end of the month, anyway. A few more weeks and I won't be your problem."

"That's not the point."

"There's nothing to settle. Just ask her."

"Why don't you?"

Gray braced a hand on the console and crowded Bronco. "And why don't you—"

"Problem, boys?"

Gray pushed away from the panel. Lt. Col. Zach Dawson hovered in the doorway. The squadron commander, the boss, he would be monitoring the mission as well as serving as the other relief pilot for the overseas flight. The last thing Gray wanted was his private life or lack of one, unrolled for the commander's viewing pleasure during the mission.

Nothing could ground a flyer faster than hints of instability in his home life. A military brat himself, he knew the mantra well. *Don't air your dirty laundry in public, son.*

He should have held his temper in check and confronted Bronco later. Too late for what-ifs. Gray smoothed his face into an easygoing grin. "No problem, sir."

"You sure?"

Gray slapped Bronco on the shoulder, his smile hitching higher. "Nothing I can't take care of during his next flight physical. You're on the schedule for later this week, aren't you, pal?"

Bronco paled. Lancelot chuckled and stuffed another cookie in his mouth.

"Then let's get this plane off the ground." Lt. Col. Zach Dawson settled into the seat behind the pilot, while Lancelot shoved aside his Ziploc bag.

Gray strapped himself into the other seat behind the copilot and slipped on his headset, grateful for the chance to lose himself in the routine. Routine had carried him through countless Desert Storm missions when he'd been the primary pilot, before he'd gone back to medical school. He could depend on it now, as well.

In a timeless military fashion, disjointed voices wafted through the headset. Checklists from pilots in front and loadmasters in back. A few more minutes and they'd be in the air. Already the escape of flight lured Gray.

Bronco was right. If there wasn't anything left with Lori, being on the mission didn't matter anyway. A thirty-seven-year-old bachelor, he had his life plan set.

He and Lori would spend a few hours together, travel memory lane and move on.

Bronco flashed a thumbs-up. "Checklist complete."

The engine drone built, swelled, vibrating the plane to life. Gray watched Lancelot grip the stick. As skillfully as a kid with a video-game joystick, he eased the throttle forward. No yoke for the C-17 Globemaster III, the mammoth cargo aircraft possessed the same stick and grace of a fighter plane. Smooth as a baby's butt, it rolled forward.

Gray wanted in the pilot's seat, to be in control, but he would get his turn in the cockpit as well as with the patients. He could wait. A small price to pay for having it all.

Having it all?

His thoughts winged back to the woman waiting strapped into one of the red, webbed seats in back. Was she nervous, elegant hands trembling? Or excited, her eyes glittering topaz? With seasoned determination he reeled his thoughts right back into the cockpit.

Forget Lancelot's home-baked cookies and Bronco's psychobabble garbage about Lori only bothering him if she still meant something to him. Gray had created the perfect life for himself where no one would get hurt.

The aircraft picked up speed, roaring down the runway. The copilot's voice rumbled over the headset. ''One hundred forty knots.''

''Committed to take off,'' the pilot acknowledged.

Committed. Damn. Even the word beaded Gray with sweat. With his messed-up past, who could blame him? Lori was better off without him.

The nose lifted off the runway.

Committed. To spending the next thirty hours learning how to forget Lori Rutledge once and for all.

Chapter 2

Lori gave up trying to forget about Gray. No way could she dodge thoughts of him while stuck in the middle of this military mission. She couldn't even manage to escape through sleep for more than an hour or two.

After thirteen hours in the air, the plane descended to the antiquated landing strip outside Sentavo. Her stomach lurched in synch. Was Gray piloting? Or one of the others?

She let memories steamroll over her. Not that she seemed to have a choice today.

Memories of meeting Gray through a mutual friend and then dancing for half the night, both knowing that someday they wouldn't go home alone.

Gray singing hokey Karaoke love songs at the Officer's Club, his husky voice growling out the lyrics. Definitely a stylist, not an artist. But so doggone charming.

Their fights about his committing more of himself to his job than he did to her. Gray was the king of keep-it-simple. Keep relationships light.

She'd needed more. She still did.

Throughout the flight, Gray had walked back to talk with all the passengers, as had the rest of the crew. Nothing special, just shooting-the-breeze chitchat. His deliberate refusal for any real conversation with her was conspicuous, thought provoking. Painful.

Damn, but she wanted to see him and have it mean nothing. She didn't want awkward avoidance that hinted at unresolved issues between them.

Meanwhile she was stuck in a webbed military seat surrounded by her co-workers, Gray's co-workers and her memories. Thank heaven in a few minutes she would have more than enough to think about assessing and loading the children.

Were her memories of Sentavo's lush, mountainous landscape accurate, or confused with other childhood "nose pressed to the car window" recollections of a different Eastern European city? Her gypsy childhood trailing her artist parents had left her with a blur of memories from cities all over the world. And a fierce need for roots that had increased with her thirtieth birthday.

A light tap gave the only indication they'd landed, followed by the drag and whine of the engines slowing the aircraft until they taxied to a stop. She gathered her backpack and trailed the others down the load ramp, her stomach flipping another loop-de-loop. Because of the mission, not the man. Right?

Liar.

Old buses littered the tarmac, parked alongside the hangar and shaded by maple and pine bowers. The hangar loomed, nothing more than a rusting warehouse with an oversize door. The children would be waiting inside, her reason for being here, and she couldn't forget that for a minute. Lori strode forward.

Dappled sunlight threaded through the dense trees, patterning lacey shadows on the pitifully thin and cracked asphalt. They'd landed on that? She shivered in spite of the near eighty-degree summer weather.

"Lori."

From behind her, Gray's voice encircled Lori like a warm blanket, like his solid, strong arms. She put two more steps between her and those hot tones before turning to face him. "Smooth flight, Major. I'm impressed."

"Thanks. Lancelot and Bronco put her down, though. The commander and I just relieved them for a few hours over the Atlantic while they snagged a nap." His eyes searched her face as if he might finally say something else, something substantial, then he held fast to his standard behavior for the day and smiled lightly.

Nothing deep.

And absolutely no touching.

"Regardless of who flew when, we're here and those children have waited long enough for a home, for families." Even with a set of affluent parents, she'd waited her whole life for a home, and the ache had sometimes seemed to consume her. God, what must those children, with such greater concerns and fears, be feeling?

Gray scratched a hand along his bristly jaw. "I'll need your help inside."

"Mine?"

"If you don't mind," he said, the best wicked grin back in place.

Ah, a gauntlet. "You're a bad boy, Grayson Clark."

"You're only just figuring that out?"

She ignored his question and parried with her own. "You want *me* to assist you for the next four hours while you check out these kids?"

"Why not? You and I can work together, probably better than I can with the others in your office, since we know each other. No sweat."

He met her with a challenging stare, as if daring her. To do what? To prove something by showing herself and everyone else they could work together, no sweat, like he'd said? Was he trying to convince himself, as well?

The mere thought scared her all the way to her hiking boots. "No sweat?"

"Of course not. We can focus on the job. I'll be getting the heavy-duty cases, greater injuries and traumatized kids. I can use your help. Put that social work degree of yours to good use. You're the boss after all. Shouldn't you take on the tougher ones?"

The kids. War orphans. How could she refuse? And he no doubt knew her well enough to realize she couldn't. "You're a bad boy, *and* you don't play fair."

He shrugged. "So tell my mom."

"A little late for that." Lori sucked in air like water. Her gaze shifted from Gray's handsome face to the landscape behind him—the rounded mountain peaks, the smattering of quaint stucco cottages. Beautiful, except half of the buildings were missing sides or bore gaping holes in their clay roofing. How many of those children in the hangar had lived here? Had they played with parents and siblings in the yard? Watched planes fly overhead?

Witnessed the devastation.

She'd seen more than her fair share of poverty and destruction in the world, following her parents from country to country. And it never failed to fist in her stomach, compacting within her a need to act, fix, change things.

Lori pointed to the hangar. "Let's get these children checked out and loaded up."

"Yes, ma'am." Gray charged after her, weaving through the crowd of military and relief workers.

Lori strode the last few feet to the shelter that housed seventy-two scared kids. Did Gray have to walk so close behind her? Too easily she could inhale that mixture of bay rum aftershave and just *him* tinged with sweat, a scent too reminiscent of summer afternoons spent making love, sleeping entangled, making love again.

She stepped inside, and any fanciful musings fell away. Controlled mass activity echoed up to the metal-beamed ceiling. The dark, muggy warehouse rumbled with voices, mingled languages, babies crying, children playing, others whimpering. The sheer magnitude of her responsibility for these seventy-two little lives nearly staggered Lori back a step into the strong support of Gray's broad chest.

She braced her shoulders and donned her training for support. More reliable, anyway. "Okay, Doc, where do we start?"

His hand hovered around her back, low, near her waist. She could feel the heat, although he never touched her as he ushered her forward.

"Atta girl. Knew I could count on you. If only you could say the same for me, huh?"

She shot a startled glance over her shoulder.

A half smile curved his mouth. "Broke the keep-it-light rule there for a second, didn't I?"

"Whose rule was that, anyway?"

Before Gray could answer, a loadmaster called to him. Tables, chairs, even a few stretchers had been set up at makeshift exam stations to triage patients. She studied one young face after another. The flight was only slated to transport ambulatory passengers.

And if someone needed care beyond what they could provide in-flight? How could she leave behind a sick child in a country where bombs and gunfire still whispered insidiously in the distance?

She refused to think about that. Gray would patch them up and board them. When it came to his job, the man was determination personified.

Lori flipped her braid over her shoulder. "What do you need from me?"

His eyes snapped to hers. "Going for a little rule breaking yourself, huh?"

She shot him her best withering stare. "In the examinations."

A self-deprecating smile flickered across his face before disappearing altogether. "Keep the flow moving, bring me a child, pass the one I just finished with over to the loadmasters so we can board them. The faster we get out of here the better."

"I thought we had four hours?"

"The sooner we're out of here, the better," he repeated. Bombs growled in the distance as if applauding him. Uniformed workers didn't even break stride. Children barely winced. "Thank God the Red Cross already gave them their immunizations and TB tests. Saved us time and the kids' irritability in-flight. For now, anything you can do to calm them, hugs, pats, whatever, will speed things along."

"Like their mothers would have done for them in a checkup." Her own mother hadn't been much for chicken soup, but she'd always ordered the best of room service. Hugs and an afternoon of cartoons rounded out the treatment. Hugs. The cure-all for kids. She could do that. Longed to do that.

"Exactly." Gray's gaze swept the roomful of children who would never see their mothers again. His cheeks puffed on an exhale. "Just do what you can for them."

"Got it."

A representative from the orphanage brought the first child forward—a toddler, not more than a couple of years old but with none of the chubby-cheeked health of the babies in Lori's dreams. Carefully she scooped him into her arms. So frail. Even needing a bath and fresh clothes, he carried that precious baby scent universal to all small children.

Cocking his head to the side, the boy studied her with dark, curious eyes. Quick as a flash, he yanked her braid.

"You're a little stinker." She grasped the tail of her braid and tickled his chin, earning a gurgling giggle. She passed him to Gray, their eyes locking over the tiny head. Their arms brushed in the exchange.

For the first time in a year he touched her, and the pure pleasure of that careless caress closed her throat. She wanted more, like a dangerous, addictive narcotic. She wanted his hands on her again.

Lori transferred the toddler to Gray and backed away.

He plopped the child on the edge of the gurney. With a broad, gentle hand he chucked him under the chin and tipped up the boy's name tag pinned to his tattered sleeper. "Well, hello, Ladislov. What a big name for a little guy."

Gray kept his tone low and reassuring as he skimmed off the sleeper, stripping the baby down to his diaper.

Those big hands were so tender with the child, Lori had to look away. "Sorry. I should have done that for you."

"Next time. We're fine now. Right, Ladislov?" Gray ran his hands along spindly legs and arms, explored a bump on the boy's head, listened to his chest, continuing the physical with relative ease until he tried to peer inside the child's ears.

Ladislov made his displeasure known.

Loudly.

He lurched off the gurney.

Gray and Lori both caught him in midair.

Lori took control and cradled the screeching child. "Hang on. I'll have him settled in a second."

She tucked her chin on top of his head and swayed from side to side, humming reassurance. The oddly domestic scenario wrapped around her and squeezed with suffocating force.

Life wasn't playing fair today, either.

The baby's shrieks dwindled to hiccuping sobs. Gray scratched his jaw. "Just sit on the gurney. Hold him, but turn him to face me and I'll finish up."

Lori hitched onto the edge, a difficult maneuver with at least twenty pounds of baby crawling to snuggle closer.

Gray braced her elbow and balanced, lifting until she perched in front of him. His hand dropped away a second too fast.

Her elbow burned.

Gray selected an instrument from the tray. "I need to check his ears. Hold his arms for me." Gray flipped the light off and on in front of Ladislov's face. "See, pal. Just an otoscope. Nothing scary, right?"

Ladislov thrust his bottom lip out mutinously and wriggled. Lori clasped the tiny hands in hers, her arms locked around little Ladislov. Gray canted toward her. He wheeled the chair forward until he was abreast with her legs.

No way in hell was she inching her knees apart for him to slide nearer. Lori angled forward.

In a horrifying flash, she realized just how close little Ladislov's ear was to her breast.

Before she could adjust the child into a different position, Gray leaned the rest of the way and slid the otoscope into the boy's ear. He peered inside. A scant two inches of air separated her breast from Gray's cheek. If she moved even the least bit...

Uncomfortable as hell, Lori held herself very still.

Ladislov wasn't as accommodating. He twisted. Squirmed. Tried to slide free.

Gray bobbed his head, keeping the instrument in place. "Hang tough, buddy," he mumbled words the child had no hope of understanding. "Almost through with this one. There's just so much wax, I've gotta..."

Gray's wrist brushed Lori's breast. Heat flooded her.

"Please, little guy." She whispered a tight plea. "Hold still."

Gray froze. His face tipped, and he peered up at her, his green eyes deepening to a glittering emerald. His brow lifted before he returned to make short order of the other ear.

With the heel of his boot, he pushed, rolling away. Far away. Not far enough. "All set."

Her shoulders sagged as she exhaled. "He's okay?"

Gray scribbled in the boy's thin chart. "Just a minor ear infection, a little fever and congestion. His ears might be uncomfortable when the plane descends, but nothing dangerous. I'll start him on antibiotics now. He'll feel better before we land." Gray passed the chart to one of the technicians and filled an eyedropper with pink, syrupy medicine. He reached for the boy. "Time to drink up, pal."

Lori passed Ladislov to Gray and couldn't stifle the taunting whisper in her mind. She'd once thought this man would be the father of her children. Now she knew with certainty this was the only child she would ever give Grayson Clark.

Damn his too charming soul.

Gray watched Lori pass over yet another newborn, her elegant hand bracing the little behind until he rested snuggly in a loadmaster's arms. She looked so damned right with a child. Why didn't she find some great guy and work on increasing the world population?

Sweat dribbled down Gray's forehead, stinging his eyes. He swiped his wrist over his brow. The hangar had turned into a furnace.

He whipped a red bandanna from the zippered thigh pocket of his flight suit. Three quick yanks and he'd knotted the do-rag around his head. "Bring on the next batch."

With inherent dancer-like grace, Lori knelt in front of a boy. She looked too good, even after being tugged, spit up on—clung to. Way too beautiful.

So much for his bright idea they should work together. He'd only wanted to prove to the crew…to himself…that he could be with her and remain unaffected.

He didn't doubt his ability to do his job, no matter the circumstances. But did she have to test his resolve to the limit? The occasional whiff of her peach scent chased away the acrid bite in the air, if for just a distracting second.

Gray drummed his fingers on a stack of ragtag charts while Lori offered nonsensical, soothing words to a child.

There wasn't anyone better suited than Lori to deal with the traumatized children he would evaluate. Odd how he trusted her more than others from the base he'd worked with countless times.

Even during the beyond-tense moment while he'd checked little Ladislov's ear, leaned too close, she'd never winced because that child needed her. Lori always put others' needs first. A bomb could have detonated, and Gray knew she wouldn't have moved.

Only he would notice the hitch in her breathing—and wished like hell he didn't know her well enough to understand its significance.

Meanwhile, his patients had to be his priority, and that included ignoring the wisp of hair sneaking free from Lori's braid to caress her brow.

Gray opened the next file. "Okay, kiddo."

As he'd done in the plane, Gray escaped into the reliable routine of his job. He evaluated one child at a time, not a chart or a case, but a person. Nikola, Antonije, Goran, Vasiliji, Jelena, each the complete focus of Gray's attention for his or her ten minutes while he checked vitals, cleansed and bandaged cuts, assessed broken teeth, ground his own teeth at the sight of a partially healed gunshot wound on an eight-year-old.

Gray passed off a chart and stretched his shoulders, glancing at his watch as his arm arced up. An hour and a half until takeoff. The walls rattled with another burst of gunfire—and something else. A grenade? Or a land mine? Did they sound closer or were his heightened senses exaggerating?

Lori didn't flinch, but her complexion downgraded from ivory to milky. Noise inside the hangar waned for five heart-stopping seconds, then resumed. Gray glanced around the warehouse and caught the commander's attention two tables over. "Can we step up the pace, Colonel?"

Lt. Col. Zach Dawson's tense nod wasn't reassuring, but Gray had been through worse. Just not with seventy-two children and Lori depending on him.

The next child shuffled forward, clinging to the hand of a soft-figured orphanage worker in a dulled-out white uniform. Gray spun his chair to face her fully and found a little girl, around three or four. Sprigs of hacked, dark hair damp with sweat curled along her round face. With those cropped locks, she'd probably been de-loused. Poor kid.

A harsh cough rumbled from the tiny chest as she tucked behind the woman's long skirt. Gray looked up at Lori. He knew when he was out of his league.

She crouched in front of the girl. "Hello—" slowly Lori reached to tap the name tag "—Magda."

Dirty little fists eased their grip on the dress. One wide, dark eye peeked warily, her cough dwindling to a raspy sigh. Lori kept her hand extended and steady.

The older woman mumbled a few words in another language, pried her skirt free and nudged Magda forward. If only they had more time to ease this kid through the exam. But they didn't. Gray stifled the rush of frustration over things he couldn't change.

Lori extended her other hand to the girl. A look of resignation crossed the tiny face. Magda dropped her arms to her sides and waited, helpless.

Lori gasped, the first substantial reaction he'd heard from her all day. Who could blame her? This kid was a heartbreaker.

She stood, small and still, her navy cotton dress a size too big and drooping off one shoulder. A grubby Barbie poked from either end of her clenched grip. Magda met his gaze dead-on, her eyes flat. A living casualty of war.

He'd seen the look too often in his father's eyes, a look

cultivated in a Vietnamese POW camp. A look the old man still carried in unguarded moments. Gray had long ago accepted he couldn't heal his father or his family any more than he could fix the real problem for these children. He could only bandage them up and pass them off to true healers like Lori.

Too many emotions churned within Gray. Complicated mishmashes of things he couldn't deal with now, didn't want to wade through ever again. Keep it simple. Give the kid a bandage and a smile. It was all he had to offer.

Lori heard the creak of Gray's chair as he shifted. She wanted to ask for his help with this child whose soulful eyes lashed at emotions already too bare after a draining day.

But she wouldn't. She could handle it on her own. Asking for help had never been her forte, anyway.

Gunfire grumbled outside. Not much time. Lori eased forward, no fast motions, and carefully picked up the little girl. She placed Magda on the gurney, then hitched up to sit beside her.

Gray pulled the stethoscope up to his ears. Magda cringed back. Lori encircled her shoulders and squeezed. "Shhhh. It's okay."

"Yeah, see." Gray held the stethoscope on his own chest.

Magda frowned. He grinned, put it on his forehead, his chin, his nose, like any mischievous kid except for that beard-stubbled jaw. Magda buried her face against Lori's shoulder.

"Ah, playing hard to get are we, little Magpie." Gray held up the stethoscope. "Look. Here's how it's done."

He reached toward Lori and paused, as if waiting for permission. She swallowed and nodded. The disk rested safely in the center of her chest, no accidental brushes. Good.

Except he would hear her heart tap dancing double time.

Heaven help her if he flashed that wicked grin of his her way, because she didn't think she could keep from blushing—or screaming.

He didn't look up.

Worse, his head bowed and he simply listened. Disk pressed against her chest, he listened without moving as if the sound of her racing heart might mean something to him. Lori stared down at that strong neck, his dark hair peeking from the edges of his red bandanna. Boyish, rugged, appealing.

Wrong.

She'd had enough of playing doctor with him for one day. For a lifetime.

Magda's hand untwined from Lori's shirt and inch by tentative inch snuck forward until she touched Gray's bandanna.

He jerked away. Magda winced. The tight lines around his eyes eased, and he tapped his head. "You like this? With that stylish 'do' you're sportin' little one, I can't say I blame you for wanting some head cover. I'd give you mine, Magpie, but it's probably soaked by now." His hand snaked into his thigh pocket. "How about this?"

Tugging free a blue bandanna, he waved it in front of her. Her brown eyes sparkled to life for the first time. Her fingers gripped the Barbie in an excited, tight fist.

Gray folded the fabric into a triangle and draped it over Magda's head. His total focus on his small patient riveted Lori. He knotted the three ends over Magda's butchered hair.

Leaning back, he smiled a full-out grin and gave the girl a thumbs-up. "Beauty."

Lori wanted to gut punch him.

How dare he be so…so…*everything.*

Her mind wandered angry paths as he warmed the stethoscope on his hand. Gray should have left her alone and let her work with Tag in his baggy flight suit. Or with happily married Lancelot. Or with Bronco, who was more like a big brother. A really big brother.

Instead Gray had to torment her with all those appealing ways that had rattled her world first time around. Except she would be smarter now, resist temptation. She would heed his warnings and the warnings of her own heart, a heart she had no intention of entrusting to Grayson Clark.

She wouldn't be fooled by his bandanna-bonding. This charming vagabond had zero interest in happily-ever-after, and she couldn't settle for less. "I think she's ready for you to check her out now."

"Okay, Miss Magpie, let's listen to those lungs." He rested the disk on her reed-thin chest, moved it around, frowned, moved it along her back, then front again, lingering longer than he had with the other children.

"Damn," he whispered, before draping the stethoscope around his neck while he used the otoscope to look up her nose and in her ears, his doctor-face smooth and expressionless.

"What?"

He palpated the glands in her neck. "Pneumonia most likely. Not to mention a vicious double ear infection. This kid's not in any shape to fly."

Horror sliced through Lori like one of those scalpels in the instrument tray. "You're joking, right? Have you listened to what's going on out there? We can't leave her here."

"Hold it down." Gray held his hands up. "I didn't say she wouldn't fly. Just that regulations say she shouldn't."

The sick twist of her stomach eased, only to knot again. Regulations. "What can you do?"

He scrubbed a hand over his bandanna and glanced at the tray of supplies beside him. "Screw the regs. Pump her full of meds. Keep quiet. Pray like hell."

She prayed—prayed for the day to end, so children like Magda could crawl into a safe warm bed, so she could crawl into her own...alone. Far away from having to watch Gray be the honorable hero of the day, saving and charming children with heartbreaking ease.

A cleared throat sounded just behind Gray. Lori jumped and peered over his shoulder as he glanced back.

Lancelot stood behind them, a ridge creased between his brows. "Problem with this one?"

"No problem." Gray filled a syringe and pierced Magda's arm before she could blink, much less cry. He flung aside the empty needle. It clattered to rest in a tray. "All set."

"Good, 'cause we're gonna have to clear out. Now. Radio report says..." He paused, his gaze flickering to Lori, then back to Gray. "We should start packing. Load 'em up and finish the rest in-flight."

An eerie quiet mushroomed in the warehouse.

Panic pierced her like that needle he'd tossed aside, seeping fear into her veins. Not exactly what she'd wished for with that prayer, but then, things rarely turned out as she hoped around Gray.

He shoved to his feet, his body humming with tension. "Roger that, Lance. Ready to roll."

Gray extended a hand to Lori just as an explosion ripped the air outside the hangar.

Chapter 3

"Incoming!"

The warning echoed through the hangar, in Gray's ears. Lori's horrified eyes met his. Too distracting.

Gray kicked aside his chair. He flung his body over Lori and Magda, pinning them to the gurney.

Braced his arms. Cursed. Prayed.

A whistling premonition increased. Incoming. Another explosion. Metal walls rattled like a drum.

Reverberated. Waned. Silence.

Then shouts and orders for evacuation zipped around them. He couldn't afford mind-numbing fear for the woman beneath him. He had to get her out. Fast. Gray hauled himself off Lori.

"To the plane," he barked. "Now!"

He yanked her up, trying to pry Magda from her arms. Spindly arms and legs held tight.

Lori shoved his shoulder. "Just go! I can carry her."

With a terse nod, Gray grabbed Lori's hand. He called on his training to overcome emotions that could dull his reactions. He bolted forward. They followed loadmasters herding clusters of children out the door. Local officials darted through the crowd, scooping up children.

Sunlight and carbon-tinged air assaulted his senses. A distant explosion plumed smoke. Damn, why hadn't he pushed to leave sooner?

He checked left, right and sprinted, Lori's hand locked in his. A few more feet to the cargo plane.

Whump, sounded just beyond the trees. Mortar fire launched.

Lori's soft hand felt too mortal in his.

Her fingers jerked free.

Panic popped through Gray like a semiautomatic. He spun to find her darting away.

Toward a weaving toddler heading for the trees.

Mortar rounds shattered the asphalt inches from her feet. She stumbled, righted herself and plowed forward, her body curved protectively around Magda.

Fury and fear discharged within him. "Lori!"

She didn't hear, or chose to ignore him, damned reckless, selfless woman.

He dodged left, putting his body between her and the spewing rounds. His boots pounded pavement in time with his heart. His left calf stung. Pain spread into a flame he had to ignore for now. He ran faster, frustration clawing through him.

She scooped up the child, balancing one orphan on each hip. Already her eyes scanned the cracked runway as if searching for someone else to save. Did she intend to carry them on her back?

Gray skidded to a stop beside her. He whipped the extra kid from her arms. He crowded behind her, nudging, urging, shielding her back with his body. "Go! Go! Go!"

"Wait!" She pointed across the runway at another group of children. "They need—"

"Damn it, woman! They're fine. Tag's got 'em. Now

move!'' he shouted over the mayhem. Hours of restraint expanded within him as he raced a serpentine path. The percussion from another blast slammed Lori back against his chest. She staggered, paused.

Hesitation could kill them. He chose words he knew well would fire her feet and distract her while they ran. ''Why couldn't you have stayed home and baked cookies?''

''Fat chance.'' Her chest pumped for air as she shouted over the latest whistle. Explosion. Trees falling, burning. More running. ''There's no one around to eat them.''

Her accusation sprayed him like shrapnel. He'd fired her more than he could have hoped. Restraints fell away on his control in the madness of the moment. ''You walked. Not me.''

''I just,'' she gasped, cradling Magda's bandanna-covered head to her breast, ''got to the door first.''

And Lori was right.

His feet found purchase on the load ramp. More relief than he wanted throbbed through him. He plopped the toddler in a seat, then reached for Magda. She plastered herself to Lori, bandanna and Barbie secure.

''Stubborn women.'' Gray twirled Lori by the arm onto the red webbing. She sat, still and poised, with Magda in her lap. Both sets of wide brown eyes promised one great big distraction.

He jabbed a finger in Lori's face. ''No more saving the world today, lady. Sit. Don't move until we get this plane off the ground.''

Not waiting for any argument, he shouldered through the swell of bodies crowding onto the aircraft.

Lori's whisper dogged him all the way to the cockpit. *Be careful.*

Operating through life solo was a hell of a lot easier.

Gray stared out at the night stars blanketing the sky beyond his windscreen. The bombing in Sentavo was a world away. Or at least ten hours past.

Lori, little Magda, everyone had made it out unharmed.

Gray didn't let himself dwell overlong on those seconds he'd stood horrified, watching Lori sprint into a shower of shrapnel. He focused on the plane, stick in hand, rudder pedals beneath his boots.

Only the fluorescent glow of the green instrument panel lit the confined space. Bronco sprawled to his right in the copilot's seat reading a paperback. The aircraft hummed contentedly across the Atlantic.

Forget autopilot, he loved to fly.

The sky had been his salvation for years. As a child he'd dreamed of flying with his bomber gunner father. Later Gray's dreams had shifted to piloting a rescue for his POW father, easing the strained lines around his mother's eyes, bringing back her smile.

But he couldn't.

He'd settled for earning her smile in other ways. He was good at that, joking, keeping things light.

After his father's return, his mother still hadn't smiled. No one did. Before long, Gray traveled the skies in his mind to escape.

He was good at that, too. Running.

Gray called in a position report. In the homestretch, they only had three more hours before landing in Charleston. The children would be whisked away to their sponsor families. Lori would go home and find some great man, bake cookies for him, make babies with him.

The thought soured in Gray's brain, not at all comforting. As a matter of fact, it was damned depressing.

Gray reached to tighten his bandanna tied around his calf over the mortar nick. The bleeding was minimal, his need for a Band-Aid nothing compared to the other pilots' need for sleep. Air safety came first.

Forget the dull ache. Ditch the morose garbage. It had

never been his style. He needed a few of those smiles for himself.

One thing he could always count on, crew dogs thrived on a good laugh, even in the middle of combat. Especially in combat.

Gray pivoted to Bronco. "Well, my friend, payback time."

"Payback?"

"Payback." Gray flipped a CD between his fingers and nodded to the makeshift CD player hookup he'd rigged into the interphone. Damn but he enjoyed flying with these guys. He would miss them when he transferred. "I feel like giving you boys a concert."

Bronco flinched. "Couldn't you limit your revenge to the physical?"

"Not a chance. You deserve my full retribution, and now that the squadron commander is snoozing away in the bunk... Well... Hey, Tag," he called into the headset. "Hear that, my traitorous crewmate? Time to pay up for your little scheduling stunt. What will it be? Eagles, Elvis, or Beatles?" Gray popped in the CD and depressed the interphone button on the stick. John, Paul, George and Ringo's crooning blasted through, Gray joining in two seconds later.

Tag and Bronco's groans flooded his headphones, followed by light chuckles. Gray gripped the stick, flew his plane, sang. Escaped.

Just behind Gray, Lori leaned her head against the bulkhead and stared at him silhouetted by panel lights. The children settled, she could afford a moment to go up front and talk with Gray. Numbing exhaustion from adrenaline letdown left her languid and mellow.

Vulnerable.

God, he was gorgeous. Mud-splattered boots braced on the pedals, he relaxed in his seat, stick in his hand, in control.

But on his terms, growling out tunes as he flew. His jaw and shoulders kept the beat. Bronco drummed percussion on the panel. Gray flipped switches, sang, piloted the aircraft.

So competent. Never serious. Always gorgeous.

Not that she'd come to check out the view. She just thought he would appreciate an update on Magda.

At least that gave her enough reason to be there so she wouldn't have to dwell overlong on the need to see him and reassure herself he hadn't been injured in their sprint to the plane.

"Gray," she called once, twice, before he stopped singing and looked over his shoulder. His eyes glittered an emerald echo of the fluorescent cabin lights.

He flipped his headset mouthpiece to the side. His thumb popped off the button on the stick. "Hi. Problems with one of the kids?"

"No, I just—" Her gaze flickered to Bronco, then back to Gray.

Bronco disconnected his headset and shoved to his feet. "Think I'll step back to the head."

Lori twisted sideways as he squeezed his bulk past. Alone with Gray, she willed herself not to fidget.

He slid a CD free from a player and gestured to the vacated copilot's seat. "Go ahead and sit."

Lori sagged wearily. Her fingers twined in her lap to keep from touching the countless buttons and switches in front of her—and to keep from shaking.

"What's up?"

"I thought you'd like to know our little pal Magda just drifted off. Her fever's down. She quit tugging her ear an hour ago. Her cough's still pretty harsh, but at least she's comfortable."

"Good. Thanks for the update. I'll check on her again when I'm through here." He nodded, eyes trained on the small holographic display above the console. ''Is she saying anything yet? Communicating at all?''

Lori grasped the safe topic with both hands, although not sure what she hoped to accomplish by talking with him, anyway. ''I tried to teach her a couple of basics like yes and no before she goes to her sponsor family. Who knows if she understood me.''

Silence and dark hummed around her.

What now? If only she could will her feet to carry her back to her seat. But the cabin was so warm, dark, soothing, and she was beyond tired. Her temple settled against the copilot's headrest as she caved in to the temptation to spend a few more minutes with Gray. How could she resist the intimacy too reminiscent of another time?

Lori pointed to the small Plexiglas screen with holographic images floating across it. ''What's that?''

''The HUD, heads up display, duplicates the instrument panel along the bottom of the windshield. It enables me to monitor the readings without taking my eyes off the sky.''

More than a little awe swept over her for the extent of his technical training in two differing career fields. ''Cool.''

A familiar grin kicked up the corner of his mouth. ''It sure is.''

He had such a great smile and a real talent for making her smile as well—even when she wanted to club his thick, gorgeous head.

Memories crackled along the air like popcorn in oil, heating to life. Dancing at the Officer's Club. Beach picnics with the crew members. Stretching out together under a blanket of stars.

''And that sky.'' She gazed through the windshield. Regular stars she viewed every night glowed vibrant shades of orange, red, green, even an arctic blue. ''Is it always this incredible?''

''Oh, yeah.'' He pointed right. ''See how much larger

the planets are? The red one there is Mars, and the green one over there, that's Jupiter."

Lori slumped in the seat and savored the beauty. She'd seen some of the world's greatest works of art growing up, had met the artists firsthand and watched them create, watched her own artist parents pour their souls onto canvas.

This beat it all, hands down. "Thank you for dragging me out of there today so I could see this."

"You're welcome."

Silence returned, heavy and full, pulsing syrupy need through her veins. The tiny quarters, dim lighting, scenic night sky, and her weary defenses didn't help one bit.

Gray flipped a switch before easing his hand from the stick. The plane glided on smoothly. "Why did you really come up here, Lori?"

He knew her too well, and that swirled a mix of alarm and excitement within her. "To thank you. To say goodbye without a big audience."

Gray looked away and tapped the CD resting beside him. "And now that you have?"

He slipped the disk on his finger and spun it with an almost exaggerated focus. As if he couldn't face her. She understood that well enough. Seeing him made reasonable thought tough enough.

Instead she watched a streak of light across the sky. Northern lights, perhaps? She stared and whispered, "How do I wake up in the morning and forget we spent the day together?"

Her words hung between them like the stars, vibrant, alive, hot.

"The same way we've gone through every day this year." He stopped the disk, set it aside, and flipped two switches on the instrument panel. "Except I'll be sitting on Bronco this go-round."

Confusion pushed through her exhaustion. "Bronco?"

"So he and the rest of the crew won't pull another stunt like this one."

"Stunt? Help me out here. Sleep deprivation must be making me slow. I'm not understanding what you're saying."

"The whole scheduling change." His jaw flexed. "They set us up."

Her body tingled, her ears echoing with the first thrummings of realization. "Set us up."

"Oh, yeah. They're probably laughing their a—" he glanced at her "—laughing their butts off over this one."

Hurt, anger and too many emotions she didn't dare explore churned overtime. She straightened in her seat. "This whole day has been a big joke."

He whipped the CD off the console and slapped it into a case. "Crew dogs never miss a chance to pull one over."

"And of course you think this is funny." Her voice tightened. Her eyes stung.

"Hell, no."

She continued as if he hadn't spoken, "Of all the immature BS I've ever heard."

"Hey, simmer down." His mouth kicked up with a pacifying smile.

Major Smiles-and-No-Confrontation-Please would just have to suck this one up. "Don't defend their sixth-grade prank." She blinked back the weak tears. "All good intentions aside, they meddled in my life, and I don't appreciate it. And neither should you."

"I don't. But it's over and done with. Working yourself into a frenzy doesn't change a thing. Lighten up, Lori."

"Grow up, Gray." She snapped without thinking. But then that was the whole point. Arguing was instinctive for them. She pressed two fingers to her temple. "Sorry. That sort of remark pretty much negates my thanks. I guess old habits are hard to break."

Gray's hand fell to rest on her knee with the familiarity

of old lovers, his eyes gentle as his light squeeze. "At least we've made it a little easier to get up in the morning."

And forget? The heat of his hand on her knee made a lie of his words. Her body refused to forget the gentle rasp of his hands along her bare skin, the caress of his mouth against the vulnerable curve of her neck, the shimmer while unraveling in his arms.

But then her body wasn't as smart as her heart.

They couldn't build a relationship on great sex alone. Heaven knew they'd tried. And failed.

She didn't bother knocking his hand aside. She simply stood so it fell away. "Goodbye, Gray."

Lori shoved away from the seat just as Bronco returned. She clenched her jaw rather than speak words that wouldn't change a thing. Like Gray said, the damage was already done. Just how much damage, she didn't want to consider until she'd slept at least eighteen hours straight and faced the morning alone.

Bronco lumbered into his seat, glancing from Gray to Lori and back again. "Yeah right, you two are history."

Gray hefted his bag and loped down the hatch steps. Lights flooded the Charleston Air Force Base runway, haloing a neon umbrella in the evening dark.

It was over.

The children would complete in-processing and meet their new families. He would go back to his work with patients and regular missions.

Two days ago that might have been enough. But seeing Lori again had started something akin to a spark on a parachute. Would his feet find ground before the whole damned thing burst into flames?

His best bet would be to haul out, fast.

Except he couldn't dodge the sensation he was forgetting something. A glance around the flight line didn't ease the feeling. Buses crowded the tarmac to transport the children. An NGO worker directed human traffic flow.

No Lori.

Past time to hit the road, he reminded himself.

Hanging out with Lori any longer would only leave him more frustrated. And he was mighty frustrated already. Just a by-product of a year without sex, of course. Not because he'd spent thirty hours wanting Lori and her peach-scented body wrapped around him.

He forced his eyes front and walked toward the crew bus. Noises meshed around him—engine whines and barked commands blended with children crying. Other children hung limp, sleeping against an adult shoulder while military personnel boarded them on the buses.

No Lori and her little Magpie.

Keep walking. His job was done. He needed sleep and a bandage for his leg. No need to risk starting something with her that he wouldn't have time to finish before he moved.

Gray stared up into the bus and resisted the urge to look over his shoulder. He and Lori didn't need more goodbyes. She would have her hands full transferring the kids, especially the one screaming up a blue streak. It sounded as if someone needed sleep as much as he did.

An image of Lori sagging against the copilot's seat flashed to mind. Beautiful, drowsy, exhausted.

Another spark flamed on his mental parachute.

She always pushed herself harder than a normal person. Lori's job wouldn't be complete until the last kid had a safe place to sleep.

Gray planted a hand on the bus and hung his head. Three deep breaths later he turned around. What was one more hour without shut-eye? She'd needed so much more from him than he could give a year ago. He could give her this now, an hour to help out and speed the in-processing.

His eyes scanned the bustling tarmac for Lori.

Shrieks beyond a small crowd increased. Lori would be there, of course, fixing the problem. Gray dodged and wove until he found her cradling a screaming Magda.

Little Magpie had found her voice.

A military nurse in fatigues gripped Magda's shoulders, attempting to lift her from Lori's arms. Like a spider monkey, Magda held tight and cried gulping sobs. Her bandanna-clad head nestled firmly in the crook of Lori's neck. The Barbie clutched in Magda's fist tangled in Lori's unraveling braid.

Gray plowed forward. "Lori. Lori!"

She turned, wisps of hair flying around her face. Pure exhaustion lined her face. Unshed tears clouded her eyes as her gaze met his. Gratitude mingled with those tears.

His whole damned parachute went up in flames.

Fatigue fell away. He wasn't going anywhere, anytime soon. Gray dropped a hand on Magda's head. "Problem?"

"She doesn't want to go." Lori's voice quivered. "And I can't make her understand."

That tiny quiver slayed him, coming from a woman who never lost control. His hand fell from Magda's head to the small of Lori's back. She felt too soft and warm under his palm. "She may never understand, and she shouldn't have to, but you're going to have to let her go eventually."

"I know." One blink would have set those tears free. She didn't blink.

Lori would go down with a fight.

Damn but he wanted to fight this battle for her. "You paved the way for me all day. Maybe I can ease this one along for you."

She swallowed heavily, still didn't blink. "Thank you."

Gray ducked eye level with Magda. "Hey, Magpie."

Her little muscles bulged as her arms locked around Lori's neck. But she stopped crying. Wide brown eyes looked at him with a wary hope that sliced right through him.

Couldn't he fly combat instead? Perform an appendectomy or two? Either would be easier.

Gray cupped Magda's head as he mumbled reassuring words she wouldn't understand. Slowly her grip slackened. He talked, his hands sliding around to grip Magda's waist.

Tiny arms and legs vice-gripped Lori.

Lori trembled. Gray wasn't feeling all that steady, either. Carefully he pried Magda free one arm at a time. The child was so small, so damned delicate with fever heating her fragile body.

Magda grabbed a fistful of Lori's hair. "No!"

A hoarse laugh tore at his chest. "Fine time to talk, little one."

Lori's trembling turned into teeth-chattering shaking. "Maybe I should ride over in the bus with her."

Then Lori would get off the bus, following Magda until her tired body fell over.

The best he could do for Lori and Magda was to make the separation quick, like jerking off a Band-Aid, except no way in hell would this one be painless. "It's not going to be any easier an hour from now, if you can even last that long. You're dead on your feet now. Let go, honey."

"Okay." Lori's voice trembled almost as much as her hands.

Gently as he could, he pulled Magda from Lori's arms. "Come on, kiddo."

The Barbie snagged in Lori's hair, extending her unraveling braid in a link between the woman and child until finally the roped hair fell lank against Lori.

"No!" Magda cried again, arms extended.

Lori lurched forward, her arms reaching to yank Magda back. Gray sidestepped and passed the child to a waiting nurse. Pivoting quickly, he caught Lori against his chest. "Hang tough. You'll only make it worse if you take her back now."

For the first time in a year, he held Lori, fitting her to

him with a familiarity that should have sent them both running in the opposite direction. She stood stiff and shaking against him. Her hair caressed his chin, teased his nose with hints of peaches and tears.

He dealt with people in pain every day. He wouldn't call himself callous, but doctors had to develop a level of objectivity to survive.

Objectivity wasn't even an option.

Over Lori's head he could only watch the nurse carry Magda to the bus. She stared back at him over the nurse's shoulder, brown eyes wide with betrayal as she cried out her lone English word. "No! No!"

Lori squeezed her eyes shut and pressed her face to Gray's neck. Cupping the back of her head as he had Magda's, he swallowed heavily and tried to calm Lori with mumbled words, soothing strokes. Inadequate offerings.

Lori's trembling built, and Gray held tighter until her first sob broke through, harsh and full. His arms tightened around her. He'd never seen her cry. Not even during their last fight before she'd left him.

He threaded his fingers through her hair and tipped his head back to stare up into the night sky. The stars seemed to wink back at him. *Not a chance of escaping here, pal.*

"Let me go." She twisted in his arms.

He held strong, afraid she might dart out onto the busy flight line. "In a minute. You're tired and—"

"If you call me hysterical, I'll rip your head off. Just let me go." She cried, kicked his shin, cried some more.

He winced at the jab to his leg from her foot and sucker punch to his gut from her tears. But he kept smoothing his hand over her hair until Magda's cries waned with the retreating bus.

Lori thumped a fist against his shoulder with only half the force she could have. "Damn you. Damn your bandannas and Beatles. And damn you for making me miss your smiles all over again."

Her drumming fist slowed. Her words pounded through him with double the power as she sagged in his arms.

The activity on the flight line dwindled to a hum in his ears. She simply lay against him—peaches, sweat and softness.

He stroked back flyaway strands of her hair. "It's gonna be okay, honey."

"God, Gray, I wish for once it really could be that simple." Her breath mingled with his.

"Her new family will be spoiling her rotten by morning. With any luck, she's young enough to forget."

If only he could say the same for himself. Gray knew without question he would never forget the disillusionment he'd seen in Magda's eyes. A look too much like the one he'd found in his father's eyes years ago.

Gray's arms tightened. He stared down at Lori's beautiful mouth and needed to make her smile more than he needed to sleep. And he needed sleep mighty damned bad. "Don't think about Magda crying. Think about her in her new room."

"In her new home."

"That's right. She'll have a home and a family."

"Home and family." Lori shivered in spite of the muggy night air. "It's more than a lot of people can claim, I guess."

"Yes, it is." He wanted to drop a kiss on her head, but settled for resting his forehead against her silky hair.

She swayed against him, and Gray realized he would have to drive her home. Lori wasn't in any condition to climb behind the wheel. She needed him, even in a small way, and that shouldn't have mattered as much as it did. "Magda will be settled by morning."

"She deserves so much more."

And so did Lori.

"I'm sorry." For wanting Lori when sex was the last

thing they needed. For not being able to give her that home and family.

For knowing he was no closer to being the kind of man she needed than he'd been a year ago.

What did he plan to do when time came to say goodbye again? He couldn't leave things the way they were. That hadn't worked for the past twelve months, and he didn't expect it to be any different now.

Before he left Charleston, he needed to fix things between them, make some kind of peace. He'd allowed the questions, the unresolved issues, the tension to hang between them too long.

He needed a game plan, but solutions weren't coming any faster now than they had a year ago. And he only had two and a half weeks to find the answer.

Chapter 4

Hadn't she learned anything in a year? Lori scavenged inside herself for the resolve to step out of Gray's arms, but couldn't find the energy. Magda's sobs echoed in Lori's weary brain until she fought the urge to cry again. More tears wouldn't fix anything, heaven knew, because she'd cricd buckets over Grayson Clark a year ago.

How easy it would be to let herself go slack and sleep where she stood on the flight line, secure in knowing Gray's arms would support her for a few moments longer.

She wasn't sure how long she did just that, slump against his broad chest and breathe in his bay rum, sweat and strength. Maybe she did drift into a twilight nap. She'd always been able to drop off easily, a talent cultivated from childhood years sleeping in hotels or apartments while partyers dodged around her.

Reality intruded, not through flight-line noises but in the strange quiet. She elbowed free from Gray's embrace and found the tarmac almost empty. A lone truck waited, engine humming, headlights cutting the night while a uniformed driver waited inside.

Lori swept a hand over flyaway strands of her hair. Enough leaning on Gray, she needed to finish her job, then go home to crash. "Where is everyone?"

"I told the crew to go ahead without me." Gray jerked a thumb toward the military truck. "SOF, uh, the supervisor of flying, will take us back."

She scrubbed a palm over her face, wiping away remnants of her crying jag. "Real professional of me to miss out on the end because I needed to indulge in a little fit of histrionics."

His hands fell to rest on her shoulders. "Only a hardnose wouldn't have been moved by what went down here tonight. So what if you needed to let go? You'd already stayed later than the rest of your team, far longer than was necessary." His fingers trailed, and he lightly squeezed her upper arms. "Cut yourself some slack."

Those broad hands warmed her, weakened her. She stepped back. "Whatever."

His hands dropped to his sides. "You ready to pack it in?"

Lori nodded. "It's going to be a long drive downtown. At least traffic will be light."

His jaw thrust forward. "You're not driving."

Irritation stirred up her second wind. "Think again."

"You're not in any shape to drive."

"Like you're any better off than I am? I can drive myself home as easily as you can." A face-splitting yawn snuck through in spite of her best efforts to swallow it. "End of discussion. But thanks all the same."

"Long missions and hours on rotation at the hospital are par for me. I'm used to it. Okay?" When she didn't answer, Gray cricked his neck to the side, once, twice, then reached to tighten the bandanna around his upper calf. "Geez, woman, why we arguing instead of sleeping?"

''It's what we do best?''

Gray glanced up at her, his eyes glittering in the night with a heat and longing that reminded her too well of what they'd always done best together.

Uh-oh. ''No way, Gray. Don't even say it!''

He gave the bandanna another yank around the mud stains on his uniformed leg and stood. ''Let me give you a ride, for old-times' sake. I promise not to pull off at the first dirt road and jump you. As tired as I am, I'd be pretty worthless anyway, and it would ruin all those better memories.'' His signature grin creased his face as he plucked his grimy flight suit. ''Not to mention we both smell pretty rank.''

Against her will she laughed. Against her better judgment she agreed. ''Just a ride.''

''Just a ride.''

''And my car?'' She tossed out a last half-hearted attempt at refusing. She truly would be a menace on the road if she got behind the wheel, and calling a taxi would take too long. Not to mention blatantly refusing his offer would say too much about her need to avoid him.

''Bronco and I can drive your car to your place tomorrow after debrief.''

Her stomach took a nosedive. She would see him again. At least they would have Bronco as a buffer.

Gray frowned. ''Unless you need a ride into work. I could—''

Come earlier alone? Not a chance. ''I moved to an apartment above the offices. My assistant is holding down the fort today and tomorrow, anyway, because of the mission's long hours.''

''No sweat, then.''

No sweat?

Oh there was plenty of emotional sweat to go around, and it carried the tauntingly familiar scent of bay rum and Gray.

* * *

At the base ops parking lot, Gray thumbed the unlock button on his key chain. The running-board lights glowed to life like a beacon in the dark as he strode ahead of Lori to open the passenger door. He reached to brace her elbow as she stepped up into the Explorer. Even weaving on her feet, she ignored him and used the hand grip and running board to lever herself inside the car.

Fine, if that's the way she wanted to play it. He kept his eyes firmly off her slim hips, not that it helped. His mind's eye remembered them well.

He circled and climbed into the driver's seat, the hint of gently musky perspiration and peaches already invading his car as well as his senses. Memories marched over him, images of choosing peach-scented lotion for her at the mall. He'd tested half the selections on Lori, working his way up inch after inch of the tender inside of her arm. Stirred into a frenzy by the time they'd reached the end of the display counter, they'd sped back to his apartment....

Gray rolled the windows down. Cranking the air conditioner, he let it blast out the oppressive heat. "Where are we going?"

Her startled gaze met his.

Double entendres stunk, and they seemed to abound around Lori. Gray chose his words carefully. "Where do you live now? You mentioned an apartment over an office. I assume that means you're not renting the carriage house anymore."

"Oh, right. I moved this year. When I landed the job to start up the offices here in Charleston, the building we use has offices on the first floor. I rent the second. It just made sense for me to live there."

"And that's where?"

Crickets hummed an evening tune while he waited. She twirled the end of her braid around her finger, one of her understated signs Gray recognized as nerves. With his reserves nearing zero, he needed to get her in bed soon.

Bed? *Damn.*

Had Freud and his infamous slips jumped in the car with them while Gray was busy ogling Lori's silky hair? "Lori? Where's your place?"

"Oh." She laughed and slumped back against the seat. "I must be punch drunk from lack of sleep. You were right not to let me drive. It's downtown on Broad Street."

"Great locale." And a long drive. He shuffled aside his own pressing need to fall facedown on his bed.

Alone. He rushed the thought before Freudian slips and double entendres could bite him on the libido again.

Slower and slower Lori twisted the end of her braid. "It's a fixer upper, but worth the elbow grease. I'm happy with it."

Happy. She'd moved on, carved out a great life for herself. Time to yank himself out of limbo. He raised the windows and slid the Explorer into drive.

Lori started fading before he reached the base's front gate. Traffic was sporadic and light, not many drivers other than truckers venturing out after twelve on a weeknight.

Gray blasted the air conditioner on his face to keep himself alert and Lori awake. "And you're happy with the job?"

"Yeah. I love it. I just hope the new southeast division makes it through its probationary period. Placing these children without a hitch will go a long way in buying us some security."

They'd never discussed her work much in the past, although her dedication was obvious. Her life-threatening sprint on the flight line went beyond dedication. "What made you switch jobs?"

"Working for the Department of Social Services was starting to wear on me. I tried to focus on the kids I helped, but there are just too many loopholes in the system. Children don't always end up where they should. Every time I had to return a child to a home my instincts told me wasn't safe, it tore me up inside." She crooked her arm against the window to pillow her head. "Maybe I'm being selfish. But there's more immediate gratification in this job, finding homes for these children, even being a foster parent in a pinch. These kids give me so much. I never forget a face." Her smile faded.

Magda might as well have been sitting in the back seat, because her tear-streaked face all but hovered between them. "You're the last person I would call selfish."

"Thanks, Gray," she whispered, "but maybe you just don't know me all that well."

Highway streetlights whipped past in bursts and fading flashes. His grip tightened around the steering wheel. "So have you found the guy who does know you?"

The question fell out of Gray's mouth before he could think to stop it. He turned another air-conditioning vent on his face because he must be groggier than he thought he was to have let that one slip.

Still he waited for her answer, not sure what he wanted it to be. After two mile markers of silence, he glanced at her. She lay limp against the door, her lashes against her cheeks, her breasts gliding in the even rise and fall of deep slumber. He'd always enjoyed watching her sleep.

Gray jerked his gaze back to the road before he landed in more than a ditch. The turnoff to his North Charleston apartment approached, Lori's place still at least a half hour away. He blinked past the grit in his eyes and stifled a yawn.

He looked at the road sign again. Without giving himself time to change his mind, he turned at his exit. She could sleep in the guest room. He would take her home in the morning.

Unlike Lori, he'd never had any problem being selfish.

Pulling into his driveway, he stared at the complex of

brick apartments from Lori's perspective, trying to see it as a home rather than a place to park his stuff. It offered direct access to the pool, gym and hot tub, nothing spectacular but serviceable, with minimal upkeep when he left for long deployments.

Nevertheless he wouldn't miss it when the packers loaded his furniture in two weeks. And the woman beside him…?

Gray stretched his neck from side to side, clearing his mind so he could get them both into the apartment.

"Lori," he called softly. When she didn't stir, he nudged her shoulder. "Lori, we're here, at my apartment."

He added the last and waited for the explosion. Nothing. Gray shook her shoulder—her soft, delicate shoulder.

She shifted away from the window and rested her cheek on his hand. She nuzzled him with a sleepy moan that sent his thoughts of sleep on a direct flight out the window.

He considered his memory to be top-notch, but no way in hell could he have remembered just how satiny her skin felt against his. She mumbled, nuzzling him again.

And kissed his wrist.

Forget waking her up. Gray yanked his hand away. He would carry her to his first-floor apartment.

Her other hand crept up his arm to cup his face. "Hey, baby." Her Southern drawl floated on the air, husky and not quite awake. "We're here already, huh?"

Gray stifled a groan. Apparently, he'd also forgotten how deeply she slept. "Wake up, Lori."

"Don't want to." Her head lolled to rest on his chest as her arms looped around his neck. "You're a great pillow, cuddly and warm."

Another part of him was far from soft but definitely on fire.

He carefully disengaged her arms. An image of untwining Magda from Lori earlier flashed in Gray's mind, effectively dousing the moment. God, he wanted this day to end.

Gray slid from the car and circled to Lori's side. He lifted her into his arms, not an easy task as she was a tall woman and dead weight. She snuggled her face right into his neck. He walked faster.

At his apartment he put her down to unlock the door. She leaned against him, her arms encircling his neck. Her small, but perfectly soft breasts seared his chest, burning away his exhaustion.

She was obviously asleep. But if the past played itself out in her dream, her next move would involve her fascination with his flight suit zipper.

"Come on, Lori, let's get you inside. Fast." Keys jingling, he unlocked the door. Lori's arms dropped away, and Gray caught her around her waist as he shoved the door open.

She grabbed his butt. "Have I ever told you how great you look in a flight suit?"

He couldn't decide whether to laugh or cry. "Hey, honey, I'm not a piece of meat, you know," he mumbled, scooping her into his arms. Too bad her touch lingered.

Her head drooped against his shoulder. "Flight suits are so hot."

"I'll make sure to share that with the folks at work."

Kicking the door shut, he strode into the living room. Dimmed lights from the vaulted ceiling illuminated a shadowy path. He limped down the hall as fast as he could, not nearly fast enough to the guest room. He lowered Lori to her feet again and swept the daybed clear of bubble wrap and packing supplies.

Warm, sleepy woman molded herself to him as he shoved down the comforter. Gray guided her onto the bed, slipped her shoes off and draped a spread over her, no lingering touches.

But maybe one last look.

Moonlight slatted through the navy miniblinds. She burrowed into the pillow, sighed, and stopped moving. Her femininity contrasted with the stark furnishings of his apartment, always had.

Wisps of caramel hair straggled across her face, one catching on her mouth. Gray brushed them aside, allowing his thumb one extra stroke across her full bottom lip.

A dark part of his mind whispered he could have her now, in his bed, in a minute—in her. Just as quickly he squashed the thought and went to his own room alone. Of course he wouldn't take advantage of her that way. As he fell facedown on his bed, already half-asleep, he wondered who he was protecting more.

Lori or himself.

His father stepped out of the cargo plane. Reed-thin, painfully thin, Dave Clark clutched the handrail as he descended the stairs onto the tarmac with the other liberated POWs.

Gray wanted to sprint forward, but hung back with the rest of the waiting families. He gripped his brother's sticky hand while his mother held his little sister.

His father's clothes hung from his shoulders like a uniform left on the hanger. Righteous indignation and rage filled Gray's nine-year-old chest. What had they done to his dad?

He didn't want to think about it. His father was home, and that's all that mattered. Gray could give back his job as man of the house. Everything would be normal again.

His feet itched to move. Gray bolted forward.

But wait. That wasn't right.

A part of his mind argued with the familiar dream. That wasn't the way it happened. He'd stayed with his mom, brother and sister until his dad limped over to them.

Except Gray could feel his flight boots pounding the pavement, the panic slugging through him. Flight boots? But he was a kid.

He ran faster. He had to reach his dad before everything

blew. The cement cracked and spewed chunks of asphalt with each round of fire. His leg flashed with fiery-hot pain. Gray dodged and wove across the runway.

His father disappeared inside the uniform. Lori appeared in his place, holding Gray's little sister.

Gray leaped forward to tackle them just as the tarmac exploded beneath his feet.

Ring.

His ears echoed with the aftershock.

Light streaming through the blinds stung his eyes. Gray stuffed his head under his pillow to smother the sound and restore darkness.

Pillow?

Ring.

He shook off the bad dream, an expected byproduct of gunfire. Most combat flyers had them, and yesterday's shoot-out in Sentavo qualified for nightmare material. Knowing didn't make it suck any less. But at least his would fade normally, as they had done after he'd flown C-130s in Desert Storm, and again after his brief stint in Afghanistan. His father's combat dreams still had the old man walking the floors at night.

Ring. Gray pressed the heels of his hands against his eyes to dispel the lingering grip of fear for his dad—for Lori.

Ring.

Gray lobbed his pillow at the phone—and missed.

Fire shot up his leg. Groaning, he rolled to his back on the queen-size bed, boot propped, knee bent so his throbbing calf wouldn't touch even the comforter.

Ring.

He snatched the phone off the cradle. "Yeah."

"Morning, sunshine."

"God, Bronco. It's still..." Gray scrubbed a hand over his bleary eyes and read his watch. "Two hours till debrief. Go pound sand."

''No, thanks.'' Tanner Bennett's too-damn-cheerful laugh faded on the other end. ''So, Cutter, what's up?''

''Nothing.''

''Too bad.''

''Not funny.''

''Now is that any way to talk to your best bud?''

His nosy best bud. Gray needed to get off the phone so he could see Lori and wash away the sour aftertaste of his dream. ''It's not fair to challenge a man before his morning pot of coffee. I'm hanging up, bud.''

''Wait. I'm calling to offer my help.''

''Help?''

''Moving Lori's car back to her place. I couldn't help but notice it parked in the lot when I came in.''

Gray resisted the urge to growl at Bronco, knowing that would only further fuel the guy's curiosity. Locker-room confidences about women, especially Lori, weren't his style anyway, no matter how close the friendship. ''Quit fishing, pal. That pond's empty.''

''So why's her car still here?''

''She was too upset to drive, thank you very much for your *help* yesterday. I already took her home.'' His home, but Bronco didn't need to know that, and forget asking him to help trade out Lori's car now. Gray stared out his open bedroom door, his eyes attracted like a guilty magnet to the closed guest room across the hall.

''You took her home? What the hell were you thinking?''

''Your concern is downright touching.''

''Hey, I'm a sensitive guy.''

Gray snorted on a laugh that set his leg on fire again. He bit back a groan.

''Are you okay?''

''Charley horse. Gotta go. See you in a few.''

Bronco's reply faded as Gray dropped the phone in the

cradle. Time to haul his sorry butt out of bed and face Lori's wrath when she realized he hadn't taken her home.

Gray untied his boots and eased them off, careful not to jar his leg. He stood, unzipped his flight suit and shook it free before dropping back to rest on the edge of the bed.

Bit by painful bit, he peeled the fabric from his thigh and tossed aside the ruined uniform. Bracing one foot on his knee, he evaluated the back of his calf. Not too bad. Specks of asphalt mixed in with the shrapnel. Hurt like hell, but he should be able to pick free what didn't soak out in the shower.

He only had to put in a half day with debrief and wasn't scheduled at the base clinic. A call to check on Magda's condition would clear his work commitments. Then he could crash on his deck for a beer and a nap in the sun.

After he took Lori home.

His dream came roaring back like the exploding tarmac.

How the hell was he going to figure out how to put the past to rest for good this time?

Maybe he should start with a simpler, less painful task, like digging shrapnel out of his leg.

Chapter 5

She couldn't decide what would be simpler, climbing out the apartment window and hitching a ride clear across Charleston or facing Gray again. Morning sun sliced through the miniblinds as Lori tucked her knees to her chest.

Gray hadn't taken her home, but then, she hadn't stayed awake long enough to give him her street address. She knew better than to blame him for not waking her. A category-five hurricane couldn't have roused her.

Of course, he could have looked in her purse, a little voice spurred her.

Her conscience silenced the little voice in no time flat. Gray had no doubt been equally as exhausted, and she'd been selfish enough depending on him.

She pressed her back against the daybed corner in Gray's guest room, the room he set aside for his family and friends. Were they friends now? Or would they say goodbye for good? Which would be harder…never seeing him again or having to face him in a platonic way, watching other women pass in and out of his life?

The bedside clock flashed eleven o'clock. She eyed the door. Was he still in his big bed? A bed she'd shared more than once.

A clump of lank hair fell in Lori's face. She probably looked like a worn-out hag, exactly how she felt. All thoughts of vanity aside, no woman wanted her ex seeing her looking like this, with wrinkled clothes, dirty hair and undoubtedly bloodshot eyes.

Time to go home through the front door—after a speedy dash into the bathroom.

Lori flung aside the navy comforter. If only her memories could be so easily discarded.

Damn it, she'd been fine two days ago. Or had she? Work dominated her life and had for a year, no relationships, only superficial friendships.

Resolutely she squashed self-doubts. She was content—*happy*—with her life. She certainly preferred her new job to her prior one with the state. Career building demanded focus, and focusing on her career helped her stop thinking about Major Grayson Clark.

Lori padded to the door, peeked out at the empty hallway and listened. A shower swooshed from behind Gray's bedroom door.

No way would she let her thoughts wander there.

She darted down the hall past his computer room to the spare bath. While she hated the thought of putting back on her grungy clothes, at least a shower would slosh away the grime. She whipped open the door and stopped short.

Resting on the edge of the vanity waited an old pair of her shorts and a Spoletto Festival T-shirt. A half-empty bottle of shampoo nestled on top of the stack. Her brand. Things she'd left at his place.

Cottony thickness wedged in her throat like a wadded T-shirt. Why hadn't he tossed them out? He wasn't a neat freak by any stretch, but he kept a clean apartment, especially for a bachelor.

A horrible thought blindsided her. Could he have let some other woman use her things?

Unable to stop the green-eyed monster from rearing its ugly head, Lori leaped forward and buried her nose in the T-shirt. It held the same detergent scent as Gray's flight suit. There were no lingering flowery fragrances to fan the green-eyed monster's flames.

Not that it was any of her business or concern.

Lori bumped the door shut with her hip, stripped out of her clothes and stepped into the tub. The shower stung her eyes as she stared at her old shampoo bottle. Soap didn't have an expiration date, like milk and bad relationships, did it?

The bottle all but seared her hand. They'd come out of more than one shower together smelling like peaches.

Enough daydreaming about Gray.

She scrubbed through her shower and toweled dry, staring at the little pile of clothes. Too bad she hadn't left behind fresh underwear, not that she really needed a bra. Hating the thought of putting on anything she'd worn the day before, Lori whipped the T-shirt over her bare chest and stepped into the shorts.

The hall echoed with her light footsteps. Gray's door stood open to an empty bedroom. Her eyes traveled to his rumpled bed, then skittered away.

Ping. The tinny sound reverberated from the kitchen, followed by a grunt from Gray. "Yeah…uh-huh…. What's her temp now?… And when do those sputum cultures come in from the lab?… Well, page me…. Yeah, thanks. I'll check back later."

Ping.

Odd. It tinkled like a spoon lightly tapping a dish, but without the rhythm or force that accompanied eating. She walked toward the kitchen.

Ping.

Lori closed the last few feet to the kitchen archway where a fresh flight suit dangled from a hanger hooked on the molding. She stepped around it to find Gray sitting at the table in his boxers and a plain, black T-shirt. His left leg lay propped on the white tiled table.

What was he doing? His broad shoulders hunched forward, blocking her view.

She inched closer. A large blue towel draped half the table. The cordless phone and a notepad rested beside a small medical kit.

And a dish with pieces of bloody metal inside.

Gray's hand extended toward the bowl, tweezers firmly in his grip, and released another fragment of metal.

Ping.

"Ohmigosh!"

Gray jerked, then glanced over his shoulder. "Oh, hey, Lori."

She rushed forward, staring horrified at his shrapnel-splattered leg. Nausea stung the back of her throat.

Flecks of metal and rock the size of peas and pinheads dotted the upper back of his left calf. Blood oozed from the small wounds already cleared of debris.

Lori grabbed the edge of the table and sank into a chair. "'Hey, Lori'? That's all you can say? You're digging chunks out of your leg and all you can say is 'Hey, Lori'?"

"It beats flinging crew dog curses your way. And believe me, hon, I've got a few of those floating around in my head right now."

"When did this happen?"

He shrugged and resumed picking. "Sometime yesterday."

Ping. She winced. Her mouth burned with bile. She'd seen worse injuries just yesterday, tending the children, but somehow this sent her stomach hurtling in roller-coaster flips.

Her mind flashed back to the bandanna tied around his calf on the return flight. In the darkened cockpit she'd seen only the bandanna and what she'd thought were mud stains. Guilt packed a heavy punch. "Why didn't you say something?"

"No need." Pick. Drop. Pick. Drop. "It didn't affect my ability to do my job. Plenty of time for Band-Aids later."

She watched with a mixture of awe and horror as he irrigated a deeper cut with a squirt bottle, pinched it closed and sealed it with a butterfly bandage. "Shouldn't you be at the doctor's office?"

He paused digging long enough to quirk a brow. "I didn't get my degree over the Internet, hon."

"Don't be a smartass, Gray. Shouldn't you have a tetanus shot or something?"

"Soldiers get tetanus shots ten times the strength of a regular dose. Stands to reason, right?" He worked as he spoke, as if the words gave him focus. "Could be hours, even days, before treatment is available in a survival situation. Think what could happen from a simple bramble scratch, followed by wading through some unsanitary sludge pit."

She shuddered.

"We're pumped full of more immunizations than you can imagine." He manipulated the tweezers around the last piece, a heavily embedded square of metal. His words slid through gritted teeth. "Son of a—"

Ping.

Gray sighed, sagging back in his chair, eyes closed.

Lori stared at those angry, red patches on his leg and thought of their dash across the Sentavian tarmac. "You were hurt running after me, weren't you?"

His lack of response was answer enough.

He'd been injured and hadn't said a word while she let him take care of her. Guilt prickled again like a mental shrapnel blast. "Could I at least finish up for you? I'm not a doctor, but I think I can handle antiseptic cream and a bandage."

His grin slid into place, a grin that stretched his too-pale face. "Sure. Who am I to turn down a little TLC?"

Lori walked to the sink and pumped antibacterial soap into her hands. Once she'd washed and dried them, along with steadying her stomach, she crossed to Gray.

He winked. "Be gentle with me."

His eyes touched on her mouth, her neck, her braless chest.

The small kitchen shrank as she realized they were inches apart, Gray in his underwear, Lori without underwear. "Can you be serious for once?"

"Nope."

The chalky pallor beneath his tanned face kept her from arguing. Of course Gray always covered his real feelings with a laugh, and right now he had to be hurting like hell.

She squeezed the ointment in long streams over his leg. Gently she skimmed her fingers over the puckered cuts. His head fell to rest against the back of his chair.

Lori smoothed the cream, covering the area he'd shaved. While she'd been indulging in silly daydreams about him in the shower, he'd been shaving his leg around shrapnel wounds. "I'm so sorry for making you run after me."

"You saved a kid. This doesn't matter."

Her fingers detoured past the shaved area to the bruise on his shinbone where she'd kicked him. His leg muscles flexed. Crisp hair rasped under the tender pads of her fingers, kindling a fire within her hot enough to waft steam off her wet hair.

Lori circled the mottled bruise. Had she really kicked him that hard the night before? "I'm especially sorry for this."

"It's nothing."

She covered the bruise with her palm as if to sear it well. "What you did for me last night wasn't noth—"

"Lori." He jerked his leg away. "Stop. It was nothing."

"Okay. Fine." His words stung like antiseptic on her already-raw emotions.

She turned her attention to his leg. His bare leg.

How easy it would be to trail her hand up his calf. The familiarity of other mornings spent in the same kitchen lured her. Her body hungered for him, like an addictive habit.

A very dangerous habit she needed to break.

Lori unrolled a patch of gauze, procrastinating until her breathing regulated again. Gray ripped pieces of tape with his teeth and passed them to her. Lori anchored the bandage, her damp hair fanning forward over his leg. His muscles flexed again.

He reached to tuck her hair behind her ear, slowly, deliberately. His eyes fell to her mouth and lingered, caressed, as powerfully as any kiss. Her breasts, aching and heavy with yearning, tightened beneath the gentle abrasion of her T-shirt.

She backed away. "How's that?"

Gray cleared his throat and swung his leg off the table. Standing, he said, "Couldn't have done it better myself."

He tugged his flight suit off the hanger and stepped into it, shrugging it over his shoulders. She watched him dress, caught in that time warp of familiarity. A quick whip of the zipper and the intimacy fell away.

She skirted past him. "Give me a second and I'll gather up my other clothes."

Gray snatched the pad from the table and tore off the top sheet. He passed it to her, fingers brushing, pausing, heating, before he sank back into a chair to pull on his flight boots.

Slumping against the door frame, Lori read the numbers jotted in Gray's nearly illegible scrawl. She flipped the paper over and found nothing else jotted. "What's this?"

"Phone number for the Medical University Hospital."

"Are you doing rounds there?" She'd forgotten flight surgeons wore their uniforms even when acting as a doctor. A startling thought stopped her short. She looked down at the phone number. Did he want her to contact him? "Am I, uh, supposed to call you for something?"

"Nope." He tucked his squadron scarf along the neck of his flight suit. "That's the direct number to the nurses' station on Magda's floor."

The blood drained right from Lori's head to her bare toes. A dull ache throbbed inside her as she thought of the scene on the flight line. "Magda?"

"I followed up with the medical corps on base who logged them in last night. Magda was transported to the Medical University. She has pneumonia. I thought you would want to know."

He'd checked on Magda. Warmth pooled low in Lori's stomach. He could be so sweet sometimes. Then his words filtered through and chilled her. "Pneumonia?"

Gray jerked the laces on his boot taut. "Yeah."

"Poor little thing." Lori crossed her feet at the ankles, as if that might somehow ease the urge to race to the hospital. Reason battled some odd instinct within her to bolt out the door, anyway. "At least she has her sponsor family with her. It wouldn't be fair for me to disrupt her bonding with them."

Yanking the laces on his other boot with a vicious tug, he grunted.

"Gray?"

He pulled the legs of his flight suit down over the boots.

"Gray?" Lori shoved away from the door to stand beside him. "She does have her sponsor family with her, doesn't she?"

His elbows thunked on the table. "No."

"What do you mean, no?"

"According to the nurse, Magda's back in the system. The couple slated to take her had tried for years to have a kid of their own. And wouldn't you know, the rabbit died while we were in the air. So now they don't need Magda anymore."

"Oh, my—" Lori bit back the need to rage at people who weren't even present. She would have given her eye-teeth for one child, and this couple tossed away the double blessing of two. "How did you find all this out?"

"Side benefit of having privileges there, and my signature is on her chart."

Lori paced around the kitchen, unable to dodge images of Magda's crying face. "I need to check in with the office to step up the search for another family so she'll have somewhere to go when she's released. I can't afford any glitches in placing these children. Neither can Magda." A scary flutter started in Lori's stomach. This kid was wriggling a little too close. Keep perspective. Don't lose objectivity. Lori ignored the warning. "I've got to go up there and see her."

"Of course you do."

"What?"

He tipped his chair on two legs, defensiveness warring with the cocky tilt of his beard-stubbled chin. "I can be through at the base and back here in a couple of hours, long enough for you to wash your other clothes, grab a nap, dry your hair, whatever. I can get you into her room. You'll learn a lot more with me along."

She stared across the kitchen into his eyes and found more of that defensiveness. She knew him too well.

Lori cupped his face in her hand. "Why can't you admit you want to see her, too?"

Defensiveness fled. A snap of anger replaced it, only to fade as quickly as it had fired. He grazed her shoulder with a knuckle, down her side, just beside her breast, bare and tight beneath her T-shirt. "And why can't you admit you still want me?"

His touch felt too good with only the thin barrier of well-washed cotton between them. His face felt too good in her hand, with barriers between them crumbling faster than she could rebuild.

She backed out of his reach. His hand dropped away as quickly as hers. She definitely knew him too well. "Still using sex to dodge the tough questions, I see."

"What can I say? You know me." He shot to his feet and grabbed a travel mug steaming hints of chicory into the air. "I'll be back from debrief in two hours to pick you up."

The front door closed behind him before she realized she should have demanded he drop her off at her car on his way. Why hadn't she?

Lori crossed her arms over her aching breasts. Apparently, she didn't know herself nearly as well as she thought she knew Gray.

Two bowls of frosted flakes later, Lori decided she needed to leave. Her clothes should be finished in the dryer soon. She sat cross-legged on Gray's blue-plaid couch and checked her watch for the fifth time in ten minutes. She'd spent most of the past hour working Magda's case from the phone.

Now she should call a cab, leave Gray a note and cut out. Her own work credentials would gain her entrance to see Magda.

And if Gray showed up at the hospital, too? They would behave like adults. She wasn't some high-schooler ducking behind the lockers to avoid a boy.

Lori swung her feet off the sofa and searched the apartment for the phone book. She roamed from the living room, through the kitchen. God, the man loved Air Force blue. His whole place was blue, wood and white. Of course he'd once told her buying a single color scheme meant he didn't have to waste time matching.

And he hadn't. No knickknacks warmed the decor. Just

precoordinated furniture. Even his bedroom linens fit the bed-in-a-bag category. Only a smattering of framed airplane prints gave hints about the man who lived there.

A home, but not quite, like the motels and transitory apartments her parents had always chosen.

Lori found the phone book in his computer room and plopped in the office chair to call the cab company. While she waited on hold, she spun in the chair. Pictures of the C-17 littered the white wall, no surprise. His degrees must be in his office on base.

Twirling another half turn revealed a dry erase board, and his first homey touch. Notes scrawled along corners around the childish artwork dominating the space. Someone had drawn a purple outline of an airplane in the middle and labeled it for "Uncle Gray."

How long had it been there? And how sweet he hadn't erased it.

Images bombarded her. Ladislov's giggle when Gray had tickled his side to get him to cough. Magda's smile because of a simple do-rag.

Lori eyed the phone. Maybe she could wait for Gray a little longer. She reached to hang up. A brass picture frame glinted in the overhead light, halting her. She snagged the photo from the desk, the phone still cradled in her other hand.

Gray's family of five clumped together on a flight line. He must have been about nine or ten, his brother and sister younger.

Lori had met his parents. They only lived an hour away and had joined Gray and her for dinner twice. There hadn't been time to get to know the couple who'd brought up Gray, but she'd liked what little she'd found.

She had to face it. He'd had a happy home life, didn't have hang-ups about kids. Gray simply didn't want home and hearth for himself. He preferred the bachelor life.

So what was she doing waiting around for him? As if to

confirm her decision, the canned music on the phone ended and the cab dispatcher's voice asked for her information.

Lori replaced the frame and gave the woman Gray's address, an address still memorized even after a year apart.

Fifteen minutes late, Gray pulled into the apartment's parking lot. Debriefs couldn't be rushed, although he'd tried. Throughout the whole meeting, he'd worked to puzzle through a way to resolve things between Lori and him.

If he had the chance.

He couldn't shake the feeling she would leave before he returned. Maybe she'd called a friend to give her a ride.

Not that it should matter. He could track her down at her place or the hospital, and they could still see Magda together.

God knows Lori had left him flat before. Why should one more time matter? But it did. He wanted her to be waiting inside for him, like the old days.

She'd stayed over more than once. Near the end, she had almost lived there as well. He'd certainly thought asking her to move in officially would be no big deal. Wrong. It had sparked another argument, one that hadn't ended with mind-blowing make-up sex.

Stuffing the past away, he whipped the keys from his car just as another car slid into place beside him—a white Chevy Cavalier just like his mother's. He wasn't a believer in coincidence or fate, but he had the sinking feeling one of the two was about to have its way with him. Gray strapped on some much-needed bravado and opened his door.

His mother's silver-blond head soon appeared over the roof. "Hello, sugar."

Dread turned his blood to sludge. His perfectly coifed mother, a woman with inbred grace, gentility and rose-colored glasses, wouldn't be able to appreciate the nuances of his current awkward-as-hell situation with Lori.

''Hi, Mom.'' He circled to his mother.

Gray skated a quick look at his apartment door. Was Lori still inside? His mother would leap straight to a wealth of conclusions he didn't even want to consider, much less explain. Not that she would even believe him, anyway.

''I was on my way to the commissary to stock up and thought I'd drop in to see you.''

''Great.''

''Why don't we step inside where it's cooler?''

Normally he wouldn't have minded. Today he would rather face a SCUD missile. ''Mom, sorry I can't visit right now. I've got to run in and grab a, uh, reference book,'' *lame, pal,* ''and head straight back out to see a patient.''

''Oh, too bad.'' She smoothed wrinkles from her dress, a grandma charm bracelet chiming with each swipe. ''I was hoping we could have an early supper together.''

''Soon, Mom.'' He draped an arm around her shoulder and tucked her to his side protectively. With genuine affection, familiar and welcome between them, he dropped a kiss on her head, almost level with his, since she wore her standard heels even for shopping. ''I promise.''

''And you'll come up to the condo to see your father before your family farewell party?''

Ah, dishing up guilt. ''Sure, Mom.''

She rewarded him with her smile. ''Good. I'll just get a quick glass of milk before I go. The traffic wreaked havoc on my nerves, and my stomach is simply churning.''

Her stomach would be served up one hefty surprise if she walked in on Lori wearing nothing but that paper-thin T-shirt and no bra. He needed to protect his mom and Lori—hell, maybe even himself. He scrambled for a solution and came up with, ''Waffle House.''

''What?''

''Let me take you to Waffle House for supper.''

''I thought you had to go?''

He glanced at his watch and wrestled with the need to

make sure Lori didn't leave, but also to divert his mother. No choice really. He had to keep his mother out of the apartment. If Lori was still inside, she would be embarrassed if not horrified, to see them. The hospital trip to visit Magda already promised to be difficult enough without tossing this into the mix. "I can always spare an hour for my favorite mom."

"What a sweet boy." She reached for her keys. "I'll just lock my car."

"No! Uh, we should take both cars so I can leave straight for the hospital."

"And your book?"

He went blank. Just like a kid caught sneaking into the house, he couldn't concoct a single excuse. All he could do was stare out over the parking lot for ideas, not that the yellow cab pulling up offered much in the way of inspiration.

The taxi inched along, closer and closer. Horror knifed through Gray. That cab couldn't be going to—

"Mom, never mind." He shut his mother's door. "You're right. Let's go together. I'll drive. Come on."

"Oh, okay."

The cab stopped in front of Gray's apartment. Surprise held him motionless for three precious seconds. Lori really intended to walk out on him a second time. Did he even warrant a note from her this go-round? Or did she just plan to slip away without a word again?

Useless anger chugged through him. He resisted the urge to charge over to the cab and confront her. Like that would accomplish anything productive with his mom as an audience.

He all but towed his mother to the Explorer. The driver honked his horn. Gray's mother glanced back over her shoulder just as Lori's gorgeous khaki-clad legs stepped through the apartment door. The afternoon sun caught her full in the face as she clutched the shorts and T-shirt to her breasts.

His butt was officially toast. There wasn't a chance his mom would let Lori get in that taxi without pumping her for information first. He couldn't have been more busted if Lori had strolled out the door wearing his boxers.

Chapter 6

Lori's feet grew roots in the sidewalk outside Gray's apartment. She couldn't move. Gray stalked toward her cab with his jaw set.

So much for her great escape. At least she could face him in clean clothes and underwear this time. She clutched the shorts and T-shirt closer to her chest like armor.

She forced her feet to trudge forward and plastered on a smile, weak at best. "Hi."

He ignored her and tapped on the driver's window. The window rolled down as Gray pulled out his wallet. He passed a twenty inside. "Thanks for coming out, but she doesn't need a ride now."

"I don't?" Lori said, more than a little miffed at his high-handedness and more than a little unsettled by his closeness.

"Sorry I'm late." He gripped her elbow and stepped away from the car.

But he was only a few minutes late, and they both knew it. He had to realize she'd called for the ride at least an hour ago. Why the pretense that she hadn't been running like a coward?

Her answer strolled over in neat heels and a tidy sundress. Gray's mother.

Lori clutched the incriminating clothes closer to her chest. "Hello, Angela."

Undisguised curiosity glinted from Angela Clark's eyes as she closed the last few feet between them. Her gray-blond hair, short and smoothly styled, glinted in the sunlight. Her yellow cotton dress glided cleanly across her figure, a few pounds past slim but well preserved for a mother of three adult children.

Her hair, the dress, her smile all made Lori think of sunshine. Angela Clark radiated energy.

The older woman clasped Lori's hands in hers, staring for five assessing seconds before she said, "It's good to see you again."

Air escaped Lori's lungs in a relieved sigh. Thank goodness Angela didn't plan to chew her out for dumping her precious baby boy. "You, too, Angela."

"Grayson, quit scowling and take us inside where it's cool."

Scowling? Gray? He always smiled.

Lori turned and, sure enough, Gray's face sported a tight-lipped frown. He couldn't be mad at his mother, so the feelings must be directed at her. She followed his glare straight to the disappearing cab.

Gray couldn't care that she planned to leave, could he? The thought was crazy—and frighteningly exciting.

With no hope of alternative escape, Lori followed Mrs. Clark to the apartment. She had no choice but to make nice with Gray's mom and her son—a son who looked too good in that flight suit for Lori's currently shaky peace of mind. Gray stepped ahead to unlock the door.

Inside the apartment Angela accepted a glass of milk from Gray and drank down a third before slowing to smaller sips. She reigned from a recliner, leaving Lori and Gray to sit on the sofa together or stand around awkwardly. They sat, awkward all the same.

"So?" Angela sipped her milk, eyes skipping back and forth between Gray and Lori. "Is there something you two want to share with me?"

"Mom, shut down the matchmaking. Lori worked with us on that rescue operation we flew yesterday. The hours were long. She crashed here, in the guest room, rather than go all the way back into town. I'm about to take her home."

"Well, that's just a shame. I was hoping the two of you worked things out."

Silence echoed all the way to the vaulted ceiling. Hands shaking, Lori placed the little bundle of clothes on the couch. How ironic to have the perfect, accepting mother-in-law, but no husband. Lori wanted off the sofa, out of the living room, out of the whole uncomfortable situation.

"Angela, thank you. I'm complimented. But what Gray said is true. There's nothing going on. We're just...old friends."

Friends. Gray winced. He wanted to grab Lori by the shoulders and demand she at least be honest. They'd been a hell of a lot more than friends. Of course even friends treated each other better than he and Lori had. He turned to her. "Would you mind if I talked to my mother alone for a minute?"

"Of course not. I, uh, could use a drink myself," Lori said, looking grateful for the excuse to escape as she backed into the kitchen.

Perched on the edge of her chair, Angela swallowed the rest of her milk. Her hand clenched around the glass, chewed-down nails turning white.

Familiar frustration welled in Gray. His mom knocked herself out worrying about her family, all the while pretending everything was normal. He couldn't do a damn thing about it except try to keep the peace and hope like hell her stomach didn't resemble Swiss cheese.

He needed to divert her before she invested more of her overtaxed energy into fairy-tale dreams of paper bridal bells. "Mom, put away the wedding planner. There's really nothing going on here."

Angela set aside her glass and swiped a pinky around her mouth. "Too bad Lori didn't get pregnant last summer, then you would have had to grow up and ask her to marry you."

"Mom!" Gray choked on a gulp of air and shock. He could have used some of that milk for his burning stomach.

She patted his face, the seven charms on her grandma bracelet tinkling. "It's okay, son. I know you have sex."

Horrified, Gray stood. Mothers did not discuss sex, not with him, anyway. "Okay, this conversation is over. Mom, I love you, and I owe you a trip to Waffle House. But we really have to leave for the hospital."

"The hospital? I thought you were taking Lori home."

Uh-oh. He shuffled like a busted teenager. "We're, uh, going to check in on a patient from the airlift."

"Patient? I thought you were evacuating—" her face was wreathed in a smile she'd passed along to her son "—children."

She cradled her bracelet to her heart as if already selecting a spot for the next little golden grandbaby charm.

Angela rose with the speed and fluidity of an Olympic gymnast. "Well, let me get out of your way, then."

She pressed a quick kiss to her son's cheek and cleaned the lipstick away with her thumb. "Bring Lori to your farewell party. Your *friends* are always welcome."

The door closed behind Angela with a resounding click.

Gray crooked his knee forward, favoring his injured leg, and jangled his keys in his hand. He stared at the door and didn't even bother chasing his mother down. She thought it was all so simple. Pretend to be happy and it became true. His family was just like the picture he kept by his desk. Full of paper-thin smiles with nothing underneath.

He would plaster one on to get through the afternoon with Lori, and hopefully find an answer to cutting ties, cleanly this time.

She deserved substantial emotions. After a lifetime of hiding his in order to face the world with a smile, Gray wasn't sure he had much substance left.

Lori stared out the Explorer window, Gray's voice filling the car as he sang along with the radio. Country today. The man had eclectic tastes and always knew all the words.

Nerves pattered double time as she wondered what she would find when they saw Magda. Couldn't he speed up?

Sometimes she wanted to shake him until he took life seriously. Other times she found his lightheartedness a welcome relief. After his mother's visit, they could both use a breather.

Time to get her head back in tune with her professional responsibilities. Magda needed a home, and Lori wasn't about to let Gray's appeal distract her from doing her best for that little girl.

Charleston came into view as they crossed the Ashley River. Hints of muggy marshland wafted in through the vents. The whole town carried the scent of humidity and history. Time-weathered steeples rose above the skyline from St. Philip's, St. Michael's, and other churches, earning Charleston its second name, the Holy City. Gray's mother had likely already booked a wedding date for them in one of those hallowed historical landmarks.

Lori tore her gaze away. A castle-like turret jutted into view from the Citadel, Gray's military college alma mater.

Sheesh, did she have to relate everything she saw to the man belting out bar tunes beside her?

All the same, she owed him an explanation. "About the cab—"

"Forget it," he said as they passed a restaurant on stilts by the Low Country's bog, the site of their second date.

"No. I won't. It just seemed…safer to meet at the hospital."

His knuckles whitened around the steering wheel. "What? You can't even sit in the same car with me for a few minutes?"

"Gray?" Water lapped high along the shore. Moonlit walk. Their third date.

"Forget it."

Anger snipped her already ragged emotions. What had happened to Doctor Lighthearted? "I don't understand. It's not like we're some kind of couple. I don't have to answer to you."

"Nope. We're not, and you don't."

She couldn't resist asking, "Then why are your shorts in a knot?"

His grip slackened, and he hooked his wrist over the steering wheel. "I don't know."

Her anger deflated. She could always count on Gray's honesty. He never kept his feelings from her, and if she didn't like them, well, at least she wasn't in the dark. "You don't know?"

"Nope." He shook his head slowly. "I just know when that cab stopped in front of my door, I was so mad at you I forgot my mother was three seconds away from walking into a damned embarrassing situation."

"Oh."

"Yeah, oh."

They passed her favorite hole-in-the-wall deli, their last date. "I hurt your feelings?"

Gray winced. "Well, I wouldn't put it that way."

"How would you put it?"

Pulling into the doctors' parking lot, he left the car running, air conditioner blasting. His face tipped to the sky, his brows meeting. Sunlight streamed over the strong planes of his lean face, his broad forehead and square jaw. Lori didn't realize she was holding her breath until her vision dotted with dizziness. Why was his answer so important?

His gaze slid to meet hers. "I understand you have to go. Just show me the courtesy of saying goodbye first this time, okay?"

Guilt pinched her breathing like a too-tight seat belt. Why hadn't she realized today echoed the past, how she'd left him, with no note, no goodbye?

How unlike her, too. She was seasoned in farewells. Why hadn't she given him something she'd perfected through countless childhood moves?

She should have known a vagabond like Gray would appreciate an appropriate goodbye as much as her gypsy parents did. People like them could turn off relationships as easily as they stamped their passports as long as farewells were exchanged.

Throat closing off, she nodded. "Okay."

After a curt nod, he reached into the back seat. His broad chest brushed her arm, and it was all she could do not to wrap her arms around him and apologize. Regardless of how their relationship had ended, no matter that she needed peace and he craved adventure, she respected this man and for the first time realized he had been hurt, too.

He twisted front with a bag in hand. "Sorry I was late today. I swung by the BX after debrief and picked this up for Magda. Maybe you should give it to her, though. She probably won't be too excited to see me after the scene on the flight line."

Lori opened the bag and peered inside.

A dark-haired Barbie peered back up at her.

Uh-oh. Now she knew why she had walked away without saying goodbye a year ago, tried again today. Resisting Gray while he wore boxers and a smile had been hard enough. Holding strong against the man who bought Barbies for babies could be a near impossible task.

After Gray picked up Magda's chart at the nurses' station, he and Lori crossed the hall to the little girl's room. He shrugged through a kink in his shoulder and shifted into doctor mode.

Urgency thrummed through him to see, treat and heal his patient. A healthy child stood a better chance of being placed. He knew that as well as Lori.

His feet slowed as an idea picked up speed in his mind like an ascending plane. Was that his role for Lori before he could cut ties and leave? Helping her advance her career?

In the past, he'd taken a hands-off approach to her job, maybe because she worked with kids. Whenever she'd shared a story about one of her tiny clients, Lori's face had glowed with a beauty and yearning that had his restless feet itching to run. Every time he had changed the subject, he knew he'd been an insensitive jerk. He'd just been so damned wary of letting her become embroiled in a scenario that would have her believing he could be a father.

Now that they were no longer a couple, he could support her in her work. Right? She'd said speedy placement of all the children would solidify her position and the validity of the southeastern branch. He could offer medical advice, contacts and encouragement until the last child was securely placed. The idea hit cruising speed and leveled off, his course set.

Lori hesitated just outside Magda's room.

"What's wrong?"

She faced the door, soft television noises wafting through. "Am I doing the right thing coming to see her? Am I being selfish?"

"How so?"

"I do my best for all the children we transport. But for

some reason that little girl got to me more than the others. What if I'm just coming to see her because I want to, not because it's best for her?'' Lori's words tumbled over each other in a nervousness unlike her. ''What if it turns into another scene like at the base? I don't want to upset her, especially when she's sick.''

''Do you want to leave?''

''No.''

''What do you want?''

Lori rolled her eyes. ''I want to take her home.''

The rest of Gray's answer came to him. He knew precisely what to do for Lori. He could find that home for Magda and give Lori the child she wanted after all, someone she could shower with her unselfish love. He didn't question the speed of his decision. Both his jobs necessitated quick assessment of the situation, followed by a solid plan of action. Both his professions also required a hefty dose of self-confidence in those decisions. ''So do it.''

''Do what?''

''Take her home.''

Lori with a child. The thought of her as a mother seemed so right, so natural. The notion grew in appeal with each passing breath.

A food cart rattled past in the silence.

''You're kidding, right?''

''Didn't you tell me you've been a foster parent before?''

''Short-term, Gray, just as a forty-eight-hour stop gap for children on their way to permanent foster placement. Nothing with such an awesome commitment.''

Commitment. The word might make him flinch, but not Lori. She could come through for that kid with ease.

Gray tucked closer to Lori to let hospital personnel and visitors stroll past. ''Then be Magda's foster mother while the system irons out the kinks with finding her a home.''

''But I work—''

''And working mothers can't have kids? You know better than that. If anyone can juggle it all, you can.'' He could see the idea taking hold in her mind with wary acceptance. He plowed forward with his next argument before she could argue or doubt. ''For now let's go inside, see Magda and play it by ear. This kid needs someone in her corner fighting for her. With any of the other children, you wouldn't hesitate to walk in that room and take on the world for her.''

Lori drew her full bottom lip between her teeth thoughtfully, then released it with agonizing slowness. ''I have to file someone's name within the next forty-eight hours or she'll become a ward of the state. I could give them mine, shouldn't be any problem. That will hold until the evidentiary hearing thirty days from now for more permanent placement. At least it will buy her some time.'' Lori pressed the heel of her palm to her forehead. ''Oh, God, I must be crazy.''

''But you're going to do it.''

''Yes.'' Determination fired her words. ''Yes. I am.''

Victory sent a charge of excitement through him that left Gray wanting to celebrate. In the best of ways. His gaze gravitated to her full mouth. Lori's pupils widened, darkened, deepened. Her breath picked up a notch, sending an answering response through him.

Gray reined in his wayward hormones. The idea was to get over the woman before he left, not make things worse. ''Let's go in then.''

He tucked Magda's chart under his arm, tapped twice on the door and shoved it open.

Magda lay listless and half-asleep in the bed, an IV taped to her tiny hand. Tubes for nasal oxygen wrapped from her nose around her ears. A grandmotherly aid sat reading in a chair by the bed while a blue, animated dog romped across the television.

Man, the kid was a heart tugger.

He had to be honest with himself. He wanted to see

Magda, too, needed to reassure himself the little imp was healthy and safe. Their parting at the base had rattled even a hardnose like himself.

The aid closed her book and smiled. Gray held up the chart. "You can take a break. One of us will buzz the nurses' station when we're ready to go."

The older lady nodded as she crossed to the door. "Thank you, Dr. Clark. I'll run down to the cafeteria for coffee and be right back."

Gray held the door open. "No rush."

The door swished closed. Anticipation hummed low as Gray watched Lori stop beside the bed rail. Gently she rested her fingers on Magda's arm. The child startled and turned her head.

Would Magda blame Lori for the scene on the runway, too? Who knew what whirled through her confused mind?

Her tiny bow mouth tipped into a grin. She struggled to sit up, but succumbed to rattling coughs.

Concern a degree beyond professional simmered in Gray. He whipped the stethoscope from his thigh pocket. He knew too well pneumonia was the leading cause of death among children in developing countries. Why the hell hadn't he considered that before suggesting Lori tangle her life and heart up with this kid? Doubts didn't come often to him, so the possibility of being wrong gripped him with alarming force.

However, looking at the two of them together, he couldn't regret his decision. Magda needed her. Lori braced a gentle hand on the child's back, soothing Magda until she could control her breathing. They were right together.

He strolled to the bed. "Hi, Magpie."

Her smile vanished. Magda's bottom lip shot out with a speed and reach his nieces and nephews would have applauded. Her mutinous glare left him with no doubt about her thoughts.

She was mad as spit. At him. Only him.

Women had long memories, and he was definitely persona non grata for little Magpie.

Gray warmed the stethoscope on his palm so she could see it and understand. "I need to check your breathing."

Magda eyed the stethoscope and scooted closer to Lori.

Lori clasped Magda's little fingers. "It's okay."

Magda sat rigidly while he slid the stethoscope on her back between the part in her polka-dot hospital gown, then around front. Her breath sounds rattled in his ears. Not a good sign, but perhaps minimally better than the day before.

"How is she?"

Gray draped his stethoscope around his neck and waggled his hand. "A little improved. Why don't you give her the present while I look over her chart?"

"Shouldn't you give—" Magda's scowl in Gray's direction stopped Lori. Her hand fluttered to rest on his arm. "I'm sorry."

"Don't sweat it," he said, trying like hell to ignore Lori's touch. "As long as she gets the toy, it doesn't matter who gives it to her."

Lori's eyes narrowed. "Damn, you're good."

A wry chuckle slipped free. "Well, hon, you haven't said that to me in quite a while."

"And then you're so bad."

Gray backed up a step. "Take care of our little friend while I review her records."

He dropped into a chair by the window, propping his boot on one knee to rest his leg. He opened the chart in his lap and flipped through pages. Lori's Southern drawl poured over him as she talked to Magda, accompanying words with gestures.

Lori mimed a cup brought to her mouth as she asked Magda if she wanted a drink. The girl nodded enthusiastically, and Lori poured her a glass of ice water.

Other word plays and gestures followed until Gray realized Lori was actually communicating with Magda through a basic, but formalized sign language. Interesting. A part of her training, perhaps? What else didn't he know about this fascinating woman?

Lori lowered the rail and perched on the edge of the bed, passing Magda the bag from the store. Gray stopped turning pages.

Magda eyed the sack warily. Her hand crept toward it, then paused. She looked from Gray to Lori with such distrust he wanted to go back to Sentavo, kick some serious butt and take a long list of names.

Her tiny hand pinched the edge of the bag and lifted. She peeked inside—and smiled.

Gray felt as if he'd found a cure for the common cold.

Magda yanked the Barbie out of the bag and struggled to rip open the box. Lori's head dipped as she helped Magda.

Lori's face shone with a natural beauty that stole the air from his lungs. Complete contentment radiated from her in waves he couldn't help but envy.

Gray watched the two of them and knew he'd been right in suggesting Lori become Magda's guardian. With their two dark heads so close, anyone could have mistaken them for mother and daughter. This was it. What he had to do to right the way they'd left things a year ago.

Finally he could offer her what she wanted. Through Magda, Lori would find that sense of home she seemed to need, the child she wanted. His last two weeks in Charleston could be spent helping Lori settle in with her new child.

Then he could walk away.

Fast on the heels followed the knowledge that he wouldn't be leaving her with some other man to make those babies. The thought stirred satisfaction—and guilt. Lori might imagine she was selfish for the least little wish, but he knew better.

He was the selfish one.

Chapter 7

Lori stepped through the hospital's automatic doors, Gray trailing her. The late-afternoon sun prickled along her fair skin just as apprehension and an underlying excitement prickled along her every nerve.

Magda would be coming home with her in two days. Stay objective, Lori warned herself. This was just another case. Another child. A very special child.

Cars roared and honked past in rush hour traffic, echoing the thundering of Lori's blood throbbing through her veins.

She slumped against the brick wall, gasping in drags of heavy air to steady her stuttering heart. "I can't believe I'm going to do this. I have seventy-one other kids to follow up on in the next few weeks. What am I thinking taking on a sick four-year-old full-time?"

Gray leaned beside her, his boot propped on the wall behind him. "You're thinking she'll have nowhere else to go if you don't."

"I know, I know. Meanwhile, I have to buy clothes, food, toys and a thousand other things before she's released from the hospital. Will she really be ready to go forty-eight hours from now? That seems awfully early."

"She'll be fine. A secure home where she feels loved is the best medicine at this point." He pushed away from the wall. Bracing a hand on her back, he sauntered beside her across the street toward his Explorer. "Where do you want to go first?"

"To get my car, of course."

"I, uh, meant shopping. Which mall?"

"You want to go…shopping?" Shock immobilized her. A car honked for Lori to clear the road.

Gray ushered her across, his hand still planted possessively on the small of her back. "I want to help you find what you need to settle Magda. This was my idea, after all, so I feel responsible."

Responsible? She'd wanted many things from Gray in the past, but grudging obligation hadn't made her top-ten list. "Thanks, really. But I can manage on my own. I'll be able to wrap things up at the office while she's in the hospital. I'll have the weekend to acclimate Magda. Meanwhile, I can work out the rest of the accommodations. We'll be fine."

"I'm sure you will." Gray stopped by the passenger door. "Where do you want to go shopping first?"

Something else she'd forgotten about Gray. He was a mule. Stubborn. Stubborn. Stubborn. While easygoing most of the time, he could simultaneously smile and dig those boot heels in deeper than oak tree roots. "You really want to go shopping?"

"With you. Yes, I do."

The thrust of his jaw convinced her. But why? "Do you want to pick up some early Christmas gifts for your nieces and nephews?"

"Sure. It beats fighting the crowds later."

"Yeah. I guess so." But a guy shopping months ahead of time? Not a chance.

He was holding back, and she didn't like it. At least they'd always been straight with each other. As he reached to open her door, she grabbed his wrist. "Cut it out, Gray."

"What?"

"This isn't going to get you an invitation back into my bed."

He slid a slow look down to her hand still on his arm. Humidity and longing weighted the air until it became almost impossible to breathe. She jerked away.

Gray regarded her through a lazy blink. "I didn't ask for one."

"Yeah, right. Why else would a man offer to spend an afternoon perusing the latest styles at Baby Gap?"

"Because I want to help. Honey, we never played games in the past. Why would I do that now?" His eyes deepened to those jewel tones that never failed to send shivers down her spine, regardless of the summer heat. "If I wanted back in your bed, you would know."

Her pulse double-timed like the hummingbird speeding through a nearby flower bed. She couldn't stop herself from asking, "And you don't want me anymore?"

He flattened his palm on the car beside her. Those glittering eyes cruised her mouth, her neck, sweeping a leisurely ride down to the curve of her hip. "I've never lied to you, and I don't intend to start now. Hell, yes, I want you." His gaze snapped back to meet hers. "I'm just not interested in having my ego trounced again."

Sympathy melted her heart like butter over a warm roll. She'd forgotten how fast he could level her defenses with his honesty.

Reality chilled her emotions, and she toughened up.

He may have been hurt by the breakup, but it would take shoes a lot bigger than her size-eights to trample Gray's pilot-doctor ego. The man had confidence to spare. They may not have played games in the past, but he was up to something today. She just couldn't figure out what.

Tenacious curiosity compelled her to let him come along so she could unravel his agenda. Surely she wasn't letting him come because some small corner of her heart whispered a hope that he might find domestic, family responsibilities weren't so scary after all. "Fine. You can carry packages for me. If you think you can handle it."

He spread his arms wide. "Bring it on, hon. How much stuff can one kid need?"

"Geez, Lori! How much does one kid need?" Gray opened the back hatch of his Explorer. With lightning-fast hands, he caught boxes and bags before they avalanched onto her narrow, gravel driveway.

Church bells chimed the hour, clanging through Gray's pounding head. Those church murals had the concept of hell all wrong. Rather than fiery flames, the artists should have depicted a day at the mall with a woman.

Did Lori really need his advice on whether the kid would look better in pink or purple? Capri pants or short overalls? And what the hell were Capri pants, anyway?

But he'd gritted his teeth, smiled and voted for purple Capri pants because they were in the hand closest to the cash register. A good omen. Right?

After changing her mind no less than four times, Lori had bought the pink overalls.

Gray's leg burned. His head felt like someone had bashed it with a sledgehammer. And if he had to look at Lori's Madonna beauty glow one more time, he was going to toss her over his shoulder and head straight for the nearest bed.

She caught a stray outfit fluttering out of a bag and smiled as she shook out the pink, flowered overalls.

Glowing like an afterburner and she wasn't even pregnant.

Gray's head fell to rest on the back of his car. Who needed a bed? Any flat surface would suffice.

Instead of finding a bed, he would get the car unpacked and toys assembled, fast, then run like crazy back to his apartment. Where fresh reminders of Lori could bombard him from every corner.

Gray swiped his wrist over his damp brow. Shade from the towering magnolias didn't offer nearly enough relief from the hundred-degree day or his thoughts. "Come on, Lori. Let's cart this up to your place."

He hefted out a box for a riding toy and lumbered through the courtyard toward the white stucco house. Like many historical homes in Charleston, the floors had been sectioned off into office and apartment spaces.

Lush ferns, dogwoods and Palmetto trees encircled the stone patio and walkway in reckless landscaping. Black wrought-iron furniture grouped around a trickling fountain topped with a stone pineapple. A book lay open and face-down on a small table, empty glass beside it. Wild abandon and peace intertwining. Like Lori.

Three treks up and down the stairs later, Gray followed her up the narrow outdoor stairway for the final time. Thank God he held the last of the loot, a Barbie dream house. Only a few more steps to watch the tormenting sway of Lori's hips.

First the mall. Now this. Penance stunk.

Wooden steps along the side of the house creaked beneath his boots. Lori's hair swayed loose and flowing down her back. He diverted his eyes.

Twenty-three endless steps later, he reached her second-story apartment. A clump of dried daisies arced over the door. Welcoming, homey, like Lori.

Man, he was in trouble.

No time to choke now, pal. He charged inside.

As if dodging land mines, Gray sidestepped the pile of packages littering the entryway. "Where do you want me to put this?"

"Right here is fine."

So she wanted to boot him out. Not a chance. With only a couple of weeks remaining until he left, he needed to make the most of every minute. "This sucker's heavy, Lori. I don't want to pick it up again. Just tell me where it's supposed to go, and I'll carry it the rest of the way."

She hesitated, then gestured for him to follow her. He dedicated his best effort not to watch her walk, instead focusing on her apartment, safer and wiser terrain.

The place unfolded before him exactly as he would have expected—elegant, eclectic, coordinated, but not a matched set to be found. Gleaming, heavy antiques and bold-patterned cushions were lightened by mismatched pottery and doilies.

A few new pieces had been added over the year. But that sofa. Yeah, he remembered her overstuffed striped couch well.

He did *not* need to be thinking about that sofa and the memories it held.

Lori shoved open a door to an airy room with ten-foot ceilings. "This will be hers. You can set the box in that corner."

She leaned back, gripping the doorknob. Their eyes collided as Gray slid past. He propped the box against a wall beside French doors opening to a balcony. Already he could imagine Magda soaking up all that light. "Is here okay?"

"Perfect. Thanks." Her brows pulled together as she studied the glassed doors. "Oh, I'll need to buy safety latches for those."

More shopping. Gray rubbed a thumb over his throbbing temple and tried to ignore the sleigh bed between Lori and him. She inched inside. The door creaked, moved, swung slowly closed. The small click echoed like a hatch slamming shut.

Lori flinched. "Old houses lean."

"Uh-huh." More likely the house was in league with Bronco to lock him up with Lori.

"Thanks for coming along." She swung two bags of clothes onto the bed.

"No problem."

"You were a great help." Hands moving in nervous activity, she folded the clothes into a little pile on the white lace spread.

"I can haul packages with the best of them." He couldn't drag his eyes from her as she performed the simple domestic chore. The bed loomed between them, threatening his control and his peace of mind, but Gray couldn't seem to shove one foot in front of the other while Lori smoothed a wrinkle from a tiny T-shirt.

"No, really." She slid the pink overalls onto a miniature hanger and hung them in an antique wardrobe. "Your advice over the Capri pants was invaluable."

Then why hadn't she taken it? He bit back the urge to argue.

Lori pivoted to face him. The mischievous gleam in her eyes set off klaxon warnings in his throbbing brain. Come to think of it, that same glimmer reminded him of when she'd asked him whether Magda would prefer sandals or clogs. Like he knew the difference.

Realization kicked him like the sucker he'd been all evening. She'd played him. "So were you testing me or trying to run me off?"

Lori's grin turned downright wicked. "What do you mean?"

"Clogs and Capri pants."

"Took you long enough to catch on."

"That's what I get for trying to be patient."

Her smile softened to something bittersweet. "I just don't understand what you're doing here, Gray. What do you hope to accomplish with this attentive boyfriend act?"

Most of the time he appreciated Lori's straightforward honesty. Today he suspected she might well have him pinned to the wall, and not in any way he would enjoy. He dodged the question as much as he could, unwilling to fess up to his motives. What would she say if she knew he was plotting to give her the family he hadn't been able to? "We may not be a couple, but we can be friends."

"I'm not so sure."

Disappointment dogged Gray with a force that surprised him. He shouldn't care this much, and that left his feet itching to run. "Why not?"

Her eyes widened incredulously. "Because...because... because of..." Her hands flailed the air as if she might find the words there. Finally she made a sweeping gesture across the bed. "Because of that."

The mattress seemed to double in size, large and inviting. But they stood on opposite sides—of the bed and so much more.

"Lori, let me share something I've discovered this past year. *That,*" he said, jabbing a finger toward the bed, "is going to be there whether we're in the same room with it or not. *That* is going to be there even if you and I aren't in the same room. *That* is just something we're going to have to live with." He pulled a tight grin. "Or rather, live without."

She twirled a lock of hair. The regret in her eyes tempted him, echoing a regret within him he understood too well. "Meanwhile, we're old friends. You need help. I want to give it. Now let's put together Barbie's dream house."

"God, you're stubborn." Lori twisted the lock of hair faster, before flicking it aside. "But you're also right."

About being friends or wanting each other regardless of time and miles? Of course, in two weeks there would be three thousand miles between them when he transferred cross country to McChord AFB in Washington. He didn't plan to go through a repeat of the past year dodging memories of Lori. The only way he could see to avoid it was to ignore how damn much he wanted her.

Gray tapped the dollhouse box with his boot. "What'll

it be? Do you want help with the seven thousand pieces rattling around in this box or not?''

Hands clenched by his sides, he waited for her answer, watched that answer shift back and forth in her eyes—for him, against, and back again. His fingers unfurled.

''Okay, let's put this thing together.'' Lori glanced at the bed. ''But maybe we ought to assemble it in the living room.''

''I always knew you were a smart woman.'' And he sure didn't intend to let such a smart woman know he would be thinking of *that* every time he looked at her striped couch.

Lori placed a tray of sandwiches, chips and sweet tea on the antique tea cart beside Gray. He sprawled on the floor beside the fully assembled Barbie house, placing stickers on a Big Wheel. His voice filled the room with low, rumbling intensity as he sang along with her Billie Holiday CD. Grayson and the blues. A potent combination.

Intense concentration puckered his brow as he centered a racing stripe. His singing dwindled until he'd pressed the edges of the decal in place.

He really had been a great help, patient even when she'd done her best to rile him with inane Capri pants and clogs in hopes he would spill his real agenda. Maybe there wasn't one. Maybe he'd meant exactly what he'd said. He wanted them to be friends. She'd learned quickly that Gray made friends with ease.

Perhaps that was the problem. Building friendships had always been tougher for her, never having had the time to hone the skill on any one person. Friendships were rare and special for her. She wasn't sure she wanted to grant Gray that much importance in her life.

After the past couple of days, she wasn't sure he would leave her any choice.

She could take a page from Gray's book, couldn't she? A light friendship would ease a loneliness in her life that work couldn't quite fill. She would certainly need a friend a month from now when Magda went to her permanent home. Could she dare hope Gray might still be there for her, not as a lover, but as a friend?

If she even wanted to entertain the thought, she needed to learn some of those friendship skills from Gray. Lori snagged an oversize tapestry pillow from the sofa and dropped it on the floor beside him.

"Here you go, friend." Lori passed Gray a plate stacked with two sandwiches.

His gaze jerked from the sofa to her. He smoothed down a cartoon speedometer before taking the dish. "Thanks."

The light brush, tingle, heat of their fingers had nothing to do with friendship. Lori resolved to ignore it.

"The least I can do is feed you a sandwich after all your help." She sat cross-legged beside him, reaching for the bowl of chips to place between them. Not as big a barrier as the bed earlier, but certainly less provocative.

Her hand glided along the restored gleam of the tea cart, like rubbing a talisman. She'd found it at an estate auction a couple of months past. She loved to think about the history of the piece, even if the roots belonged to someone else. "I really do appreciate your help. I would have been up all night just reading the instructions."

"This was a cake walk compared to assembling toys for seven nieces and nephews last Christmas."

So he'd spent Christmas with his family. She'd wondered. Her parents had flown into Charleston, their hometown, for the holidays. She'd spent the whole week thinking about how Gray had once suggested they take a Christmas cruise together.

Lori bit into her turkey sandwich. Or was it ham? It tasted like paste. She swallowed the dry lump. "You probably think I'm crazy to buy all this for a kid who'll only be with me a few weeks. But I didn't have more than a few toys on hand, and those were just for babies stopping through for a few hours.''

''Every kid deserves toys.''

''And friends. I need to find other children for her to enjoy these toys with. They're not half as much fun if she plays with them alone.''

''Of course.'' He ate a quarter of his sandwich in one bite and chewed while he peeled, then placed a sticker on the bike's handlebars. Long fingers so adept at flying and healing applied stickers as if they were of mammoth importance.

To Magda they would be, and his care touched Lori—too much.

''I just don't want her to have to wait, you know? She's lost so much already. She can take all this with her when she leaves.''

''Sure she can. If you rent a trailer.'' Gray tore off another quarter of his sandwich, applied the last sticker and crumpled the backing paper. ''Done.''

With a fluid toss, he pitched it into the empty box and leaned against a chair to finish his sandwich. One muscular leg stretched out in front of him, his injured leg crooked at the knee. Long, lean, and so sexy her eyes ached.

Lori set aside her plate and reached for the basket of dollhouse furniture. Slowly she arranged the kitchen table and chairs. ''I have to confess, this was a purely selfish purchase.''

''How so?''

Gray crunched a chip and chased it with a swallow of tea—so at ease, when she felt like an overwound kid's toy. Lori gulped her tea.

''It would have been more practical for me to buy Magda smaller toys, things easily packed and transported. But I always wanted one of these, a huge dollhouse that wouldn't fit in the trunk with the luggage.''

''You moved around that much? I thought your parents

just traveled frequently but that you grew up in Charleston."

How could he not have known? Had they really spoken so little to each other they didn't know even basic family history? What a sad testimony to their short but intense time together.

"Charleston was our home base, sure, a place to rest when we stopped in to recoup and repack. If the mood struck, they hung out for a month or two to paint." She arranged a tiny sofa and chair around the miniature television, then sifted through the basket for yard furniture. "We usually spent about nine months out of the year traveling. There were gallery showings, guest lecturer stints, artists in residence for a semester at this college or that one. We were on the road a lot."

"What about school?"

He put aside his glass and focused on her, wrist propped on his crooked knee. His complete focus was heady stuff.

She wondered why she wanted to tell him now, needed to share a part of herself when she should be feeling more defensive than ever. Funny how a day of shopping and Gray's undivided attention could mellow a woman.

"Sometimes we relocated long enough for me to enroll for at least part of the year, other times the nanny home schooled me. I didn't lag behind." She placed the lawn furniture around a pool and little swing set. "Don't get me wrong. I'm not complaining. They loved me and made sure I had what I needed. They could have dumped me off on a relative, but they never did. It couldn't have been easy carting a kid and a nanny along. And it really was an educational way to grow up. I saw more, experienced more, lived more by ten than most folks do in a lifetime."

"But?"

"There were times..." Feeling like an ungrateful brat, she paused, running her fingers along the empty basket before setting it aside. "On my eighth birthday I wanted a backyard party with lots of friends and a really big dollhouse.'' Lori placed Barbie and Ken on the lawn furniture and put Skipper on the swing. ''I got a pocket travel dollhouse and a picnic in front of the Eiffel Tower. Not a bad trade, all things considered, huh?''

Gray smiled but didn't answer. Instead he tapped the dollhouse, then the bike. ''Guess that explains why you were hell-bent today on picking the biggest and heaviest toys on the shelf.''

She studied him through narrowed eyes, impressed anew. ''You're a perceptive man.''

A dimple dented his right cheek. ''Nah, just one who got quite a workout lugging that loot up the stairs.''

Rocking back on her heels, she surveyed the fully furnished Barbie house. Perfect. Maybe it was silly or even selfish giving Magda the things she'd wanted as a child, huge toys, a large airy room…unconditional love. All the same, she couldn't stop the twitter of excitement over bringing Magda home. Home. That said it all.

Lori shifted to Gray and cupped his face in one hand. ''Thank you.''

He cleared his throat. ''For what?''

''For coming with me. For pretending to be interested in Capri pants and clogs. For being my friend.'' She leaned over the bowl of chips and pressed a kiss to his mouth. Just a simple kiss between friends, she told herself. Nothing wrong with that.

A one-second lip brush was all she intended. She meant to pull away. But she didn't move. Neither did he.

Chapter 8

He should pull away, and he would, in a minute. Or two. If only he could find one ounce of willpower to resist the temptation of Lori's full lips beneath his after so many months of starving for a taste of her.

A soft moan floated between them. From her? Or him? Her small fist fell to rest on his chest—and unfurled.

Willpower became a scarce commodity.

That one touch of their lips, one simple caress of her hand filled him with so much more than possibility. It was a promise. He didn't have to question how good it would be between them.

He knew.

And that knowledge fired through him with memories of steamy summer nights dedicated to exploring every inch of Lori's beautiful body. Discovering what made her cry out with pleasure. Hoping that if they found enough pleasure together she might forget he couldn't give her what she really needed.

Lori's hand curved up around his neck.

What the hell was he doing?

Gray tore himself away from her, his breathing ragged over nothing more than a near-innocent kiss. Damn, but she'd gotten to him with her gorgeous stiff upper lip. She could make the best of anything, even being dragged around the world by parents who were too absorbed in their jobs to realize what their lonely kid needed. She deserved better, then and now.

Lori stared back at him with fogged and confused eyes, so unlike her normally confident self. They'd never even opened their mouths, and he wanted to toss her down on the Oriental rug. He wanted to tangle his body and life with hers in ways they'd only just begun to explore in their three months together.

They'd traveled this route before, and it hadn't worked. He didn't even want to consider why their breakup had kicked him harder than any of the others, and for him, there'd been plenty. He stunk at long-term relationships, another reason the transient Air Force lifestyle suited him so well.

Even if he and Lori fulfilled the momentary promise, it was just that. A moment. Lori hadn't wanted to live with him in Charleston. She sure as hell wasn't going to give up her job and follow him to Tacoma, Washington, for however long they could survive a relationship this time.

Gray rocked back, the ache in his leg almost as powerful as the one in his boxer shorts. He needed to get out of her apartment, now, before he lost what little control he had left in his depleted armament.

He shoved to his feet. "I should go."

"Gray?" Barbie's dream house loomed behind her.

He made for the door. Bat out of hell took on a whole new meaning.

"Gray?"

His boots stopped, but he didn't turn. The mantel clock

ticked in the silence while he waited. Finally he pivoted on his boot heel to face her. "What, Lori?"

She sat on her feet, brows knit together. "How can you do that?"

"Do what?"

"Just shut it down and walk away?" she asked, holding up a trembling hand as she rose slowly to her feet. "I'm dying here, Gray, really hurting. I can barely stand, much less walk."

He did *not* need to hear this. If he gave in and offered her comfort now, he wouldn't walk away until morning. And he'd be damned if he would hurt her that way again. "Lori, honey—"

"How do you do it?" Her voice trembled as much as her hands. "I sure could use one of your easy smiles right now."

"So could I," he mumbled, trying unsuccessfully to look anywhere but at Lori's molten-hot eyes. Where was the wide-open sky when a guy needed it?

Lungs working overtime, Lori stared at Gray, wishing she understood him. One thing was blatantly clear. The man was itching to leave. And that hurt, increasing an ache already deep, hungry and selfish within her.

It also made her damn mad. How dare he blast back into her life, then walk away leaving her shaking and needy? She'd already blown the friendship. She might as well have something from him, something to make the pain stop, even if only for a while.

An unrelentingly logical part of her argued she should stop and think. Passion and anger weren't the best emotions to fuel decisions.

For once she didn't want to be logical. She wanted Gray. On the floor. Now.

Hands on her hips, she advanced a step, determined to get what she wanted for a change. "Well, Major? I asked you a question. How do you do it? Teach me. I want to know how to entice you into having no-commitment sex with me.''

Gray stumbled back as if he'd been gut shot. ''Seems like you're doing all right on your own, hon.'' He rubbed the back of his neck, his eyes traveling a slow ride over her body. ''Yeah, you're doing just fine.''

That lingering look flowered a bloom of feminine power within her, and she sashayed forward. ''I was fine...until you showed up again.''

''We can't go back now.''

A fresh burst of anger fired her feet across the rug. Lori stopped inches away from Gray. ''You think I don't know that? I hate it. Hate it that I still want you. Hate it that you've exploded back into my life, my senses, my mind all over again.'' She watched him wince, knowing full well her words simultaneously stabbed and caressed, a dichotomy of pain and pleasure that had been signature to their relationship almost from the start. ''Gray, I may hate it, but that doesn't make me stop wanting you.''

''Geez, Lori.'' His voice strangled off as he raised his hands in surrender. ''Don't go there. Not now.''

''Don't go there? I could have used those sage words of advice five minutes ago. One stupid little kiss and I'm a mess all over again.'' The heat of him reached to her, wrapped around her with a pervasive power she couldn't avoid. She held both palms up in the scarce space between them. ''Hands still shaking, Gray.''

He clasped her hands in his. ''Stop it, Lori.''

''No, you stop it.'' Her voice rose as she struggled to jerk free.

He held tight. ''Stop what? You're not making any sense. I was trying to leave.''

''You were running away. That's different.''

''What would staying have accomplished? The two of us making a mistake.''

''At least it would be an honest mistake. We've always

had that, right…honesty?'' She closed the last step between them. With each gasping breath, her breasts brushed him, touched him, tempted him as well as herself. ''Can you honestly say you don't want me?''

A dark smile kicked up the corner of his mouth. ''Oh, honey, I want you.''

''Don't you laugh at me.'' Lori tried to tug free again, her arms straining.

''I'm not.'' His grin twitched.

His ever-ready smile pushed her over the edge. That damn gorgeous Barbie house hadn't helped, bringing up memories and dreams best left dormant. Why couldn't he be serious for once?

As if that wasn't enough, she'd circled right back around to a discussion of the past, remembering all the hopes she'd once pinned on Gray. Seeing those sexy hands sticking racing stripes all over a Big Wheel had been too explosive.

She'd be damned if she would cry herself to sleep tonight like some pitiful sap. She had better plans for finding forgetfulness.

Gray had known they couldn't spend two minutes together without stirring emotions too deep to bear, yet he'd insisted they spend the day together. Well, now he could suffer the consequences. And she looked forward to making him pay—for hours, naked, on her sofa just like old times.

Lori broke free. ''You *do* want me. At least give me that much.''

''Damn straight. I said just that in your guest room not three hours ago.''

''Fine,'' she snapped the word out like a bullet. ''Then let's do it, pal.'' Lori yanked her shirt out of her pants and whipped it over her head before giving herself time to change her mind. ''Me and you, on the sofa, let's tangle it up right now for honest, steamy, screaming sex.''

Gray looked as if that gut shot might be leveling him. His eyes glowed to life, warming over every patch of revealed skin. Her hair tickled along her back, and she imagined his hands there, soon.

He closed his eyes, swallowed heavily. Lori waited, hope and an odd fear curling through her like tendrils of smoke. He opened his eyes, resolution radiating in waves.

For or against? She couldn't decide what scared her more, his staying or leaving. Lori's breasts tightened in anticipation beneath her ivory silk bra. Her stomach twisted like a wrung-out sponge reminding her what a hollow victory this would be. "Gray?"

"Negative."

Devastation crashed over her, chilling every inch of her bared body. "What?"

Slowly, he shook his head. "No. You deserve more than this, and you know it. I should go."

Should go? Not *going* to leave.

Should go.

She aimed straight for that tiny chink in his defenses. "Let me decide what I deserve. I'm not asking for anything beyond right now. What's holding you back, Major, if you really do want me?"

She grabbed his wrist and flattened his hand to her waist. On contact they both flinched. Had lightning sparked through the room? Her toes tingled. Even the roots of her hair seemed to crackle.

His palm trailed from her waist to her belly, halting on the vulnerable place just below her rib cage. Skin to skin, they yearned. She didn't have to ask or wonder. His need transmitted through that simple caress in a communication she hadn't forgotten in a year apart.

Her eyes slid closed as she savored his touch, the heat, familiar warmth. The backs of his fingers trailed up, slowly, between her breasts, along the tender curve of her neck, sliding into less fiery terrain to cup her face.

Then his hand fell away.

Lori swayed forward before regaining her balance. Her

eyes fluttered open to find him watching her, intently, too aware of what he was doing to her.

"Why?" she demanded.

He grazed his knuckles over her cheek. "I like you."

The tingling changed to an icy shower, painful, like water on an electrified body. "What?"

"Yeah, I want you. But I like you, too. How's that for honest? I like you too much to do something I know will hurt you." His fingers curved to cup her face again with a tenderness that scared her more than passion. "You want me to be the bad guy here so it's easier for you when we say goodbye. I can't do it, Lori. Not again. You're going to have to do it on your own this time."

He dropped a kiss onto her forehead, once, twice, and stepped back. "I'll see you in two days when Magda's ready to be discharged from the hospital."

Gray turned toward the door. Lori watched him walk away and knew nothing would stop him this time.

As if to taunt her with the possibility she might be wrong, he paused. "And, Lori?"

"What?"

"Please wear a shirt."

Gray pulled the door closed behind him. He sagged against the porch rail, hands braced on his knees, and struggled for air. His heart jackhammered against his ribs.

Lord have mercy, that woman knew how to make her point.

His throbbing body screamed at him to go back inside and take what she offered, consequences be damned. The wall between them did nothing to block the vision of her wearing just a silk bra and miles of whiskey-brown hair.

Her small but firm breasts had always fitted perfectly into his hands, just as her body fitted perfectly against his. After a year apart, he hadn't found any woman who came close to knocking him flat the way she did with one smoky-eyed look.

He'd searched, determined to get over her, but ultimately turned down any and every invitation.

Gray straightened and stared at the closed door. He shoved away from the rail, toward the door and reached for the knob.

Carved wooden letters spelling out *Welcome* mocked him from the twist of homey daisies arching over the door.

Damn.

His hand fell to his side. Sliding back into bat-out-of-hell mode, he charged down the stairs.

He had two days to douse his libido before he and Lori picked up Magda from the hospital. Each pound of his boots on the steps echoed his prayer that Lori would wear not one, but two shirts.

Lori wore a turtleneck. The sleeveless ribbed cotton swept all the way up to her neck like a breastplate of armor.

She tucked the shirt into her straight-cut olive pants and considered pulling on a short-sleeved silk blouse over it. Then tossed it aside. Two shirts would be too obvious. The last thing they needed was a reminder of her stupid, fruitless stripping stunt.

Magda wouldn't be released for another hour, but Lori had finished up work for the day and planned to leave early for the hospital.

Coward.

Not that she was dodging Gray or trying to skip out. She'd left a message on his answering machine for him to meet her at the hospital.

Big coward.

Okay. So she was a great big chicken, scared and flat-out embarrassed to see Gray again without an entire hospital staff acting as a distraction.

And if he followed her home after she picked up Magda? A four-year-old would make a fine chaperone. How much could he upset Lori's equilibrium with a needy child in tow?

Of course, her parents had always managed romance, even with her around. Images of them flashed through her mind like a movie reel on fast play.

Her mother and father walking hand in hand down the Champs Elysées, while Lori skipped behind. The vivid red of her mother's lipstick as she leaned to kiss Lori good-night before a night on the town. A postcard from her father of Trevi Fountain, the trip a private celebration of their thirty-fifth anniversary. Her parents had been wildly in love, still were, and everyone who saw them knew it.

What was wrong with holding out for love?

Not a thing.

An essentially pragmatic part of Lori also acknowledged she needed a different kind of love than her parents had found. As much as she loved her parents, she was realistic enough to know there wouldn't have been enough time or energy left over in their lives to care for more than one child, certainly never a child with Magda's problems.

Love was better put off for another time and place. Magda needed her.

And what did Lori need?

She needed to wear two shirts after all.

Grabbing the extra silk blouse and a welcome-home gift for Magda, Lori left her apartment. She locked the door, turned to the stairs and stopped.

Gray sat sideways on the bottom step, boot pressed to the wall across from him. His head lay back against the porch post, his eyes closed. He'd once told her that doctors cultivated a talent for snagging catnaps when and where they could. Obviously, he'd meant it.

How long had he been waiting for her? Had he shown up early in case she cut out, just as she was doing? Or had he stayed outside because he didn't want to be alone with her?

Both thoughts tilted the porch beneath her feet.

Lori eased down the stairs and nudged him with her toe. "Time to go, flyboy."

He didn't budge. Rush hour traffic crowded the one-way side street beside her driveway. A carriage tour slowed the flood. The Belgian draft horse clomped by at its own pace while a tour guide droned on about earthquake bolts on houses.

"Gray?" she whispered in his ear.

No response.

He was out so deeply, she could step right over him and leave while he snoozed, oblivious to all around him. But that wouldn't be a nice thing to do, and they'd hurt each other enough already.

Lori sank to the step above him and sat. Unable to resist the lure of his coal-black hair, she skimmed her fingers across his brow, smoothing back a lock. There wasn't much to stroke, his military cut leaving little on his head. Of course, that also left more of his face and neck for her to view and admire.

She traced her thumb over his brows, then his eyes, leaned forward and stole one last kiss for her memory cache, a quick kiss guaranteed not to wake him, then stood again.

She tapped him with her toe, more firmly this time. "Wake up, Sleeping Beauty. Time to go."

The honeyed tones of Lori's voice pulled Gray from sleep. He started, snorted, his boot dropping to the step.

"What?" He looked around, blinking his eyes to clear his groggy brain, before his gaze landed on Lori.

God, she was beautiful. Not pretty or cute or even gorgeous. Just damned beautiful. Her hair flowed around her shoulders, and both of those shirts couldn't stop the image of that same hair rippling around her bare skin two days prior.

Gray cleared his throat, if not his thoughts. "You all set to go?"

"Anytime you're ready."

He stood, stomping his feet and shaking his flight suit back into place. Eye level with Lori, he stared at her full, damp lips. Not wise. His gaze shot up to her eyes, her wary eyes. He'd made such a mess of things earlier, he couldn't blame her. "About before—"

"Stop! Please." She held up a hand, pausing just shy of touching him. "There's no need to say anything. You and I have the uncanny knack for making fools out of ourselves around each other. What's one more time? Chalk it up to the whole crazy hormone thing we have going and leave it at that. Keep it simple."

He frowned. "Yeah, I guess."

Lori picked at her overblouse and smiled. "See, two shirts. I'm armored and ready to resist your incredible appeal."

He'd always liked her open approach to life. No games or hidden agendas or wallowing in complaints, just face life head-on. His smile kicked in. "That's my girl."

But she wasn't and they both knew it. Their smiles faded.

Gray stepped to the walkway. "Let's get moving. There's a little girl waiting to come home."

An hour later Gray drove back to Lori's apartment, Magda buckled into a car seat in the back of his car. Lori sat beside her talking softly and pointing to different landmarks as they drove past. Magda babbled a phrase in her own language, her new Winnie the Pooh clutched tightly.

At Lori's apartment, Gray unloaded Magda's tote bag of pajamas and the other toys she'd collected while in the hospital. Lori walked ahead up the stairs, Magda perched on her hip. They made a postcard-perfect picture, so why wasn't he happy yet?

The little girl's hair had been trimmed and smoothed into a new elfin do, loose curls fluffing around her face. She could have been mistaken for a boy, except Lori had outfitted her in plenty of pink. The pink overalls patterned with flowers and hearts left no doubts about Magda's gender.

She was a darn cute kid, even when she plastered that tiny scowl across her face every time she looked at him. As if in synch with his thoughts, Magda blasted a glare over Lori's shoulder, a dare that seemed to say, *Try and pull me loose this time, buster.*

He smiled an apology he hoped she understood, but likely didn't. While he'd rather not be glowered at as if he'd killed the Easter Bunny, Gray couldn't help but applaud Magda's spunk after all she'd been through. She would need it to adjust to a new culture, new language and a load of other challenges. Lucky for her she had one hell of an advocate in Lori.

At the door Lori attempted to juggle Magda and dig out her keys, but the child wouldn't loosen her grip to be put down. "Can you take her?"

"Like she'd go for that. Give me the keys." Gray unlocked the door and shoved it open.

He followed them in while Magda frowned her next message. *Hey! You better not live here, too.*

Gray kept trailing them inside.

Magda eyed the door as if encouraging him to use it, now.

"No can do, kiddo," Gray muttered. "I'm planning to hang out for a while."

Lori turned. "What?"

"Nothing. I'll put this in her room while you show her around."

"Sure. Thanks."

Gray found himself walking faster to Magda's room. He placed the miniature suitcase by the dollhouse, then shifted restlessly from foot to foot while he waited. He'd brought them home. Shouldn't he be itching to leave?

But he wanted to be there when she saw the Barbie

house. He wanted to find out if she would squeal like his niece Jessica or dance around the room like his nephew Trey.

He wanted to discover if Lori sang bedtime songs like his mom did. His father had sung along, too, before he'd left for Vietnam. Funny how he'd forgotten that. Of course, his younger brother and sister wouldn't remember at all. Gray shrugged off the kink in his neck along with the memories that had put it there and focused on Lori.

Nothing wrong with pitching in during the transition, just like he'd planned. The more he helped Lori bond with Magda, the easier it would be when he left Charleston.

A childish cough sounded from the hall. Gray turned and found Lori silhouetted in the doorway, Magda's hand clutched in hers. Chocolate and cookie crumbs stained the corner of Magda's mouth.

She stared at the dollhouse with wide eyes. She glanced at Gray standing beside it, and her mouth quirked to the side. *Wanna get outa my way, big guy?*

Lori urged her forward. "Come on, Magda. It's yours."

Her cocoa-colored eyes darted to the Big Wheel parked in the corner as if considering it for an alternative, given its distance from Gray. Then her gaze skated right back to the house.

Taking pity on the kid, Gray stepped away and sat on the edge of the bed. Magda let go of Lori's hand and sprinted forward, Lori strolling behind. The little girl dropped cross-legged in front of the house and pulled one doll after another from the basket.

Hands clasped loosely between his knees, Gray watched. Couldn't stop. He'd built the house that made her happy. Her tiny smile brought a rush that rivaled the first time he'd mastered a barrel roll in pilot training.

Magda lined up her dolls on the floor, a cough rumbling in her chest. Lori sat on the floor and pulled Magda onto her lap. Magda smiled up at her, pressed two fingers to her lips and gestured forward.

"You're welcome," Lori said to Magda, then grinned at Gray. "That was sign language for thank-you. When I visited her in the hospital, I taught her some basic signs. There's a whole movement out there for teaching sign language to babies. It's supposed to lessen their frustration until they can talk in formalized language. The same premise works with international children who don't speak English language yet. She's picking it up so quickly. I think she's really smart."

Gray stifled a grin at Lori's maternal pride, predictable and sweet. "I'm sure she is."

Lori licked her thumb and reached to swipe cookie crumbs from Magda's cheek. "I should have offered her something healthier like a cheese stick or an apple, but I just wanted everything to be perfect for her."

"One cookie won't kill her."

"Is that your official diagnosis, Doc?"

"Yes, ma'am. Give this kid a cookie a day."

"With milk."

"You bet." Conversation fizzling, Gray waited. For what? He didn't know.

Silence echoed through the room, broken only by the toll of church bells, a car horn, a cough from Magda.

Lori smoothed a hand over Magda's tufting hair and smiled a polite dismissal at Gray. "You probably have things to do, work or something. You can go now."

Magda chose just that moment to glance up. *Yeah. The door's that way.*

Gray took in the two of them, their faces so close together, so right, and knew he wasn't needed. His mission was over for the day. Magda and Lori were settled, not that it seemed to make leaving any easier.

He shoved to his feet. "She's allowed quiet play at home

for the next five days. She can play with other kids out in public after that."

"Thank you. I've already got a sitter lined up to help with the times I can't work up here."

"Watch for fever, chest pain, worsening cough."

"Gray, I have the instructions from her pediatrician."

"I'll stop in tomorrow to listen to her chest."

Her eyes flashed as if she might argue, then the flame died. "Thank you. I appreciate it."

"Be careful that she doesn't get too worn-out."

"I'm going to help her into PJs in a minute." Lori rested her cheek on top of Magda's head. "We'll be fine. We're going to eat supper and watch a video. A little Disney should go a long way toward keeping her still and starting her English lessons."

"That sounds great."

Gray waited for an invitation to join them. He enjoyed a Disney flick as much as the next guy. The family's designated Disney dude, he'd sat through Cinderella three times when his niece Jessica was stuck in bed with the chicken pox.

Propping a boot on the bed rail, he waited through another cycle of cars passing beneath the window.

Lori didn't ask, just plucked at her shirt and held her foster daughter in her lap. Hair flowing around them both, Lori tucked Magda closer into the perfect mother-daughter picture. A picture that by his own choice didn't include him. "Well, enjoy your video."

"We will."

"Call me if you need anything."

"We'll manage."

Magda clutched a handful of Lori's hair possessively, her tiny jaw thrust stubbornly.

"I'm sure you'll be fine. Just in case, call me, okay?"

"Okay."

He knew she wouldn't. Lori never really needed anyone. The thought of being free should have made him happy, but somehow it fell short of the target.

Chapter 9

"Gray!" Lori's panicked voice vibrated through the phone. "I need you!"

"What's wrong?" Dreams of whiskey-brown hair and long legs fell away as Gray jackknifed up in the bed.

"She's crying and coughing and she can't sleep and I don't know what to do for her. God, Gray, what was I thinking? I can't handle a sick kid who doesn't even speak enough English to tell me how she feels. They'll have to find someone else before the hearing next month. I can't do this. I really—"

"Calm down. It's going to be fine." Although, if it had Lori flustered, it must be pretty damn bad. Gray's gut fisted. "Does she have a fever?"

"Ninety-nine point six."

His gut eased its stranglehold. Gray relaxed against the headboard. "Okay. That's manageable. No need to head straight for the E.R. yet. Any trouble breathing?"

"No."

"Did you call her pediatrician?"

Sound waves crackled for three heartbeats.

"I'm sorry." Lori's voice steadied and chilled. "I shouldn't have bothered you in the middle of the night. Goodb—"

"No!" Gray closed his eyes and wondered if he would ever figure out how to dodge the land mines that seemed to surround Lori. "That's not what I meant."

"I shouldn't have woken you up. I just— Never mind."

"Lori—"

"Go back to sleep, Gray. I'll call her pediatrician."

"Lori!"

"What?"

"I'm on my way."

Her sigh shuddered through the phone. "Thank you."

Gray whipped on a pair of shorts and a threadbare Eagles concert T-shirt. He slipped on deck shoes without socks, tucked his medical bag under his arm and sprinted for the door. He told himself there was nothing to worry about. He'd checked Magda thoroughly before she'd been released from the hospital. The kid was okay.

Lori wasn't, though. Her trembling voice reverberated through his mind.

Damn it, he should have insisted on staying. He'd let his pride shove him out the door when she'd needed him.

He slid into his car and revved the engine. Tires squealing, he tore out of the parking lot.

Intellectually, he knew guilting himself out was bunk. Children went home from the hospital every day without an inhouse doctor to pull baby-sitting duties. Parents managed.

But Lori never asked for help.

Gray accelerated through a yellow light and made the half-hour drive downtown in under twenty minutes.

Taking her stairs two at a time, he charged toward Lori's apartment. With each pounding step he told himself to get a grip. In a couple of weeks he would be three thousand miles away from Lori and Magda. He wouldn't be here for late-night panic calls. He needed to settle them in and cut ties.

Lori tore the door open before he could knock. His fist paused in midair.

Not that he could find much air.

Lori stood before him, dressed for bed. Flowered women's boxers hung low on her hips as if the lightest tug would pull them free. A white tank top plunged too low for his comfort level. Tiny roses dotted the neckline, magnetizing his attention where it had no business straying.

Forget hankering for her in silk or satin, he had the hots for cotton, especially when it clung to Lori's gentle curves. Her hair tangled in a wild disarray around her shoulders. He'd seen the look before. Only, he'd been the one to put it there with his hands.

His gaze settled on her eyes. Her panicked eyes. Heat fell away.

"Thank God you're here." Lori shoved a harried hand through her hair. "She's back in her room."

Childish sniffles, followed by a hacking cough echoed down the hallway. Not the rumbling cough he'd expected. Gray frowned. "Lead on."

He followed Lori as her bare feet padded along the hardwood floors, then over Oriental runners. Each twitch of her hips taunted him, those baggy boxers defying gravity by staying in place.

Lori rushed ahead to Magda's bed and perched on the edge beside her, smoothing a hand along the little girl's back. The door creaked shut behind him.

A cool-mist vaporizer hummed on the bedside table. It wafted a hazy sheen around Lori, like that fuzzy lighting used to illuminate heroines in the movies.

Gray ripped his gaze away. Time to slip into doctor mode, fast, best for everyone.

Magda lay curled on her side, coughing until she gagged. She stared at Gray, hostility replaced by pleading. *Fix me.*

He'd seen that same message in the eyes of countless patients. *Please, fix me.*

It never failed to thump him somewhere around what a woman might have called his heart.

However, the plea in those two tiny brown eyes, echoed in Lori's larger set of matching ones, leveled him. Like an upper cut right to the solar plexus.

He'd wanted to be needed. No doubt about it, Lori and Magda needed him now, so much so that he didn't think three thousand miles would be far enough away to make him forget their pleading eyes.

Lori didn't want to ponder overlong on why she'd needed to call Gray. Surely calling the pediatrician would have made more sense. But hearing Gray's voice on the other end of the phone had shaved the edge off her panic. His arrival had pared it down further to an almost manageable level.

Almost.

Magda hacked her way through another choking cough, and Lori's panic returned full force. She always managed, always. This vulnerability scared her to the roots of her hair.

Like a fool she'd called the last man she should have. The only face she could envision through her claustrophobic fear. For Magda's sake, Lori would lean on him. For the moment.

Gray sat on the opposite side of the bed from Lori and pulled out his stethoscope. Gently he lifted Magda from under the covers. ''Cool to the touch. No spiked fever to worry about.''

Lori pressed her trembling hands to her shaking knees. ''That's really good. Right?''

''Absolutely.'' Shoving aside the shoulder on Magda's Winnie the Pooh nightgown, he listened to her chest and back. "No rattling breath sounds to indicate a relapse. But something's going on with that cough."

Magda whimpered, and Lori almost groaned in time with frustration.

Gray scrubbed the knuckles of his fist over his chin. "If she could just tell me where it hurts."

Lori straightened, inspiration lighting now that her fear had eased to a more manageable level. "She can. Sign language, remember?"

"How would she tell me where it hurts?"

"That's a new one, kind of tough, but we'll give it a go. Let me see your leg."

"Huh?"

"Your injured leg. Stretch it out on the bed."

Gray extended his leg, his brow furrowed. Lori grabbed his ankle. A mistake. His warmth, the bristly hair, the flex of muscles and bones beneath her touch scattered her thoughts like fall leaves. Warning herself not to linger, doing it anyway, she turned his leg so the bandage faced out. "Magda?"

She turned to Lori, wide eyes blinking.

Lori pointed to Gray's bandage, gave an exaggerated wince. Then she placed her pointer fingers facing each other and waggled her hands. "Hurt."

An image of Gray sprinting across the runway after her flared to life in Lori's mind. When had he been wounded? She'd never even seen him stumble. He'd just come for her without a care for himself.

Lori pointed to Gray's leg again, plastering on a pained expression, not a difficult task at all, and repeated the gesture. "Hurt."

Another image flamed to life, of Gray dragging her onto the plane. His injury must have been excruciating by then. Instead he'd focused the intensity of those glittering emerald eyes on her. He'd been mad as hell.

Her memory overlaid a sheen of concern in his eyes,

even fear for her mingling with his anger. Had it been there before? Or was she only remembering what she wanted to?

That bandage glared at her with agonizing brightness. She needed for him to go before she started crying all over his wounded leg.

Lori pointed to Magda and made the "hurt" symbol. "Magda hurts?"

Magda frowned, and Lori raised her hands to explain again. Then Magda's face cleared. She pointed to her stomach, placed her pointers together and wiggled her tiny hands, mimicking Lori's gesture. Magda repeated the process again, a questioning look on her face.

Lori nodded. "Yes, your tummy hurts." She turned to Gray, feeling as if she'd saved another orphanage full of kids all over again. "Her stomach hurts!"

They'd figured it out, together, an accomplishment too heady for her comfort level.

Gray nodded. "Okay, we're getting somewhere."

With any luck he would dose Magda up and be on his way. He could pack his bag and take those too-tempting muscular legs out of her apartment before she started dreaming up late-night thoughts. She didn't think she could take much more of barely dressed Gray while moonlight cast a yellow hue a little too like candlelight romance.

Lori tucked Magda under her arm and asked Gray, "What can you do for her, Doc?"

"Doc," Magda parroted.

Gray grinned and ruffled Magda's hair. She ducked from his touch and patted her hair back in place. Lori offered him an apologetic grimace. "Sorry."

"No problem. Let's just focus on finding out what's wrong with her. At least I know where to start looking." Gray placed his hand on her belly, palpated lightly and frowned. Magda flinched, doubling over. He rested his stethoscope over her stomach. His eyes widened. "Uh, oh."

Magda coughed. Groaned. Gagged.

"Lori, move!" Gray scooped the little girl up and ran full-out to the bathroom, positioning her head over the toilet bowl with only seconds to spare.

Lori trailed after them helplessly.

Gray held the back of Magda's neck and looked at Lori. "Not pneumonia this time. She's just got an old-fashioned case of the stomach flu."

"Stomach flu." Relief diffused the tension from her, and she slumped against the bathroom door. Adrenaline gushed through her in waves, leaving her with an absurd urge to laugh.

So much for concerns about late-night passion and mood-setting moments. If Magda's green pallor was any indication, Lori had a long night ahead of her and romance wasn't even an option.

Four hours and countless loads of laundry later, Lori sagged onto the floor beside Magda's bed. She leaned her head against the mattress with a weary sigh.

She needn't have worried about ending up in some unexpected, mind-numbing clench with Gray. They'd both been too busy taking turns cleaning up after Magda.

It was a miracle there weren't more only children in the world. How did parents ever find the energy necessary for the sex to make another baby?

Who'd have thought taking care of one sick kid could suck the life right out of a person? They hadn't even been dealing with anything life threatening. Just a simple stomach flu like the one going around the base.

Lori watched Gray as he strode through the bedroom door. Thank God she'd had his help.

Doubts slunk in with insidious force. How was she ever going to manage alone? How easy it would be to succumb to the temptation of calling for his help over the next month. A dangerous mix of alarm and anticipation fizzed within her.

Gray dropped down beside her, having just changed into clean workout clothes from his car. "Any noise from our little patient?"

"Nope. She's sleeping, for a while at least."

"Probably worn-out."

"She's not the only one."

Propped open, the French doors ushered night breezes and sounds inside, clearing away the dank, sick-room odor and replacing it with a tantalizing intimacy. Bells chimed four times, the distant rush of waves echoing from the harbor a few blocks over.

Lori shifted toward Gray. "I didn't even think to ask. You're not on call are you?"

"Not until Sunday."

"Oh, good. Thank you for coming. I know I don't have any right to ask—"

"I want to help. I've told you that already."

And he had helped, so much. His steady calm and frequent smiles had lent her a confidence she needed. "I don't know what I would have done without you."

"You would have managed."

Maybe, but his smiles had helped more than he could know. More than she wanted him to know. "I don't really have that much experience with kids. I never had younger cousins around, never baby-sat."

"I guess not, with moving so much."

"I feel like such a fraud. What do I know about taking care of a child long-term?"

"You've been a foster parent. You have training."

"Short-term placements. And all the textbook training in the world can't teach me how to deal with this for real. She's counting on me, for so much more than food and a temporary place to sleep." A gust ruffled the sheers on the French doors, swirling the room with hints of ocean and marsh. Warmth and hints of bay rum waited an arm's reach away. "What if I screw up? The stakes are so high here, and I'm all she has."

"Parents make mistakes, Lori, but you've already got the tough parts figured out. Some people are just born to be parents."

"And some aren't?"

"Some aren't."

Frustration edged away wiser constraints on her mouth. "Why, Gray?"

He pinched the bridge of his nose. "Lori—"

She forged ahead, in spite of him, maybe to spite him for once. "Why do you think you're not meant to be a father?"

Finally she dared to ask the question that had tormented her for over a year. Of course, now she no longer wanted to know for herself, but some lucky child deserved this man as a father. She didn't linger overlong on the thought of the woman who might give him that child. "You're great with kids. Look at how you deal with Magda. And I've heard you talk about your nieces and nephews. You obviously adore them."

"That's different."

"Because they don't come with a wife?"

"Partly." He met her gaze dead-on, honest as he'd always been, even when it hurt.

Lori swept aside the shards of pain his single word had sprinkled over her and hated that he still had the power to wound her.

So he didn't want a wife.

Not that she wanted the position. She needed a man who wasn't afraid of commitment, a steady man who wanted to put down roots and build a life rather than play games and sing Karaoke until the end of time.

But how she would miss his smiles.

Why couldn't she have smiles and constancy wrapped

up in a package that sent her heart stuttering like it did with a simple look from Gray? ‘‘So you’re just a confirmed bachelor who plans to shower Barbie dolls and Tonka toys on other people’s kids for the rest of his life.’’

‘‘It’s better that way.’’

‘‘Why?’’ she demanded, confused, angry and more curious than she wanted to be.

He twined a length of her hair around his fingers, linked to her but not touching. Gray stared at the simple lock as if it might hold the answer. Slowly he released it, one strand at a time. ‘‘Why do you want to know? It won’t accomplish anything.’’

Good question. She struggled for an answer. ‘‘Aren’t we both trying to find a way to say goodbye to each other? You talk about helping me with Magda, but I think there’s more to it than that.’’ His eyes darted away from hers, confirming her suspicions. She stifled the unproductive disappointment and charged ahead. ‘‘Is that what this is all about? Putting the past to rest for good?’’

‘‘Seems like you know me pretty well after all. Maybe you can tell me why I don’t plan to get married.’’

‘‘Ever? Not to anyone?’’

‘‘Ever.’’

All confusion about the two of them aside, she couldn’t help but ache at the thought of Gray spending the rest of his life alone. ‘‘If I knew the answer, Gray, we wouldn’t be sitting here right now.’’

Would he respond? While always truthful when he spoke, he sometimes opted for silence or covered the moment with a laugh and a smile. Would this be one of those times? A lone car drove past, and she almost gave up. What difference would it make, anyway?

Gray scratched a hand over his heavy, five-o’clock shadow. Lori prepared herself for his lighthearted quip.

Not a smile in sight, he said, ‘‘My dad.’’

Confusion muddled her tired brain. ‘‘Your father?’’

''My father was a POW in 'Nam.''

''Oh, Gray, how awful.'' She had to touch him. Taboos be damned, she couldn't let such a revelation go past without contact and comfort. Lori laid her hand over his on the floor. Gray twitched, but didn't pull away.

She searched in the dark for something to say, but he hadn't given her much to go on. ''I knew your father was active duty Air Force, but you never told me.... How long?''

''Four years overseas. Three of them in the camp.''

Lori stroked his fingers one at a time. ''You must have been young when he left.''

Tendons and veins bulged and rippled along the top of his hand. ''I was five. Davis was three. Mom was pregnant with Mary Ann.''

''Your poor mother.'' *Poor young Gray,* she thought but didn't dare say. Instead she linked their fingers without giving him a chance to say no.

His jaw worked double time. ''Damn straight.''

''But your father came home.''

Gray's grip tightened, painfully. ''Yeah, he came home.''

''What happened?'' she asked, then wished she hadn't. His hold slackened, and he slid his hand free.

''He finished out his time in the service, retiring at thirty years.''

''End of story?''

''For him maybe. It didn't matter to him what it cost my mom to see him put on that uniform every day. It didn't matter that it almost killed her to send him off to fight in other conflicts around the world.'' Gray pinned her with eyes that glittered in the dark like the fluorescent lighting of his aircraft. ''It didn't matter because the military is in his blood. It's a calling, something he couldn't turn his back on no matter what it cost. Even if it cost him his family.''

''But your parents are still together. They're still a family.'' She tried to take his hand again, offer something to smooth away the harsh lines she'd never seen on his playful face before.

He gripped her wrist and held it between them. ''Lori, your training should have taught you better than that. Just because two people live together and exchange a few vows doesn't make them a family. We haven't been a family since he walked out the door to Vietnam.''

The bitterness in Gray's voice stopped her cold. She'd asked for this, thinking there had to be something more beneath the songs and smiles. But she hadn't expected an intensity that almost scared her. For herself or him, she wasn't sure.

The vaporizer chugged in the silence. He carefully released her arm with exaggerated control.

Gray looked out the French doors as if searching for something in the night sky. ''I'm just like him, Lori. Whether I'm a flyer, doctor, or a ditch digger, I'm going to do it in the military. It's in my blood. Some men can juggle it all, family and service. I'm not one of them. I'm too much like my father, too driven, too selfish. And I won't do to any woman what he has done to my mother.''

''How do you know if you haven't tried?''

''Who says I haven't tried?''

Steamy air weighted her lungs until she couldn't find the breath to talk.

''I tried twice. Desert Storm wrecked one relationship.''

She inhaled that thick air, but it did little to ease the band constricting her sides. ''And the other?''

Silently he stared back at her with the answer they both already knew. Did she want him to say it? What would it gain either of them?

He looked away, and the moment passed. Lori deflated against the bed.

Gray was damn right she'd picked up a trick or two about human nature in all those counseling courses. Her every professional instinct shouted there was more about his father and his family than Gray was sharing. Even so, his set jaw as he stared out at the twinkling sky told her it wouldn't do any good to push him. He'd spilled as much as he planned to. End of discussion.

Lori rested her head against the mattress and closed her eyes as if that would somehow block out visions of the man beside her. Regardless of the rest of his story, he'd made it clear. He had his reasons for staying single. He had plenty of commitment in his life. He'd just committed himself to the Air Force.

Knowing that should have freed her.

It didn't. Instead of hearing his words, she saw his eyes, the flash of pain that had likely not been as well hidden in the young boy.

More than anything, she wanted to cradle that child to her and make his world right. She wanted to comfort the man and thank him for finally sharing a part of himself with her, even if it scared her more than a little and pushed them farther apart.

How sad something that should have sent her hot-footing it away only made her want to hold him even more.

Legs stretched out on the floor in front of him, Gray stared through the French doors for what seemed like hours. He'd tracked air traffic, civilian and military, as it circled the city, any distraction to keep from thinking about what he'd told Lori.

He listened to the whir of the vaporizer, Magda's slight but steady snore, Lori's even breathing as she slept beside him.

Gray turned to look at her, the edge of the mattress rubbing along his neck. Lori slumped asleep, propped in the corner created by the end table and mattress. Her arm draped up to the bed, her hand on Magda's arm.

Unable to stop himself, he reached to rest his hand on

top of Lori's. She didn't wake, but still laced her fingers with his. He held on to her soft hand and stared out the door again.

He hadn't meant to tell her so much. There was so much more he could have said. Not that it made any difference except to leave him feeling as if he'd taken a load of shrapnel internally.

Lori had just listened and held his hand, like now. She gave to others even in her sleep. Just like his mother.

And he'd pushed her away. Just like his father.

Gray freed his hand if not his thoughts.

God, he was tired. He'd monitored patients through the night before. What was it about this particular mother and daughter that drained his reserves more than a wardful of patients? She'd bombarded his defenses until he'd stupidly indulged in morose psychobabble garbage.

Time to shake it off, pal. If he was that tired, then Lori must be past exhaustion. She needed to be in her own bed.

Gray stood and checked Magda, careful not to wake her, then scooped Lori into his arms. Just like a few days before, a year ago, she snuggled in for a secure fit. Thank heaven she slept on though. He wasn't up to resisting any more of her groggy gropings.

Limp with deep sleep, Lori didn't stir during his walk down the hall to her bedroom. He lowered her to her bed and tucked her under the covers with lingering hands.

Lori's towering four-poster canopy bed enticed him to stay. The door finished its swing in, the lean of the house and gravity at work until the door clicked shut as if defying him to leave. A bottle of peach lotion waited on the bedside table like an invitation to remember things he could never forget, anyway.

Lori's hand trailed down his arm and held fast to his hand. "Stay. Sleep."

Did she know what she was offering? Or was she talking in her sleep again, trapped in the familiarity of a year ago?

Gray found her eyes open, fairly clear. Her touch was steady and warm. "Stay."

He thought of mentioning Magda as an excuse, but beside Lori's bed the nursery monitor glowed with a single red light. Magda's gentle snuffling floated through the device. He would hear her if she called out from down the hall.

Too tired to argue or pull his hand free, Gray lay beside Lori. On top of the fluffy comforter. No use tempting fate. He would just grab a little shut-eye in case Lori or Magda needed him, easier than making the cross-town drive again.

Taking care of Magda, then falling victim to Lori's gentle prodding left him more wiped out than he'd been after a Desert Storm mission. Gray closed his eyes and hoped like hell combat-induced dreams wouldn't chase him into sleep.

Chapter 10

Lori settled deeper into the most incredible dream. And it involved plastering herself against Gray's warm, solid body.

Surrendering to the dream proved irresistible. She'd been so long without. Without him.

Her hungry hands climbed over his back, along the rippling cut of muscles and pure man. Her fingers itched with impatience to feel *him,* not the well-worn T-shirt. A frantic trek to his waist brought her to the hem of his shirt. She tunneled inside.

Skin to skin she touched him. Her face buried in his neck, she inhaled, snuggled closer, pressed her lips to the delicious salty taste of his shoulder. She kicked her down-filled comforter to the foot of the bed so she could cuddle closer.

Gray groaned. Somewhere in her hazy mind she heard him, felt him turn his face to her.

"Lori?"

Instinct guided her mouth to his before he could say more.

Searing, hot need painted vibrant reds and blues on the backs of her eyelids. Heat combusted within her, sleep evaporating. Her hands paused, tensed. What was she doing? Other than almost passing out with pleasure just because she had Gray's mouth against her, fully, finally.

She thought of pulling away. For all of one practical second.

Lori twisted her fingers in his hair and yanked Gray closer. Hard. No doubt, remnants of sleep clouded her judgment. She didn't care. How could she think, much less reason while her legs tangled themselves with Gray's?

She worked her lips over his in a silent, demanding plea he couldn't miss, hopefully couldn't resist. Opening, urging, she traced her tongue along his mouth, then nipped at his bottom lip. Again, harder.

His lips parted with a hungry growl. Bold, strong hands clamped along her back, one on her waist, the other between her shoulder blades, both firm and insistent.

Forget about deluding herself into thinking that sleep muddled her reactions. She knew exactly what she was doing and simply couldn't stop.

The past year slid away as their tongues tangled, tasted, tempted. Her hands remembered he liked the brush of her thumbs just below his jaw, along his collarbone, over his small, flat nipples. Gray traced a tantalizing touch down her spine, one vertebra at a time until she was ready to scream with the need for more, had done so often before. He had to remember, too, and that stirred her to a near frenzy as she thought of what would come next.

If only they didn't stop.

Gray rolled her to her back, anchoring her to the mattress and the moment as she stared up into his glittering eyes. Her shirt scrunched up. His followed. Gray's bristly chest rasped her breasts to agonizing tightness. Her fingers crawled down his back, found their way into his shorts and gripped his taut buttocks.

His shorts inched low on his hips, hers following as Lori rocked against Gray. With frightening ease, they recaptured their familiar rhythm. Together, but frustratingly incomplete as two layers of cotton separated them.

He was such a great kisser, and Lori loved to kiss. Loved to kiss him, loved to look at him. Her leg hooked around Gray's hip, and he grabbed the back of her knee. Their boxers inched lower, his as well as hers, with Lori's every restless, needy wriggle. The hard, hot length of him pressed to her, so close, so intimate. No longer feeling cotton, just Gray, she savored that moment of delicious realization just before…

He slid in.

Full, thick pressure filled her, stretched her. The pleasure of it, after so long without, shimmered to an almost painful intensity, and she screamed her release into his mouth.

Gray's shoulders tensed beneath her palms. His eyes opened wide.

She stared back for at least ten racing heartbeats, joined, connected, throbbing, neither of them moving.

Deep within her, she felt him, wanted more of him. Her hands trembled on his back. Had he meant to be here, inside her? "Gray?"

He tore himself from her, growling as he flung himself onto his back. Air washed over her body, nearly freezing her, disappointment finishing the job. Just when she thought she would die from the loss, the hurt, he reached for her. Gray gathered her to his side with hands far from steady, reassuring her that all was not lost.

Her fingers skipped a determined path down his chest. "Come on, flyboy. Don't crash and burn on me now."

His chest pumping, he turned to her. A pained smile stretched his face. One of his shaking hands swept back

Lori's hair from her face. "Hold on while I regain control of the jet. She's quite a handful today."

Her fingers walked lower. "I'll say."

Gray's eyes slid closed as he groaned, his fist knotting in her hair. "Lori, slow down, hon. You're killing me here. I need to think."

Forget slowing and thinking. Reason could well land their feet back on the floor. "Wanna play wounded Allied pilot and saucy French nurse?"

"Only if I get to be the pilot this time."

Laughing, Lori rolled on top of him, enjoying the lazy trek of his fingers down her spine. "I'm willing to negotiate."

Sex with Gray had always been fun, and she'd missed it. More than she could have imagined. "Please don't say you *like* me too much to finish this time. I might well have to hurt you."

"No intentions of stopping, hon. I believe we're both way past that right now." He cupped her hips in his hands, keeping her a safe distance above him. "Just taking care of details first."

"Details?"

"Birth control."

"Birth control?" Old arguments stampeded over her. His refusal to consider marriage. Her need for children to love. Her decision to go on the pill to buy them both time to think and explore their feelings.

"Are you still on the pill?" he asked, a desperate edge darkening his words as his grip tightened on her hips.

She'd begun taking them just before their breakup, and had promptly thrown them in the trash after. Eating an entire bowl of raw cookie dough hadn't come close to making her feel better as she'd stared across the room at the wastebasket where she'd pitched her pills and dreams.

Lori flipped onto her back. "I'm not on the pill."

"O-kay." He slung an arm over his forehead as he

rushed on, ''Condoms, then. Or a diaphragm's fine. No diseases here.''

Of course she didn't have any, either. Abstinence had ensured that. It also fostered a lack of readily available birth control. ''There's nothing here, Gray. No birth control.''

His cheeks puffed on a heavy exhale as he straightened his clothes. ''I'll just run to the store—''

''No.''

He sagged back. ''Okay.''

What? She could barely breathe, think, talk, and he gave up with a simple ''okay.''

''Okay? That's it?'' She slugged his arm, hard. ''You could at least argue with me! Pretend to be disappointed, you damn jerk!''

The seasoned warrior rubbed his arm with an exaggerated grimace. ''Why should I be disappointed? It doesn't have to be over.''

Were all men jackasses? Or just this one man she had the unfortunate luck to want more than air? Lori turned away.

His arm snaked around her waist, and he flipped her to her back, looming over her. ''We'll do without birth control this time.''

Shock twisted her stomach. He couldn't mean what she thought. He couldn't be willing to risk pregnancy. He never had before. Never.

Heaven knew she wasn't ready to risk it. Not now.

A year ago she might have caved to the moment, to the beautiful image of Gray's laughing green eyes peering from the face of their little boy, but now... Things were more confusing than ever.

''It wouldn't be fair, Gray.''

''Shhh.'' His lips nipped along her collarbone, over her breasts.

She tried to shove his hands away, weak halfhearted pushes. ''We can't take that risk.''

"No risk." He kissed her stomach, rasped his beard-stubbled face over her skin before toying along the edge of her boxers with his teeth. "I'll take care of you, honey."

Realization seeped into her, leaving a bitter, metallic taste in her mouth. Of course he didn't mean to risk a pregnancy with her.

How many times would she make a fool over herself with Gray? Lori grabbed his shoulder to stop him, promising herself she meant it this time.

"We can't. For more reasons than pregnancy." Anger, frustration and old-fashioned heartache made her words harsher than she'd intended.

Wincing inside as well as out, Gray rested his forehead against Lori's smooth stomach. Of course she was right. He'd just lost it. Waking up with her in his arms had wrecked his remaining defenses. Thank God Lori had come to her senses.

Not that it made him feel any better. He hurt. Bad. He needed to touch her, taste her, more than he'd ever needed anything.

And that scared the hell out of him. Their need for each other a year ago had been so strong it nearly destroyed them both. He hadn't thought he could ever want anyone as much as he'd wanted her then.

One night back in her bed proved him wrong.

Lori slid out from under him. Braced on his elbow, Gray watched her charge toward the bathroom as if racing for a fallout shelter with incoming imminent. Those blasted boxers hooked low on her hips. Still, he could feel the moist heat of her clamping around him as it had for that brief moment when he'd lost his mind and slipped inside her.

Stupid. Wrong. Incredible anyway.

His arm gave way, and he slumped back onto his pillow. Her heat and peach fragrance still clung to the tangled sheets.

A shuffling, then coughing noise broke into his concentration. Gray frowned, looked around, his gaze landing on the red light glowing from the nursery monitor. Thunking his forehead, he mentally kicked himself. How could he have forgotten about Magda a few feet down the hall?

Never had he let his personal life interfere with his professional responsibilities. If he were totally honest with himself, he considered Magda more than just a professional obligation. Each hospital checkup with his pint-size patient had only edged her further into his heart. Now she was Lori's child. That alone made her special, no matter how many mind games he played with himself about keeping his distance.

Gray heard the shower swish on just as Magda coughed again. Raking his fingers through his hair, Gray reined in his thoughts and libido. No easy task, but necessary if he hoped to make it through the morning.

He shoved to his feet and lumbered down the hall. Opening Magda's door, he found her sitting up in bed, her eyes wide with early-morning groggy confusion. Her hair spiked in at least three different directions. Bed head, his mother called it. Magda eyed Gray and clutched a Barbie in her fist. Tenacity and wariness mingled in her little eyes. She had spirit no language barriers could disguise.

Yeah, she was a special kid.

"Hi, Magda." He entered slowly so she wouldn't bolt. She needed peace while she recuperated. After the life she'd likely had, the kid needed peace—period.

"Magda?" He extended his hands. "Let's go see Lori."

"Yori?" Huskiness from coughing distorted more normal childish tones.

"Yeah." He nodded. "Lori."

He held his hand out and waited while she scrambled from under the covers. Her legs dangled over the edge of the bed, her bare feet not quite touching the floor. Gray reached to take her hand. With rabbit speed, she jumped down and scampered past him.

Apparently, her trust wasn't easily won.

Kids didn't forget and forgive as easily as some thought. He knew that well enough from his own childhood. He hadn't understood the change in his father until he was an adult, and then it had been too late. They'd grown too far apart.

Gray shrugged off depressing thoughts. Too much soul picking wouldn't accomplish a thing. He needed to remember that, before Lori had him spilling his guts all over her priceless Oriental rugs again.

He followed Magda to Lori's room, silence echoing from the bathroom. He rapped two knuckles on the bathroom door. "Lori?"

Magda skirted past him to press her ear to the door.

"Lori?" he called again, then decided he'd better warn her about Magda. Lori had been spitting nails when she'd charged to the bathroom. Magda didn't need to overhear the tones from angry fallout that belonged squarely on his ears. "Magda wants to talk to you. She's right here."

"Gray." Lori's voice wobbled.

Was she crying? Guilt clubbed him. His brow fell to rest on the frame. He should have checked his libido at the door before he'd crawled into bed with her. "Lori, are you okay?"

"No. Go away. Please."

Like hell he would leave her crying over him. "Not a chance. Cover yourself, or whatever you need to do, because I'm coming in." He gave her a five count and hoped the door wasn't locked so he wouldn't have to pull some lame John Wayne stunt. "Now."

He pushed the door open and found Lori sitting on the bathroom floor swaddled in a bulky white bathrobe. Her green pallor answered his question before he could even ask.

Lori blanched. "Stomach flu."

* * *

Gray stretched out on Lori's sofa and channel surfed. She had been too incapacitated to turn down his offer to watch Magda for the afternoon. Lori had started to protest. Then her face had turned seaweed green and all arguments died as she'd shoved him out of the bathroom and slammed the door in his face.

For the best, since he still wasn't all that steady after their near miss earlier, and he needed time away from her to regain his footing. Taking care of Magda offered a perfect distraction until he could leave. After an hour he and Magda had arrived at an armed truce. As long as he didn't pick her up, she was fine.

They'd had breakfast, Magda's a bland diet of dry toast in accordance with her own stomach flu recovery. She'd eyed the cow cookie jar with longing as if to say "Yori" would have given her one. He'd held strong. Not too difficult since he didn't relish the idea of mopping up that cookie later.

Now Magda played quietly on the rug while Lori slept the day away. He'd hauled the Barbie house into the living room so he could catch the ball games.

Not a bad gig.

Magda seemed to be a low-maintenance kid, and she didn't want his attention anyway. Which stung a little more than it should have. Kids always liked him. He was the favorite uncle. The Disney dude. King of Barbies and Tonkas.

Gray thumbed the button until he found the cartoon channel and pitched aside the remote. Good thing Lori was totally out of it. Memories of her passion-dazed eyes, her playful touch swirled through his mind. He didn't have much left in the way of reserve ammunition around her.

So much for his clean break.

When he'd checked on her earlier, her weak smile of appreciation had slathered on the guilt. Who'd have thought she would turn weepy over a pack of crackers and a cup of tea? Weren't women supposed to want roses and Godiva chocolates?

Of course he'd given her those a year ago, for all the good it had done them.

Lori was grateful for such damned unpredictable little things. That stabbed at him. She deserved more. She deserved everything. The house, the kids and a husband who could commit to something more than the next piece of rank on his shoulder.

He thought of the next assignment and its assurance of his promotion to lieutenant colonel within a year. Tomorrow would start his last week of work at Charleston Air Force Base, his final flight scheduled for Friday, his party at his folks' condo on Saturday.

His parents. Damn. Gray sat up. He'd promised his mother he would stop in over the weekend.

Gray snagged the phone from the end table and punched in the number. Listening to the call go through, he watched Magda march her Barbies in front of the dollhouse.

The ringing stopped.

"Sergeant Clark's quarters," his father's clipped voice answered. Even retired and living off base, the old Chief Master Sergeant never shed his military routines.

"Hey, ol' man, it's me. Could you put Mom on?"

"Sure, son." The phone clattered to rest. "Angela..."

And that was it. The standard conversation he could expect with his dad. He wasn't sure anymore if it was his fault or his father's but didn't much care, other than it seemed to bother his mother.

The phone crackled with muffled sounds of his parents talking while he waited, watching Magda. She mumbled in her own language, and he resolved to find a translation dictionary. Some familiar words flowed through the gibberish, like "Mama" and "Papa."

Could she still have memories of her real parents? Her file hadn't held much information, except that her mother and father, both local schoolteachers, had died about eighteen months ago in a village raid. With no other living relatives, Magda had been placed in the orphanage.

She slid a smaller doll into the swing, the "Papa" doll behind pushing. A fist tightened around Gray's heart.

Of course she would have memories, spotty but real. His nephew remembered the color of a car they'd sold when he was two. Gray remembered his father—

"Grayson?" His mother's voice jolted him back to the present. "Where are you, sweetie?"

"Hi, Mom, still in Charleston. Sorry, but I'm not going to be able to make it out there this weekend. I'm, uh, with a patient today." Not a lie, but good thing his mom couldn't pin him with those laser, lie-detector eyes or he'd be busted for sure. If he didn't keep her diverted, she'd be talking about his sex life again. "And I'm on call tomorrow."

"Oh, well, work has to come first," she chirped, ever the good soldier.

Gray grimaced. "I'll still be over next Saturday for the party."

"And we'll be at your little ceremony on base Friday."

Magda folded the "Mama's" legs and sat her on the tiny porch steps. Lori would have a field day analyzing the doll play unrolling before him.

Gray yanked his attention back to the phone conversation. "You don't have to come to that, you know."

"We wouldn't miss it. Your father's looking forward to it."

Yeah, right. "Okay, then."

The little girl doll swung higher. Magda giggled and squealed, sounds Gray had never heard from her before. Perhaps if he looked into an interpreter, Lori could collect those memories for Magda and record them for when she was older. Magda squealed again.

"Who's that?" Angela asked.

Busted. Apparently, his mother's radar extended through telephone wires. "Uh, my patient."

"You're still working with those children from overseas?"

"Uh-huh." Keep it simple and get off the phone. "Look, Mom—"

"What about that little patient you and Lori were going to check on?" His mother's bracelet jingled over the phone. "Are you seeing her?"

"Yeah."

"I thought she wasn't supposed to be in the hospital more than a couple of days."

Might as well spill it before his mother concocted something more convoluted than reality, although he couldn't imagine what that might be. "She's home. Her foster parents backed out, so Lori stepped in. She called for a consult when Magda got sick."

"Magda," she sighed, her grandmother bracelet chiming. "What a sweet little name."

He could almost hear the jeweler's engraving tool etching out the name on a new charm for his mother's bracelet. "She's a sweet kid."

When she wasn't scowling at him.

"I'll bet she would enjoy playing with all those other children at the base party Friday."

Seconds ticked by while Gray clamped his teeth together. Magda moved the papa doll as he pushed the swing. She should remember her father had played with her. Every kid should have happy childhood memories.

His own father had been big on camping trips and parks when Gray had been a boy. Of course, looking back now, Gray realized that's probably all their budget would allow. Those simple vacations made for good memories. Odd how he hadn't thought about them in years.

"Grayson? Are you still there?"

"Yeah, Mom."

"Why don't your father and I pick up Lori on our way to base? Then she won't have to bother with the guards and registering her car at the front gate. Where does she live?"

"Above her office, but Mom—"

"If the two of you are back together, you really need to make the most of your time before you leave."

He and Lori a couple again. He could see how his mother could come to that conclusion.

Had Lori gotten the same idea from all the time they'd spent together? He'd told her they weren't going to start anything. But he'd seen that softening in her eyes when he'd told her about his father, then again when he'd brought her those lame crackers.

Somehow he needed for her to realize what he'd said about his job was true. Maybe a trip to the base, combined with time spent with his parents might help her to understand.

He ignored the annoying voice that insisted he was scrounging for excuses to spend more time with Lori. "Okay, Mom. I'll ask her and see what she thinks."

"Maybe she would also like to come to your family party on Saturday—"

"Don't push it, Mom. We're talking about Friday. Magda can have fun with the other kids. Lori and I can say goodbye then. But no family party."

"Of course, sweetie. Gotta run. Tell Lori we'll pick her up at four on Friday."

"Mom, I'll let you know," he repeated, not that she seemed to be listening. The dial tone hummed in his ear, so he disconnected. Somehow his world had taken an out of control nosedive, and he wasn't quite sure what to do to level it back out.

He would worry about his folks and Lori later. First, he had a recovering kid to watch. At least with Magda he knew where he stood. No surprises there.

She hummed and moved the papa doll. The Magda doll flew higher in the swing, and Magda laughed again—only to stop short.

With a swift sweep of her hand, she knocked the swing sideways. Her words dwindled to odd noises. Swishing sound effects with her mouth. Crashing noises.

Like bombs.

Gray straightened. The father doll fell to the ground. Magda tugged the smaller doll from the swing. She gripped the mother and child dolls in one hand and ran them across the yard.

A cold core, like a lethal lead ball, lodged right below Gray's sternum. The mother shoved the child under the tiny kitchenette table and ran back outside to the father.

Another crashing sound from Magda.

She dropped the mother doll to the ground.

Magda folded her hands in her lap. Silence echoed as it always did in the aftermath of battle.

Gray blinked once, twice, wanting to deny what he'd seen, but he couldn't. Magda had acted out her parents' death. He had no doubts. Her story likely didn't differ from many other children's, but that didn't ease the clutch of anger inside him or the fierce urge to protect her.

Unable to stop his feet, he slowly walked into the room. Magda looked up at him as if she'd known all along he was watching.

Careful not to startle her, he sank to one knee beside her and stared into her dark-brown eyes, bottomless eyes that had seen too much too early.

She glanced down at her "parents" then back up at Gray. *Fix them.*

He heard her, as clearly as if she'd said the words, he heard her. The weight of responsibility crashed on his shoulders like a seventy-pound survival pack.

There were at least a couple thousand people in Charleston better equipped to handle this moment than he was.

One of them slept in the next room—incapacitated with the stomach flu.

The moment to act was now. No time to wake Lori or consult a slew of child psychologists. Magda needed him, perhaps more than she'd needed him days ago in Sentavo.

Gray looked at the mother and father doll and thought of his own parents. During his father's years in 'Nam, Gray had dreamed of flying overseas to bring his father home.

Life would be normal again. His mother wouldn't go to bed alone, her eyes so exhausted even a kid could notice. Once again the familiar nighttime calls would sound from down the hall as his father hollered a laughing roll-call/lights-out for the kids.

Magda stared up at him with such wary hope, her "parents" lying beside her tiny bare feet. Right or wrong, he had to do something. Inaction wasn't an option.

One at a time Gray lifted the mother and father, dusting each off in turn, smoothing back their hair, silently offering up a prayer for the parents of the child by him. Side by side he placed them on the dollhouse bed and draped a miniature blanket over them.

Then he prayed like crazy again that he'd done the right thing. Surely an image of them asleep, even if forever, had to be better than visions of them dead in their yard.

Lori would be able to come up with a better answer later. For now he'd done the best he could. Hopefully, it was enough. Gray waited for Magda's verdict.

Magda cocked her head to the right. Rocking forward on her bottom, she leaned into the dollhouse. She pressed her fingers to her lips and touched the face of the father doll. She repeated the gesture with the mother.

Gray sucked air down his closing throat.

Magda turned to him, fingers pressed to her lips. For a second he thought she meant to kiss him, too. Then her fingers simply gestured forward as she'd done in communicating with Lori.

Thank you.

There wasn't enough air in the room to expand his constricted lungs.

Gray dropped a hand on top of Magda's shorn head, all the comfort she would likely allow from him. A familiar, but no less powerful, fire burned inside him, and he knew that if Lori were watching she would finally understand his single-minded commitment to his career.

This was why he served. For the people who couldn't fight for themselves and right the wrongs in their lives. He flew, he fought, he healed, whatever he could.

Because he didn't know how to do or be anything else.

Chapter 11

Maybe Gray would consider leaving the Air Force.

The ridiculous idea gnawed at Lori with tenacious determination.

She stepped from the shower, feeling almost human—at least well enough to watch Magda now. How wonderful it had been having Grayson with her through the night when Magda had been sick. Then taking care of Magda while Lori had slept, sleeping on the couch himself the second night until she'd recovered.

She couldn't hide from the truth. She wanted him back in her bed. Not that she had a clue where they were headed. They likely wouldn't head anywhere as long as she had to compete with his job. Which brought her back to her crazy, tempting thought.

Gray leaving the military?

She knew better. Hadn't he told her the military was his life?

But her mind couldn't help wandering along scenarios of him settling in Charleston, opening a practice, maybe serving time in the reserves. Reservists didn't move around or pull nearly the same number of hours. Weekend warriors, she'd heard them called.

He could stay in Charleston near his family, where he'd spent more time than anywhere else in his life. If there was one place he might put down roots, this was it. She would have the time to get to know him as she hadn't when they'd first been together. The man who brought her crackers and watched over Magda entranced Lori as much, if not more, than the man who had given her smiles—and the sex of a lifetime.

Gray leaving the military.

The idea spun in her mind with taunting power.

Fantasy. Pure fantasy. Changing Gray would take away much of what fascinated her. A Catch 22 since so many of the things that enticed her were the very traits that made any relationship between them unworkable.

Time to get dressed and take care of her responsibilities with Magda. Lori tossed aside the towel and opened her antique wardrobe. She'd had such great plans for their first day together, hours full of finger paints and paper dolls.

Gray had done more than his share. More than dishing out food and playing with Barbies, he'd dealt with heavy-duty emotional fallout.

His eyes dark with worry, he'd checked in on Lori with toast and a recounting of Magda's dollhouse revelation once Magda had drifted off for an afternoon nap. His handling of the incident had been worthy of any play therapy session with a certified counselor.

While she felt guilty for not being there for Magda, she couldn't fault the way Gray had managed. And honestly, it felt so good to have someone to share the problem with.

She slipped on a long, cotton sundress, a straight-cut burgundy favorite of hers that matched her painted toenails. She combed out her wet hair and swiped lip gloss over her mouth for color. Gray had always been fascinated with her mouth.

She stopped midswipe. She wasn't actually dressing up for him, was she?

Duh. Of course she was.

No matter what they said about learning to say goodbye, she was rapidly realizing she needed additional time to sort out her feelings. The more she learned about Gray, the more confused she became. Wary but resolute, Lori opened her bedroom door.

Gray's latest serenade wafted from the kitchen. ''Old MacDonald had a farm. Eeeee-yi, eeeee-yi, oooooh.''

Lori smiled. Enthusiasm had a musicality all its own.

''And on that farm he had a cow.''

''Cow!'' a hoarse, childish voice echoed.

Magda. Lori's heart tripped over itself, her feet following suit as her knees turned to pudding. She flattened her palm against the wall.

''With a moo-moo here,'' Gray sang, Magda joining in with off-key harmony for animal sounds. ''Moo-moo there.''

Lori rounded the corner and paused unseen in the doorway. The scene before her was so beautiful it hurt her eyes almost as much as her heart.

Magda perched on the edge of the counter clutching the cow cookie jar in her lap. Her clothes didn't match, clashing stripes and polka-dots from differing outfits, but she was clean, a red bandanna tied around her head. Gray wore the blue one this time.

Dropping pieces of bread into the toaster, he simultaneously serenaded into a wooden spoon. ''Here a moo, there a moo...''

He afforded Magda equal ''microphone'' time as he sang. She kept the beat, her tiny heels drumming against the cabinets.

Gray danced his way around the kitchen as he cooked

oatmeal and set the table. Jogging shorts displayed his muscular legs flexing with each weaving step.

He might as well slide her right into that toaster along with the next round of bread, because at the moment she was toast. He had her attention, completely, just as he'd done a year ago when he'd smiled at her that very first time.

Even more so.

Lori stepped into the kitchen. "Well, Doc, is this a duet or can anyone join in?"

The impromptu concert stopped. Gray set aside his spoon, his expression unreadable.

Magda squealed and held out her arms. "Yori!"

Lori scooped Magda off the counter and hitched the little girl onto her hip. Magda snuggled closer with total ease and trust. A child's unconditional love certainly was a powerful thing. Lori rested her cheek on Magda's bandanna, Gray's bandanna, the mix of the two of them doing odd things to Lori's heart. She stared at Gray across the kitchen. "Thank you. I seem to be saying that to you a lot lately."

"You okay now?" He shuffled from foot to foot.

A flutter of unease stirred in her chest. She knew that caged look in his eyes, the rhythm of those restless feet, too well. "Can't handle the heat of a morning-after kitchen, huh, big guy?"

Gray's feet stilled. His gaze collided with hers, linking them as firmly as that single moment he'd slid into her body. He'd set her up with the perfect morning-after breakfast, and now he was bowing out instead of joining them. She forced herself not to look away.

He turned first, spooned oatmeal into two bowls, dropped slices of toast on the plates and transferred the butter from the counter to the table. "I wish I could stay longer, but I've got rounds at the hospital."

His excuse was valid. Why then couldn't she shake the disappointment because he wouldn't be spending the rest of the day with them? Or shake the sense that he didn't want to. "Sorry. Of course you have to go. We've exhausted our house-call quota."

"Yeah, well, duty calls." His feet picked up their itchy pace again.

Magda on her hip, Lori followed Gray into the living room where he hooked his gym bag over his shoulder and charged for the door. On her porch he paused. "I've been thinking."

So had she, thoughts of waking up in his arms, of feeling his hands on her, of his being inside her.

Of never having him there again.

Could she actually be considering giving them another chance? There was also Magda to consider. Lori could so easily see herself serving as a foster parent beyond the one-month evidentiary hearing.

Maybe if she and Gray talked this time, rather than just jumping into bed whenever they didn't agree, they might solve something. Or at least keep from getting hurt again no matter how it turned out. She was wiser now. She would walk in with her eyes wide open, unlike her fairy-tale ideas of a year ago. "Thinking about what?"

"Magda should spend some time with other kids."

What a wake-up call. She'd been selfishly dreaming of time with him, and he'd been nobly considering Magda. "I'm looking into play groups once she's better."

His feet shuffled their restless dance. "Can you get off early Friday?"

"Maybe." Caution made her ask, "Why?"

"There's a crew party after Friday's flight. Other kids, children of crew members, will be there."

He *wanted* her there with the other families? One look into his eyes told her how important this was to him, and her knees went weak. Surely only because she hadn't eaten anything other than crackers and toast in more than twenty-four hours.

"All right." The words fell free before she could stop them, but she didn't call them back.

"Great." His gaze ping-ponged around the porch, before settling on her again. "My mother and father can pick you and Magda up."

His parents? Casually Lori grabbed the railing because the house seemed to have tilted even farther to the left, leaving her decidedly off balance. "Your parents?"

"You won't have to deal with the hassle of getting on base."

"Gray, I'm confused—"

"Guess I didn't make it clear. We're all meeting on the flight line first, then heading over to Lance's for the party."

"Oh, okay." She hadn't really meant confused about the plans so much as just what he was trying to accomplish. Her stomach was a mess all over again, and it had nothing to do with the stomach flu.

Gray dropped a kiss on Magda's bandanna-covered head, then cupped Lori's face in a farewell caress. For a minute she thought he might kiss her, too, and she couldn't find the will to move closer or away.

Instead Gray broke the moment with a nod. "Thanks, Lori. *Finit* flights mean a lot to us flyers."

"*Finit* flight?"

"Final flight. That's what we call a guy's last flight before he leaves a base. Everyone gathers on the runway for a farewell party. A fire truck hoses down the guy after he lands. It's all a part of Air Force tradition."

"Leaves? Who's leaving?" She hoped it wasn't Bronco or Tag. She knew how much working with them meant to Gray.

He scrubbed a hand across his blue bandanna. Was it her imagination, or did the fearless warrior look worried?

"Me. Lori, I transfer out of Charleston to Washington in another week and a half."

Gray stared straight into Lori's wide eyes and waited for the inevitable disillusionment. Which he got. In spades.

What he hadn't expected was her flat-out surprise.

He'd thought she knew. He'd talked about their need to say goodbye. He'd made it clear they had no future. Hadn't he?

Quit lying to yourself, pal.

Whether consciously or subconsciously, he'd been vague. Likely because he'd known he would get just this reaction. His transfer ended it for her. After hearing about her gypsy childhood, he knew talk of cross-country moves would send her underground.

Which was what he wanted. Right? So why hadn't he told her up-front? Damn, but he hated questions. He needed answers and action. He needed to leave.

Then why couldn't he make his feet move?

The silence between them stretched, broken only by an occasional passing car, the trickle of water from the garden fountain, the call of mockingbirds.

He'd done it again. Hurt her. In spite of all his great plans, he'd brought disillusionment right back into those brown eyes.

"Doc?" Magda's hoarse voice croaked.

Her voice jolted through Gray's confusion. His gaze jerked to Magda. "What, Magpie?"

She peeked at him from the security of Lori's neck and smiled. "Moo-moo, Doc. Moo-moo…cow?"

Something else entirely different jolted through Gray this time, an emotion so strong it jabbed right at his chest. "That's right, Magda. The word is *cow.* You're a smart kid."

Lori wasn't the only one who could be hurt by his choices. It would have been easier for Magda if he'd let her go right on hating him. Like Lori probably did now.

Somehow, in the span of a week, he'd twisted his life right up with these two. Their matching brown eyes would haunt him all the way to Washington. Not in the least certain what he would say, he still had to try. "Lori, I'm sorry, hon, I thought—"

A car horn drowned out the rest of his sentence. Gray twisted to look over his shoulder and found…

His parents.

Their Chevy Cavalier slid in behind his Explorer. His conversation with his mother came crashing back around him, his unwitting revelation of too many details about how he'd spent his weekend. He shouldn't be surprised by her visit, only that it had taken her twenty-four hours to drop in.

What surprised him most was that she'd managed to convince his father to come along. Gray braced his shoulders. God, he didn't need to deal with his father today.

His mother tucked a hand in her husband's arm and waved up to the trio on the balcony porch. "Hi, sugar! Lovely morning, isn't it?"

Of course she would have to catch him leaving Lori's house—in the morning. His mother had whipped out that maternal radar again. It must be some kind of holdover from his teenage years. He didn't even waste time wondering how she'd tracked Lori's new address.

Gray pulled a pained smile. "Morning, Mom. Dad."

His mother waved for him to come down. "I've got some things in the car. Your father could use help unloading."

He shot Lori an apologetic look, her face now a blank slate. He heard her footsteps behind him as she followed him down the stairs. Of course she wouldn't make a scene in front of his mother.

And neither would he. He had to make the best of it for everyone. His mother was a mama on a mission.

Gray thought of Magda behind him. More likely, his mom was a grandma on a mission. She intended to meet the little imp and would no doubt have Magda charmed in minutes.

Then he would be out of Lori's life again, Magda losing her new "grandma." How could the kid be expected to understand why all the grown-ups in her life suddenly faded away? He sure as hell hadn't understood about his own father—a man who'd never fully returned home.

Gray shoved aside thoughts of his own childhood and focused on the present. Time to head his parents off at the pass. Gray didn't intend to let Magda or Lori suffer any more losses in their lives.

Lori trailed Gray, resisting the urge to punt his too-damned-cute behind all the way down the steps.

Damn Grayson Clark for ruining her day. And damn him again for whisking her right back into his emotional revolving door.

One minute he plied her with more TLC than even her own mother had ever provided. The next, he broke land speed records running for the door.

Then he unrolled the family dinner invitation. Followed by the equivalent of "Been nice reminiscing. Catch you later, hon. I'm headed for Washington."

She wasn't sure she wanted any part of his little farewell gathering. She'd said enough goodbyes to the man to last her a lifetime. If she weakened and went with him to the party, would she weaken further and follow him right to Washington? Even if by some crazy fluke they worked things out, how many more farewells would a life on the move include?

On a day that had already taken a swan dive into the pits, she now had to dodge his matchmaking mama and pretend she didn't want exactly the same thing Angela did.

The closer Lori drew to the Clarks, the tighter Magda's arms locked, reminding Lori she had greater concerns than her own. Snuggling the tiny girl closer, Lori pressed her cheek against Magda's. "Sweetie, it's okay." Lori pointed to the couple stepping from the car. "Doc's mama and papa. Do you understand? That's Doc's mama and papa."

Magda's brow furrowed, but her hold relaxed ever so slightly. Lori slowed to wait in the courtyard. Shading her eyes with her hand, she watched Gray and his father unload a casserole dish, a Tupperware container, and a small cardboard box from the car.

Side by side, there was no mistaking the father-son resemblance. A broader, weather-worn version of his son, Dave Clark was still a striking older man, his full head of salt-and-pepper hair closely trimmed. The resemblance to Gray was there, but superficial only. The similar features didn't look the same without the smile.

Of course, Gray wasn't smiling, either. The two men didn't exchange a single word. No father-son thumps on the back. No quips or discussion of Sunday ball scores. They just quietly unloaded the trunk.

Echoes of Gray's confidences whispered through her mind, of Gray telling her about his father's three years spent in a POW camp. The few times she'd visited with Gray's parents last summer, she'd only seen Dave Clark as a reserved, somewhat brusque man. Now she wondered if he might have once looked more like Gray than she'd originally thought.

Angela swiped the travel wrinkles from her mint-green dress. Men following her, she called out to Lori, "Hello! What a gorgeous morning. Hope you don't mind that we stopped by unannounced. We couldn't help indulging in a drive after early-morning services."

"Hi, Angela. Dave. Of course you're welcome—"

"Mom, this is all nice." Gray plowed right over her words with uncharacteristic rudeness, dishes cradled in his hands. "But I need to head into work, and Magda's been sick. Lori, too. They both need quiet and rest."

"Oh, now that's too bad, son. Good thing they had you to take care of them. We didn't plan to stay long, anyway.

I just had to get a peek at this little one.'' Angela tugged her silent husband and his cardboard box toward Lori. ''Grayson told me on the phone yesterday that you stepped in to take Magda when her foster parents backed out. Since we grandmas always have extra toys on hand, I thought you could use a few to tide you over.''

''How thoughtful. Thank you, Angela, really. Both of you.'' Lori smiled at Dave Clark and tried not to think about how Gray might look just like his father in twenty years. Except she wouldn't be around to see the change.

''Afternoon, Lori.'' Always a man a few words, Dave nodded and hung a step behind his wife.

''It's good to see you again. Thanks for driving all the way over.'' Lori traced a bare toe along the dusty stone path. *Awkward* didn't even begin to cover it. How did one talk to the parents of an ex-lover? ''Would you like to come inside for lemonade?''

''No, thank you, dear. We really won't stay but a minute.'' Angela dipped a hand inside the Tupperware container and pulled out a cookie for Magda. ''What a cutie pie you are, sweetie.''

Magda clung tighter to Lori's neck. Lori's hand dropped protectively to cup Magda's head. ''I'm sorry, but she's had so much change. And she doesn't speak English yet.''

''Of course she's shy.'' Angela placed the cookie on top of the container, strategically within Magda's reach. ''Not a thing in the world wrong with that. I vow Mary Ann didn't let go of my leg until she was five. We'll have plenty of time to get acquainted come Friday.''

''Mom, about Friday—''

''Angela, I'm not so sure we'll be—''

''Dave, honey. Set the box on the bench over there.'' Grayson's mother stepped away as if neither of them had even spoken. Magda squirmed to get down, eyeing that cookie, stomach flu obviously long gone.

Angela waggled her hand toward the duo of wrought-iron benches by the fountain. With a nod, her husband lumbered over and set the box on a bench, taking his place beside it. He relaxed back in the seat, eyes trained on the trickling fountain.

Gray stepped forward. "Mom—"

"Son, why don't you run those dishes upstairs before that chicken pie spoils in this heat?"

He hesitated as if searching for some way to dodge the inevitable. Finally he pulled another pained smile. "Sure, Mom. I'll be right back down so I can walk you to the car."

After Gray climbed the steps and disappeared into her apartment, Lori turned to the older woman and tried again. "This is so thoughtful, but I don't want you to misunderstand the—"

"Shush, now!" Angela waved for silence, her eyes carrying a hint of melancholy. "Just hush up and let a mama dream. All right, dear? I know this is very likely not going to play out the way I want. But maybe you can indulge a meddlesome, worried mother for just a minute longer." Angela paused for a breath, then smiled. Her hand drifted up to her mouth. "Oh, Lori, look."

Lori followed Angela's gaze over to the black iron bench. During Angela's minirant, Magda had slipped away to stand beside Dave.

One by one, the older man quietly passed toys to the solemn-eyed little girl. A rainbow-striped ball. A Cinderella coloring book and box of crayons. A Raggedy Ann doll that looked suspiciously new with a dangling price tag.

Angela tucked her hand in the crook of Lori's arm. "He was always so good with our boys when they were little. Just like that. So patient."

Magda scooted forward, stretching up on her toes to peer inside the box. She eyed Dave warily, and when he nodded, her hand snaked inside the box. She pulled free a stuffed white-and-black Snoopy dog that had seen better days. Definitely a well-loved toy. Magda scooched up onto Dave's lap and continued to empty the box, one treasure at a time, all the while keeping her Snoopy snuggled under her arm.

Angela's bracelet jingled as she pressed a hand to her chest. "My goodness, Lori, does that ever bring back memories. Grayson's younger brother, Davis, was a cuddler like I bet you were." Angela sighed. "But Grayson, Lord have mercy, that child could wiggle. He never could hold still for more than five seconds at a time. The peculiar thing was deep down he wanted, even needed, those hugs much more than Davis."

Lori swallowed the urge to run up the stairs and lock herself in her apartment before Angela unveiled anymore heart-wrenching peeks into Gray's past. Instead of running, Lori changed the subject. "Magda seems to have taken a liking to the dog. I hope your grandchildren won't be upset that it's on loan for a while."

"They won't miss it. That's one I had tucked away. It was Grayson's. He slept with that Snoopy every night when he was a baby." Angela gnawed the corner of a nail absently. "He took it back after his father deployed to Vietnam."

Magda nested under Dave's chin, her eyes drooping as he patted her back. Lori couldn't help but think of how much living the man had missed with his own children.

Tears dulled Lori's vision without warning. She should have run when she'd had the chance. She was way out of her league in holding strong against the emotion-tugging powers of Angela Clark.

The older woman's hand fell back to her side. "So, dear, should we pick you up for the *finit* flight party at four or closer to four-thirty on Friday?"

Lori took in the determined gleam shining from Angela's eyes. There wasn't even a chance of avoiding that party. "You don't play fair."

The door slammed shut above, just before Gray charged down the stairs, a determined look on his face.

Angela studied her son for a lingering second, then turned back at Lori. "Mothers rarely do when their children need them."

Chapter 12

Gray gripped the stick and flew. Beach music pulsed through the interphone. No one argued or grumbled. This was his flight.

But he wasn't singing. The shock on Lori's face when he'd told her about his move kept blindsiding him.

Damn it, he needed to fly the plane.

Air-to-air refueling demanded concentration. Twenty-five thousand feet in the air, he eased up behind the tanker that would off-load the gas they needed to complete the mission.

Routine grounded him as he maneuvered the stick and mumbled through steps he'd completed hundreds of times before. "Visual references…lined up. Bump the throttles—Oops, too much. Pull it back. Wings level. Got good closure. Back…off…it and…level it right there." Gray called to the copilot, "Refueling checklist complete?"

Bronco slapped his checklist closed. "Roger. Checklist complete. Two green lights. Tanker ready to pass some gas."

"Uh-huh." Not in the mood for crew dog exchanges, Gray had let Bronco's lame jokes slide all day.

The tanker's long metal boom, an enclosed gas hose, dropped, connected, and the two aircraft flew in tandem twenty-two feet apart. Gray settled in for the forty-five-minute refueling with none of his expected excitement.

Refueling offered the greatest challenge in Air Force flying, short of combat, and he couldn't even find a song he wanted to sing.

Damn.

Gray adjusted his air speed.

Bronco stretched in the confined space. "Done any house hunting up in Washington yet?"

"Nope."

"But you've got a couple weeks permissive leave to look, right?"

"Uh-huh."

Bronco shifted in his seat, drummed his fingers on the panel. Shifted again. "Sure hope those firemen down there got the right hoses hooked up for you. Remember when they sprayed Sasquach with the yellow foam? Guy looked jaundiced for a week."

"Yeah." On a normal day Bronco was talkative, but the guy was downright chatty today with no signs of letting up.

"You're gonna pull some awesome Pacific trips with this new assignment. Temporary duty to Hawaii. Guam. Philippines. Japan. Great shopping."

Shopping. Thoughts of Barbie houses and Capri pants made Gray flinch.

"Hey, Cutter?"

"What?"

"You'd better talk to me, man, or I'm going to yank these throttles, knock you off the boom and then tell everyone you screwed up refueling on your *finit* flight."

Gray shot a quick glance at Bronco before returning his

concentration to the plane flying in front of him. "Sorry. Were you talking to me?"

"Funny."

"Hey, Lance," Gray shot over his shoulder to the senior pilot in the instructor seat. "You actually let your copilot talk?"

"Sorry. He snuck that in while my mouth was full. Really great cookies today. Want one?" The bag rattled behind Gray's shoulder.

"No, thanks."

Silence settled over them, broken only by sporadic calls through the headset. Not at all like times he usually flew with these guys.

Tag was best of the best, one of the old guard. Lancelot had a great set of flying hands, a solid pilot, even if Gray didn't hang with him much outside the airplane. Rumor had it Lance's party habits, combined with job stress, had put his marriage on the line more than once. But he had an air sense Gray trusted.

And Bronco. Damn, he would miss the big, chatty guy.

Of course these guys would be his choice for his *finit* flight.

His *finit* flight, a tradition chock-full of celebration and other rituals central to the "fight hard, play hard" so he could "fight harder the next day" mentality of all soldiers. And he wasn't enjoying himself in the least because he kept thinking of Lori.

Would she be on the ground waiting for him?

She'd said she would, for Magda to say goodbye. For good.

They hadn't spoken all week, but she hadn't called to cancel, either. The flight had taken off before his parents would have even left to pick her up, so he wouldn't know if she'd come until he taxied down the runway.

There wasn't a thing he could do about it now. Might as well plaster on the smile and put on a good front. "Hey,

Lancelot, did you hear what they said about Bronco at the last training meeting?"

Lance chuckled, picking up the teasing thread as any decent crew dog would. "Refresh my memory, Cutter."

"Something about copilot upgrades to aircraft commander. And how he'll never get one...because he talks too much!"

Lance coughed into the headset. "Almost made me choke on a cookie with that, Cutter. Good one, huh, Bronco? Or should we change your call sign to 'Motor Mouth'?"

"Upgrade me and it won't be a problem," Bronco growled, then fell silent. Before long, the big guy was squirming predictably in his seat. "Hey, you're making up that stuff about the meeting—right?"

"Whatever you want to tell yourself." Gray jumped into the familiar routine of crew camaraderie. Everything would be fine. He'd just experienced a ripple, a mental air pocket, before he leveled out. "Got any more cookies back there, Lancelot?"

Gray reached over his shoulder, downed the cookie, then decided he'd tortured Bronco long enough.

"Hey, Bronco." He winked. "I'm just yanking your chain. Get over yourself."

"I knew that." Bronco sniffed, then grinned.

Gray decided he should take the same advice for himself. He'd fallen into the trap of letting things get too complicated, and he knew better. The sky unfolded before him, cloud after cloud whipping past. Keep it simple. Just him and the sky—

Wham.

The pop reverberated through the aircraft. It echoed, like a baseball bat to the side of the plane. Gray's hand convulsed around the stick.

Fog rolled into the cockpit. An ominous white cloud churned, filling his rapidly fogging brain.

Rapid.

Rapid decompression.

His mind flashed with thoughts of Lori waiting on the ground. Lori, smiling because of a silly cracker.

No time to bite out a curse or waste on distractions. Training kicked in. He had less than twenty seconds of useful consciousness left.

Gray stared up at the refueling plane ahead of them and smashed the disconnect button.

"Breakaway! Breakaway! Breakaway!" He whipped the quick-don oxygen mask over his face.

A deep inhale started to clear his brain. "Rapid dee," he barked over interphone. "Everybody on oxygen and report up."

"Copilot up on oxygen."

"Instructor pilot up on oxygen," Lance called.

"Loadmaster up."

"Bronco, tell center we're descending to ten thousand feet." Gray clipped orders over the headset. He rammed the stick forward. Nosedown the plane dived, faster, rattling, increasing vibration, gaining speed as they descended toward breathable air.

His mind clicked through causes, everything from a popped seal to an explosion. He couldn't evaluate until they reached ten thousand feet. If they got there.

Lori's face flashed in front of him again at absolutely the worst time. He did not need distractions. Not now. And Lori had always been the biggest distraction he'd ever known.

The plane rattled louder, noises picking up, whining. Clouds whipped past the windscreen.

Still Gray couldn't shake thoughts of Lori. He could almost smell peaches. Was this what guys like Lance and the squadron commander, all those married flyers went through every time they faced danger?

If so, he didn't want it. Thoughts of Lori's horrified face

if he died tormented him with each plummeting mile. He'd wanted her to understand, but hadn't imagined he could throw her right into the sort of pain his father had given his mother.

Damn. Damn. Damn. His crewmates counted on him to do his job, to protect them, and all he could think about was Lori. And the ground closing in at three hundred and fifty knots.

Lori hitched Magda higher on her hip and tried to soothe her with a combination of bouncing and swaying. It wasn't working. They'd been out on the flight line too long and any child would be restless.

Magda had already climbed up and down the small set of bleachers by the line of parked planes at least fifty times. The allure of strolling around their corner of concrete had long ago palled for the four-year-old.

A summer breeze lilted along the open airfield and through Lori's loose hair, offering relief from the stored heat drifting up from the cement. At first Lori had worried a return to the base might upset Magda. But Magda's wariness had faded each day as she bonded with Lori—with a speed Lori understood well since she felt the same. She knew there wasn't a chance she would be giving Magda up at the hearing in a few weeks.

Magda squirmed to get down, not in the least bothered by her surroundings. Too bad Lori couldn't find some of that reassurance for herself. She still wasn't certain why she'd come. For Magda? To find out what made Gray shut himself off from any life other than flying and medicine?

To see him one last time before he left?

A tinkling sound broke through her thoughts. Angela Clark's bracelet sounded from Magda's fist.

Lori knew exactly why she'd come. Grayson's mother was just as persuasive as her son.

Magda jingled Angela's bracelet again, Gray's mother

having passed it over fifteen minutes earlier in hopes of calming the wiggling child. Lori had long ago exhausted her bribe supply of gummies and juice boxes.

"Lori?" Dave Clark extended callused hands. "Let me take her."

"Dave, she's not at her best." Lori hesitated, not wanting to impose.

The older man gripped the child's waist. "Grayson couldn't sit still to save his soul when he was a boy. I think I can handle this tiny scrap."

"If you're sure you don't mind?" Lori handed her over with reluctant relief. The kid seemed to have doubled in weight since they'd arrived well over an hour ago.

Angela straightened Magda's hat and matching ladybug-patterned dress. "Of course he doesn't mind. Dave loves babies." A fond smile lit her face, a smile so like her son's. "He was always toting the boys around on his back when they were small." Her smile faded. "Of course he missed Mary Ann's baby years, but she was right about Magda's age when he came home."

All those lost years. An image of young Gray curled up with his stuffed Snoopy dog slipped right up and past Lori's defenses. "Thanks, Dave, my arms were ready to give out."

"No problem." He shifted Magda onto his shoulders so her feet dangled on his chest. Angela pointed to different sites on the runway—cars, trucks, flags—and chanted the words to Magda.

Lori glanced around the tarmac at the other fifty or so waiting people. Maybe one of them would have an answer for the delay. Most of them she recognized from a year ago. Tag's family waited to the side, his wife and two teenagers. Other servicemen milled around in flight suits.

Captain O'Connell, one of the other flight surgeons, stood with the squadron commander and ground crew. Of course, Kathleen O'Connell didn't look at all peaked from her stomach flu bout. If anything, she looked tanned and healthy in her flight suit.

A military doctor, she was just the sort of woman Gray should be seeing. They would have similar goals with a mutual understanding of the job and its demands.

Lori had no reason to suspect there was any relationship between the two of them. Still she couldn't stop the stab of jealousy at comparing herself to Kathleen and finding herself lacking.

Just when she decided she would have to swallow her pride and ask Kathleen for an update, Lori's gaze lit on a late arrival. Lance's wife, Julia, stepped from a military truck, clutching a champagne bottle.

"Thanks, Lieutenant," Julia called breathlessly. "Lance would have had a cow if I wasn't here. Not a pretty sight, let me tell you!"

In a flurry of short, blond curls and yards of whispery cotton, Julia Sinclair rushed across the flight line. Lori had thought they might develop a friendship a year ago, but there hadn't been enough time. Another disappointment. She could have used girl talk and someone to share her bowl of consolation cookie dough.

Lori tapped Angela's arm. "I'll be right back. I'm going to say hello to someone."

"Of course." Angela didn't even look away from Magda. "We'll be fine."

Lori looked up, but still no sign of an airplane. She pushed through the crowd and called out, "Julia. Over here."

The woman turned, frowned, then smiled, waving. "Lori, wow, you came! Lance said you might, but well, men can get things all messed up so I didn't know for sure. I put you on the party count, anyway."

"Thanks. I hope we haven't caused any extra trouble."

"Not at all. Everything's done and waiting." Julia fanned her face with her hand, shuffled, shifted her handbag over her shoulder. Nervous energy radiated from her in waves to rival the heat steaming from the runway. ''I thought for sure I would be late. I had to transfer all those deli meats and cheeses to real platters, then stuff the plastic ones deep in the trash. Bury the evidence, you know? Can you believe Lance actually thinks I cut all that stuff up with my own little hands? Sheesh! But who am I to disillusion the guy?''

Lori laughed, looking up at the woman who topped her by at least three or four inches. Julia had a way of making her presence felt in a way that had nothing to do with her near-six-foot height. ''I guess it's lucky for you they're running late.''

Julia tugged her necklace up to read the watch face. ''I guess they are, aren't they? That happens. It's probably nothing.''

''Of course.'' Lori grasped for something to say, anything to keep the conversation alive so she didn't have to think about the delayed aircraft. ''It's nice of you to put together the picnic for Gray.''

''The local deli and I can throw one heck of a party. Your little one will have plenty of kids to play with. Most of the families are joining us back at the house. Gray has a lot of friends here. We're going to miss him.''

''Hmmm.'' So would she. He'd left his mark on her life. She couldn't walk through her apartment without thinking of him. She'd fed a whole box of crackers to the birds so she wouldn't have to look at the packs and remember Gray.

''It's not often they get to fly with one of his kind.''

Where was he? ''What do you mean?''

''A flyer flight surgeon.''

''What about Captain O'Connell?'' Lori nodded to the woman across the runway. ''I thought she was a flight surgeon, too.''

''She is, but didn't Gray ever explain the difference? He probably didn't want to brag. A flight surgeon is a doctor who specializes in medicine pertaining to flyer ailments. Only a few of them are actually flyers themselves, about a dozen I think."

"A dozen?" Lori answered absently, scanning the horizon, searching for a dot, each minute weighing on her. Wind stirred, swirled, plastering her silk wraparound dress to her body. "Here?"

"No. In the Air Force."

Julia's words sank in, slowly, heavily. A flash of admiration mixed with a wayward twinge of pride. Only a dozen people in the entire Air Force held that distinction, and Gray was one of them.

There wasn't a chance he could give it up. That doused the last of her hopes, banked though they may have been. No reserves or weekend warriors after his stint in Washington. He'd charted his life.

A rumble sounded in the background. Lori straightened, her breath catching as she searched the sky and runway. Was that the plane? She jerked to look over her shoulder.

Hangar doors growled open, not aircraft sounds at all.

Sirens split the air.

Numbness fell away.

Fire trucks tore out, six of them screaming across the tarmac toward the runway.

Lori stopped breathing altogether. She looked around frantically. Gray had said a fire truck would hose him down, a tradition for *finit* flights, but he hadn't said anything about six trucks with sirens.

Julia's pale face didn't calm Lori in the least. Just as she started to search for Gray's parents, a handheld radio crackled, blaring loudly enough to be heard over any flight line pandemonium, "Wolf One, this is command post."

Lori followed the noise to a small group between the bleachers and line of planes.

The squadron commander, Lori searched for his name

and couldn't find it, raised the radio to his mouth, "Yeah, Wolf One here, over."

"Sir," the radio broadcast, "Lifter one-three has declared an in-flight emergency. Experienced a rapid decompression. They're on twenty-five-mile approach."

In-flight emergency. Just the words horrified her. Lori held herself still, desperate to absorb and decode every word.

"Roger that, command post. Rapid decompression. And the crew?"

"No injuries."

No injuries. Lori clung to those words as tightly as she held Julia's arm. When had she grabbed it?

"Roger," the commander barked. "Send Foxtrot over to pick me up at spot twelve. I'm heading out for landing. Over."

Seconds later the commander leaped into a truck. Sirens blaring, it followed the fire trucks past the line of parked planes next to the lengthy runway.

As quickly as that, her world rocked.

Lori felt a hand on her shoulder and startled. She found Gray's father standing behind her, Magda still on his shoulders jingling Angela's bracelet.

"He'll be fine, Lori." Dave held his wife's hand, her face pale but in control. "Rapid dees happen all the time. The trucks, the noise, it's all procedure. Since he's only twenty-five miles out, he'll be here in minutes. Probably landing in less than five. Should be breaking the horizon right about...now."

Like magic, a speck appeared.

Lori exhaled. She pulled the fragmented pieces of her reason together. What right did she have to accept comfort, anyway? She wasn't anyone to Gray, not like his parents beside her. And Julia had a husband to worry about.

That didn't stop Lori's heart from punching her rib cage or her hands from shaking.

Julia's hand fluttered to rest on Lori's arm. "Really, thank goodness it's just a rapid dee. Those can be absolutely nothing big."

Lori looked around at the fire trucks positioned along the runway. If this was "nothing" she didn't want to consider "something." How could they all be so blasé?

The plane roared closer, growing larger. She started breathing again. Her pulse only raced double time now, not too bad.

Julia laughed a slight wobble. "I remember once when Lance came home and told me—"

Angela cleared her throat, shooting a pointed look Lori's way. "Save that one for another time, dear."

"Ooops, sorry, just nervous chatter." Julia clutched the champagne bottle to her stomach. "We'll all laugh at the party."

Of course they would. She could always count on Gray for a laugh, and in minutes he would surely step from that plane as carefree as ever. "I'm fine. Dave, do you want to pass me Magda?"

"Let her stay."

Lori held Magda's foot, anyway, needing the comfort of contact. Eyes trained upward, Lori watched the plane near, slow, touch down.

Relief turned her limbs to oatmeal. Thank God she wasn't holding Magda because she surely would have dropped her.

Engines whined as the aircraft slowed, fire trucks pacing alongside. The cargo plane turned, heading toward them.

Dave nodded. "That's good."

"What?"

"If it was a serious emergency, they would have stopped on the runway. But they're still coming over. That's good. Probably nothing more than a loose seal."

Swallowing twice, Lori tried to moisten her gritty mouth.

The lumbering aircraft neared. She could even see Gray through the window, his headset on as he parked the plane.

Lori inhaled deeply, the exhaust-tinged air stinging her lungs with each gasp. This was nothing, she reminded herself. Just a little in-flight emergency, practically an everyday occurrence for him.

She would have a heart attack by the end of the week.

Handling a crisis had always been her strength. Why was she freaking out now?

Because she was helpless. Out of control. There was nothing she could do in a situation like this, and she needed control over her life after so many years of chaos.

The side hatch door opened. A firefighter in his silver fire suit waited, firehose poised and ready.

One at a time crew members ambled down the few steps onto the runway. Burly Bronco. Too-pretty-for-his-own-good Lancelot. Steady Tag.

Finally Grayson.

His smile as bright as the sun glinting off his airplane, he loped down the stairs.

"Congratulations, Major Clark," the firefighter shouted. "And farewell!"

The blast of water caught Gray full in the chest. His laugh rumbled over the flight line as he stumbled back from the force of the crystal-clear water.

Bronco grabbed a bottle of champagne from a cooler, popped the cork and launched into the deluge, pouring the bottle over Gray's head. Sun shimmered off the fire hose spray, sparkling rainbows into a nimbus around them.

She'd heard Gray when he'd said the military was his life, but until now she hadn't really understood.

The transient lifestyle, the edge-of-the-seat action, the battle-forged camaraderie, Gray would never give it up. More important, he couldn't. Even if Gray somehow managed to overcome his resistance to commitment, this really was it for them unless she could find a way to accept his life in the military.

The spray slowed and dripped to a halt. Jostled from behind as people raced past, Lori steadied herself. Gray's parents, other uniformed flyers charged toward the plane. Julia dashed forward. Bottle in her hand, arms waving, she sprinted to her husband.

Gray hefted Magda from his father's shoulders and tossed her in the air. Water dripped down his gorgeous face as he caught her. Hooking her on his hip, Gray scanned the crowd. The party converged around him, in-flight emergencies long forgotten by everyone.

Except for Lori.

She didn't feel much like partying.

Chapter 13

"We need to talk." Gray waited for Lori to answer, but she stayed silent, jamming the key into her front door. Streetlamps threw shadows across her profile, or had he put those there?

Some days sapped the life right out of a guy.

Magda lay slack against his shoulder, exhausted from the party. He shifted her more securely and waited for Lori to answer.

The celebration had gone off without a hitch—well attended, lasting hours past the schedule. Magda had won hearts as she taught her new friends a mixed English-Sentavian version of "Old MacDonald."

Lori's perfect smile had charmed his friends. He couldn't complain, except he recognized that smile. He'd invented it, after all.

Lori was upset. No one else had noticed. He couldn't miss it.

The trip to base should have offered her closure, saved her from being hurt when he left so he could shake loose the unrest dogging his heels. Instead he'd done the very thing he'd sworn never to do. He'd started an ulcer gnawing in her stomach just like the one his father had given his mother.

Gray had flown countless incident-free flights. Not today, not when he'd really needed to. A damned popped seal had blown his whole plan, and now he needed to fix it.

For two open, honest people, they'd danced around the real issue long enough, and time was running out. "Lori? Did you hear me?"

She spun to face him as the door swung open behind her. "Okay, fine. Let's talk."

The tight pinch to her full mouth told him clearly he wouldn't get anywhere with her tonight. No need to step straight onto the land mine. He would have his hands full dodging the less obvious ones. "Not now. Not while we're both wired. Not with Magda around."

And not with the moonlight caressing Lori's fragile jaw and glinting off golden streaks in her hair, hair he wanted to bury his face in while he buried himself in her. The open door taunted him with an invitation to Lori's room and peach-scented sheets. "Definitely not here."

"Well, Major Clark, that pretty much rules out all the options because I have a child to put to bed."

The marshy wind toyed with her hair, gusting strands over him. Options dwindled until he finally settled on the one place guaranteed to douse romantic thoughts. "My folks are having my brother, sister and their families over tomorrow for a farewell party."

"I know. Your mother invited me. Twice."

"I should have warned you. Sorry." The more he thought of going to his parents' for the day, the more he warmed to the idea. He would show her a good time, let them end on a positive note. And maybe if she spent more time with his family and saw his parents together at home, she might understand his need to stay away from her. "I want you and Magda to come."

Her brow quirked, Lori-spunk firmly in place and stirring his exhausted body wide awake. She also looked three seconds away from telling him to go pound sand.

Gray plowed over the silence before she could speak. "Come with me for the day. My mom can watch Magda. We'll talk without distractions."

"Wasn't today enough for you, Gray? It was for me."

She was giving him his walking papers, a chance to end it here and now. But he couldn't do it. Wouldn't do it this way. "We can't leave it like this. At least at my folks' we can find some time to talk—"

"Won't your mother think—"

"I'll take care of my mom. This isn't about her." He lifted Lori's hand and held it loosely in his, studying the fragile bones with an odd sort of objectivity. He knew the names of every bone in that hand. Just regular bones. But infused with Lori's vibrancy, they were beautiful, unique. "We have to talk."

Bells chimed eleven times—or was it twelve—while he waited, already lining up his next argument. Gray shifted Magda more securely on his shoulder, arm hooked under her bottom.

Head bowed, Lori stared down at their clasped hands. "I guess if the king of keep-it-simple wants chitchat, it must be pretty bad." She tugged her hand free and pressed it to her stomach. "We tried so hard to avoid this."

"Too much like last summer."

"But worse."

"Worse?"

Her mouth twitched with a reluctant smile. "We didn't even get to have sex."

Her words punched him square in the libido, and he could only laugh. His body hurt like hell from the rapid decompression. His head wasn't much better off, and still he ached for her. He wanted nothing more than to crawl into Lori's big bed and sleep tangled together.

Instead he laughed at himself and the colossal mess he'd made of his attempt to forget her. Lori joined him until she sagged against the balcony rail, swiping her wrist over her eyes.

He took her hand again and wouldn't let her pull free this time, instead tugging her to him. Her tear-filled eyes met his, stealing the breath from his lungs more effectively than any rapid decompression.

"Oh, God, don't cry, honey. Everybody's fine. No one got hurt today." He brushed his thumb along her cheek, absorbing a lone tear.

"That's not why I'm crying."

"I'm not worth it."

Her chin tipped up. "I know that."

"Of course you do."

Unable to resist, not that he'd ever had much luck resisting Lori, Gray skimmed his lips over hers, kissed her once, then again. A nice safe twelve or so inches separated them. He couldn't get closer or any more intimate, not with a sleeping kid on his shoulder.

Adrenaline letdown in the aftermath of his hazardous flight left him susceptible. He wanted those warm sheets and Lori's soft arms around him. All those moments when he'd thought he might never see her, kiss her, touch her again hammered down on him.

Too much emotion. He needed to pass off the sleeping kid and get away from the temptation of Lori and those welcoming daisies arched over her door.

Easing his face away, he nipped her full lower lip one last time and stared into her stormy eyes. "Come with me tomorrow. I have a reason, something I want you to see." He would come up with something by morning. "I know I've asked a lot. But do this one last thing for me."

No answer had been this important since his first pilot

training check ride. His fingers worked a massage on her scalp, a silent plea for her to relax and trust him. A smart woman wouldn't.

"Okay."

Relief made speech tough. Thankful Lori had checked her brain at the door for once, he passed over the sleeping child. He should have offered to carry Magda inside, but he needed to keep his feet firmly on the other side of Lori's threshold since he was already on shaky ground around her. "I'll pick the two of you up around noon."

"I'll be waiting with both my shirts."

Apparently her brain had checked back in, and just in time. Intelligent thought seemed to be in short supply for him. If he didn't pull it together before he picked her up in the morning, he might do something they would both regret. If he hadn't already.

What in the world could Gray want to show her? They crossed yet another bridge over the intercoastal waterway to his parents' seaside condo.

He'd been so serious the night before, so unlike himself. She couldn't resist his invitation. After spending the entire party with her stomach in an uproar over the possibility that Gray could have been hurt, could have—

Blinking quickly, she focused on the glittering ocean.

She simply couldn't walk away. Not yet.

Beach music pulsed low, Gray humming if not singing. Magda drummed her feet against her car seat in time as she stuffed French fries into her mouth, a Happy Meal box on her lap. Gray had detoured to buy it for her even when Lori insisted Magda could wait. The stubborn man had pulled into the drive through anyway and bought himself a Big Mac, too.

Used to winning, more comfortable being in charge, she found his quiet mulishness an odd challenge. Funny how she'd been so focused on the playful exterior a year ago, she'd missed deeper implications of his determination. His resolution no doubt had carried him through in achieving two such ambitious career goals.

What else hadn't she noticed about him?

Like the annoying way he kept popping his knuckles and flexing his feet. Why couldn't he have worn long pants instead of those khaki shorts? Muscles bulged along his bare calf with each flexing stretch. "Could you stop that, please?"

"What?"

She stared pointedly at his cracking fist and feet.

His hand paused midcrack. He straightened his fingers and shrugged, his untucked plaid shirt rippling over his broad shoulders. "Oh, yeah. Sorry. Just working out the bends."

"The bends?"

His fist curled, finishing off the popping in the silence as Gray stared at her legs.

"Eyes on the road, Major." She tugged her silky sundress over her knees. Why in the world had she worn a dress to a picnic? She'd convinced herself she would be cooler, ignoring the fact that Gray had told her countless times how he liked seeing her legs bared by a dress.

His hands clenched and unclenched again around the steering wheel. What was he doing? Murmurs of residual panic still taunted her. "Gray? Are you okay? What are the bends?"

He shrugged again. "Just a byproduct of a rapid decompression. The air in your system expands. Now that I'm back at regular pressure, all those air bubbles in my joints are shrinking."

"Does it hurt much?"

"Yesterday's incident wasn't bad." He dismissed it with a wave. "We got on oxygen fast, descended quickly. No sweat."

All that stress and pain from something he claimed was

a "simple" in-flight emergency? As if there could be such a thing. What other rigors did flight life put on his body?

"But does it hurt?" she asked, already knowing the answer and not sure why she felt the need to push her point. Perhaps she needed him to reach out to her with more than a smile. Any woman with an ounce of nurturing instinct couldn't resist a man in pain.

Gray flexed his ankle and almost suppressed his wince. "I've treated patients with worse."

Lori blinked through a sting of tears that wouldn't accomplish anything. In fact, tears had landed her in that tender kiss the night before that still tingled along the roots of her hair.

When he'd kissed her, she'd considered pulling him into her house and not letting him go until sunrise. Or maybe until several sunrises. But she'd been too emotional to risk an encounter with Gray, and more than anything, she hated weepy displays.

Admonitions from her parents fluttered through her mind. *Dry your eyes, Lorelei, sugar. There's a new adventure right over the next border.*

She'd always scrubbed away those tears and tackled the next challenge, a small part of her fearful that if she lagged she would be left behind. She couldn't regret her upbringing, as it had made her stronger and independent—skills that earned her respect in her job, and she loved her job.

But she wouldn't say it was her life anymore, not like Gray's military career. "Can I ask you something?"

"Like you've ever held back before."

"Good point." She chewed on her bottom lip, caught his transfixed stare on her mouth and stopped nibbling before they ended up in a ditch. "All that talk about the military being in your blood, I hear you. But why not just serve as a doctor? Why do you put your body through all this? We've spent less that two weeks together, and you've taken a leg full of shrapnel and had the air sucked out of your body."

His calf flexed. "I thought about getting out."

"You did?"

"Right after Desert Storm. I worried I might turn into my old man and decided to try med school. I'd considered it before, but flying tugged me, too. Confused the hell out of me sometimes when I was growing up." He spiked a hand through his hair, all the combing his short cut needed. "Six months into med school, I knew it wasn't going to work. Not the way I'd planned. Med school was the right choice. But not civilian life."

The Explorer wove a winding path through the clusters of condos—thatched wooden buildings shaded by towering oaks and hanging Spanish moss. Sunlight dappled a Hansel and Gretel breadcrumb-like trail alongside the road. What a beautiful place to call home. "Okay, so you're not getting out of the military. But plenty of other guys can fly that plane. You don't have to do everything. You're a doctor, Gray. Why not make your mark in the service that way?"

"There's the fundamental difference in the way we military people think. Every one of us honestly believes we can make a specific difference or we would have gotten out long ago. Just as I have to be a doctor, I have to fly." In front of his parents' condo, he slid the car into park. Gray released the steering wheel and flipped his hands over. "Could another set of hands have gotten Magda out of Sentavo? Maybe. But maybe not. It doesn't really matter, since knowing won't change a thing. This is what I do."

The intensity in his eyes scared her. Fascinated her. How could she not admire him? Want him.

Her hand reached up to his jaw, and she allowed her fingers the pleasure of caressing his beard-stubbled face. Just as she considered tracing his bottom lip....

Magda flung her Happy Meal toy on the floor. Lori blinked away the moment.

She twisted to retrieve the toy, pausing to straighten Magda's strawberry jumper and blow a kiss. Seeing Magda so happy and excited, Lori couldn't regret joining Gray for the day. The little girl deserved so much more from life than she'd seen so far.

Lori spun back around as Gray's family poured from the front door like water from an emptying aqueduct—a younger, heavier-set version of himself, his mother and his lanky sister, along with in-laws, nieces, nephews…

She lost count as they gushed down the steps. Envy nipped her, followed by a hefty bite of anger. She would have traded a hundred Barbie house dreams to spend an afternoon in a family like this.

Realization tingled over her as she wondered if she hadn't done just that.

Lori tapped her toe on the porch, launching the swing in motion. She cradled Magda in her lap, the gentle rocking as soothing for Lori as the child.

An ocean breeze bowed the rushes along the marshy coastline, then detoured through the lower deck screened-in porch. The precious perfume of baby shampoo and sunshine twined around her.

She'd had an awesome day.

Damn.

Every minute had been exactly as she would have wanted—*if* Gray had brought her to his parents' home a year ago as a precursor to a proposal.

Instead he'd brought her to say goodbye.

Irritability swept away her contentment. Maybe she could bang around some dirty pots in the kitchen. Lori turned to Angela seated at a rattan table with a glass of milk. "I feel guilty sitting out here while they're doing the dishes."

"Fair's fair. We cooked. They clean. They're probably almost done, anyway. Just enjoy holding Magda. They grow up too fast." Angela sipped, bracelet jingling as she replaced the glass. "Thank you for coming today."

"Thank you for including us."

"That's not quite what I meant, dear."

"I know."

Footsteps hammered on the overhead deck as the men and children thundered down the wooden plank steps, fanning out onto the yard. Gray tossed a football underhanded to his brother as they divided into teams along the shore.

Magda squirmed in Lori's lap. "Doc!" she squealed and pointed. "Doc!"

Gray turned, smiled and gestured for Magda to join them. "Send her on out. I'll watch her."

Lori eased Magda to the ground and walked her across the porch, the sticky hand so dear clutching hers. Lori nodded, pushing the door open. "Go ahead, sweetie."

Magda bolted forward, arms pumping, her strawberry jumper a blur as she sprinted toward Gray. "Doc!"

"Hey, Miss Magpie. Come be on my team." He tied a bandanna around Magda's head and dubbed her his copilot. Game calls, teasing shouts and laughter drifted through the screens.

Lori sank back to the swing, wrapping her arms around her waist, her lap too empty. "It's so idyllic here."

"I'm a lucky woman."

"Yes, you are."

Angela nudged her milk away and fished a roll of antacid tablets from her pocket. Absently she thumbed one free and popped it in her mouth. "But it wasn't all luck. I've worked hard."

Ah, finally the other shoe drops. She'd wondered when Angela would weave in her bid for a new daughter-in-law. "Of course you have. Relationships are work."

More than even she could tackle. She'd worked like crazy to earn Gray's love a year ago, just as she'd worked to gain her parents' attention, and it still hadn't changed a thing. Of course she knew him better now. Should she have worked harder to understand him then rather than simply judging?

Angela rolled the pack of tablets between her fingers as she stared out over her family. ''There were times I wasn't sure we could hold it all together, but we did. I'm very proud of that.''

Gray launched into the air, catching the football. Ball tucked to his chest, he snagged Magda under the other arm. He ran, the little girl squealing as her bandanna-covered head bobbed with each jostling step. His powerful legs pumped, those khaki shorts leaving too much muscled thigh in view for any normal woman to ignore. Lori's emotions were anything but normal around Gray.

Draining another swallow of milk, Angela waved to her older son as he sprinted past. Her hand fell to her lap. ''I'm going to miss having him close.''

Me, too. They'd been apart for a year, yet she'd taken a strange comfort in knowing she might run into him, could drop in if the crazy notion took hold. Which it had. She'd almost caved more than once.

Angela stuffed the antacid roll in her pocket. ''You do know you've gotten closer to Grayson than anyone else ever has. Probably closer than he's let even his own family get.''

Lori fidgeted on the suddenly uncomfortable wooden swing. ''I'm not sure we should be—''

''Why not?'' Gray's mother raised her hands and leaned back. ''I realize we don't know each other well, but time's running out. Consider it one last desperate measure from a concerned mama.''

While Lori wanted to be resentful of the intrusion, she understood motherly concerns better every day. Parenting brought a host of worries with all those blessings, and she wouldn't trade a moment of it. She'd just never expected to tackle it alone.

An ache lodged firmly in her stomach, and she eyed the glass of milk with longing. "How did you do it, Angela?"

"Do what, dear?"

"Send Dave off to work every day not knowing if he would come home, and if he did what kind of shape would he be in?"

"He wouldn't have given it up for me." The older woman turned away, her head gravitating toward the solitary man walking along the shore. "And I never asked him to."

"You're a good wife." *Better than I could be.*

"No, I'm a very greedy one. You asked me a question, and you deserve an honest answer. How did I do it? It was better than the alternative. Not having him at all. I faced that for four god-awful years." Angela paused for a steadying breath. "I'll take what I can have of him."

What could Lori say to that? Not a darn thing.

Angela gripped the armrests and eased to her feet. Her hands whipped wrinkles from her cotton day dress. "Time for a drink check before everyone dehydrates."

"I'll help."

"No need, dear. You sit tight and relax. I'll be right back." Angela turned the power of her smile on Lori, almost covering the concern in her eyes.

Gray thought he was so much like his father. Why couldn't he see he had bits of his mother in him, as well? He had her smile covering an iron will.

And that stubborn fool had just scored another touchdown. His uninhibited victory dance tripped right over Lori's already tender emotions.

He'd broken her heart once. He was well on his way to doing it again. How she wished she were like Angela, able to take what she could before he finished her off once and for all.

Gray had offered half measures, living together, accept whatever the future held. She'd existed that way her entire childhood, with an unsure future, holding second place to her parents' jobs. She wanted better for herself—and for Magda, because she wouldn't be able to let that little girl go. Ever. No more foster parenting. Lori wanted to file for adoption. Magda was her daughter.

Lori's gaze strayed unerringly toward two bandanna-clad heads. Why did Gray have to look so very much like Magda's father?

Lori stilled the swing and watched Angela speak to Gray before she joined her husband. Clasping Dave's hand in hers, she tipped her face up to him. Love glimmered from her like the sun glinting off the lightly cresting waves.

God, she wanted that for herself, just once. Her gaze gravitated back to Gray, and she couldn't stop from wanting it with him. Hadn't Angela said there were times to just take whatever she could from life?

While she couldn't see living the rest of her life that way, maybe she could adopt the attitude for one selfish day.

He'd wanted to make the most of their last day before they said goodbye. Well, she had a damn good idea of how they should spend their last night together.

Chapter 14

His father looked different cradling a sleeping Magda to his chest. Dave Clark sprawled in his leather recliner, remote in his hand as he channel surfed. Magda snoozed away with her familiar kid snore.

Gray had expected an afternoon with his dysfunctional family would send Lori running screaming for the woods. Instead he'd seen the Clark clan through her eyes and found a few surprises of his own. Nothing radical, just softening touches around the edges.

When had his parents started holding hands again? His father had actually spoken more than three-word sentences to his children and grandchildren.

Staring at his father, Gray leaned a shoulder against the archway into the great room. What else had he missed?

He'd missed finding a chance to talk with Lori alone, since she'd spent the entire day surrounded by his family.

Gray stopped his mother in the hall, away from nosy nieces and nephews. "Hey, Mom. Do you mind watching

Magda while Lori and I go for a walk?'' Like he really expected his mom to argue.

Penciled eyebrows rose. ''Of course not. Hold on a minute first.''

Angela bustled from the room, then rushed back in breathlessly, her arms full. ''Here.'' She shoved a beach bag and a blanket against his chest. ''Do take your time. Stop and stargaze.''

Oddly enough, he'd planned just that.

Gray juggled the blanket until it draped over his arm and peered in the bag warily. Two sodas, a box of crackers and a can of Cheez Whiz rattled around inside. As far as impromptu picnics went, it wasn't half bad.

He indulged in a much-needed grin. His mom hadn't been nearly this accommodating during his teenage years when he'd been desperate to get any number of girls alone in the woods.

His smile tightened. Her help had come a little too late, not that telling her would accomplish anything. He dropped a kiss on his mother's cheek. ''Thanks, Mom. We'll be back in an hour.''

''No need to rush!'' She waved him off, bracelet jingling.

He walked up behind Lori in the great room as she watched a movie with his dad and two nieces. Lori sat with his niece Jessica in front of her on the floor, braiding her hair. Gray leaned, his mouth two inches shy of her ear. ''Lori?''

''What?'' She glanced over her shoulder at him, their faces a whisper apart. Her pupils widened, darkening her eyes to the near black he'd only seen while deep inside her.

''Let's go for a walk. Magda's asleep with my mom and dad watching her. We won't be gone more than an hour.''

No lie there, as he couldn't trust himself alone with her for too long.

''All right.''

No arguments? Not that he planned to question his luck.

She twisted the rubber band in place on his niece's hair and stood. Careful not to disturb the movie watchers, Lori stepped over his other niece and a bowl of popcorn. As she passed Magda, Lori's hand trailed over the girl's back in an unconscious, affectionate pat. Gray's father shot them an absent wave without looking away from the television.

Gray held the door open for Lori. She tapped the blanket and bag. "Planning a picnic?"

"Mom insisted. It was easier to take it than argue. Hope you're a fan of Cheez Whiz." Gray glanced down at Lori, trying to gauge her reaction to his mother's blatant matchmaking after he'd promised to keep a lid on it.

Lori's eyes crinkled in the corners, her chest shaking with barely suppressed laughter. Damn, how had he made it through the past year without her? The Washington move loomed over him, leaving him with none of the usual excitement he experienced at a new assignment.

He extended his hand. She stared, her brow puckered like Magda's when she tried to decide between a healthy cheese stick and a gooey chocolate cookie. Lori's face smoothed, and she rested her soft hand in his.

It felt almost as good as sex.

Okay, not quite that awesome. But damned good. Even a small measure of Lori's trust was a powerful commodity.

She linked her fingers with his, and they walked across the parking lot toward a patch of woods away from the water. "You have a wonderful family."

"Thanks." Not perfect by a long shot, but who was he to throw stones? Bottom line, he loved them.

"What made your parents decide to settle here?"

"It's Mom's hometown. Retiring here was Dad's payback for all those years of moving around." Their arms swung between them as they left the parking lot to stroll along a narrowing sandy path. "We lived nearby anytime

Dad went overseas so Mom would have family to help out.''
''Family's important.''
Sliding into silence, they walked and Gray wondered what the hell he would say to her when they stopped. Parking lot lights faded, the night darkening to warm shadows cast by stars and a harvest moon. He tugged his hand free and palmed her back as they trekked over a hill, past a battle ground marker.
Almost there.
Sprawling pines blocked the condos from view, closing them off from the world. ''This is it.''
She dusted her toe through dried pine needles while he whipped out the blanket, fluttering it to the ground. He waited for her to sit. Lori studied the blanket as if its quilted pattern held secrets to the universe.
''Lori? Problem?''
She shook her head. ''No. I was just thinking about something your mother said.''
Did he even want to know? Cheez Whiz might be a safer option.
Or maybe not.
In days past, they would have found better uses for Cheez Whiz than wasting it on a cracker. He dropped the sack. ''What words of wisdom does Mom have for us today?''
Lori shrugged. ''How about we call a truce for tonight? No talk about matchmaking or goodbyes. Just you and me. One last evening together.''
He lifted a lock of her hair and rubbed its silky length between two fingers before releasing it into a gliding rest against her breast.
Not a bad place to be. ''Sounds good to me.''
Lori sank to the blanket, kicked her sandals free and drew her knees up. Her silky dress pooled around her. Gray hunkered down onto the blanket beside her, wincing as last

twinges of the bends creaked through him. Pine needles cushioned the ground beneath the blanket. His back propped against a weather-worn oak, he stretched his legs in front of him, his feet only an inch away from her hip.

Wind lifted Lori's hair. "Did you bring me out here to see your etchings, flyboy?"

Gray snorted on a laugh. "If I had, you'd already be on your back."

"Or you would be on yours."

"Now there's a thought." He grasped her bare foot, his thumb rubbing the arch. When she didn't pull away, he draped his other wrist over his bent knee and pointed. "That star right there. Betelgeuse. It was the first one my dad taught me. Even before 'Nam, Dad had a low tolerance for noise. When family gatherings got to be too much for him, he would bring me out here with him. He taught me about celestial navigation."

"What a beautiful memory." Her chin fell to rest on her knees.

A year ago she would have leaned back in his arms.

"We didn't have a lot of money, but he spent time with us." Gray targeted another star with his finger and continued squeezing her foot gently. The heat and softness of her surged up his arm. "That one there. Polaris. You could follow it straight over the North Pole and down to Vietnam."

"And you went there in your mind." She stared up at the star, her voice as sure as if she'd watched him sit in his special spot all those lonely nights as a kid.

"At least a thousand times." His head tipped back against the rough bark. The stars shimmered and blurred. "God, Lori, he was a mess when he got home. What they did to my dad..."

Gray tried to swallow but couldn't.

A rustle from the blanket pulled his attention from the sky. Lori tugged her foot free and crawled toward him. Her knees straddled either side of his extended legs as they sat face-to-face.

The swirl of peach preceded her lips by a millisecond.

She cupped his face in her hands, pressing her mouth to his, firm, grounding him. Right now the sky held little allure as Lori threw herself against him like a warm barrier against painful memories.

He whispered against her lips. "I'm going to miss you so damned much. The past year—"

"Stop it." She kissed one eye. "Stop talking." Then the other eye. "We're not any good at farewells, anyway." She kissed his mouth.

Popcorn. She tasted like buttery popcorn and Lori, and he wanted more of her.

Gray bit back words, surprising words that would beg her to go with him to Washington. She'd turned him down a year ago. Why would now be different? And if she accepted? If anything, he should protect her by keeping his damned mouth shut.

Or otherwise occupied.

He tasted, drank of her, like a drug, potent and healing. Lori, the real healer, and as always he took from her. But, damn it, with his defenses in the negative numbers, he couldn't turn her away yet.

Her lips worked over him, open, tongues twining. Close. Not close enough. Gripping her hips, he drew her securely onto his lap. Her sundress caressed the top of his hands, Lori's silky skin and satiny panties tempted beneath his touch. Chest to chest, hearts thudding, he held her and stole more, everything she would give him.

Trailing up her sides, his fingers splayed, cupped and lifted her small breasts. A perfect fit, filling his hands and senses with the same incredible rightness he'd experienced the first time he'd touched her.

Impatient hands, hers and his, shoved open the vee neck of her wraparound dress and popped the front clasp on her bra. No more waiting, he closed his mouth over one nipple, already peaked and ready for him.

Humid air and need prickled beads of sweat along his brow. Lori sipped them from his skin.

He wanted her. So simple. So everything.

Always, *always* it had been explosive between them, and he was tired of running from it. He wanted the rockets, explosion, the damn fireworks she offered.

Thought became difficult, if not impossible when she touched him. Playfulness had always come after a combustible release. He wasn't feeling at all playful. A year without her had left him struggling to level out, when he wanted nothing more than to soar out of control.

His hand snaked under her dress again and found the smooth bare skin of her hips, waist, stomach. He explored the line of her panties with one lazy finger, two barely there scraps of satin attached with fragile straps. So very Lori, conservative and in control on the outside, seductive satin and heat underneath.

He traced the whisper-thin straps, traveled down, slipping inside. She moaned into his hair, her breath a hot caress against his scalp.

She shoved him back against the tree, determination in the firm force of her hands. He knew her moods well. Competent, resolute Lori had set her mind on a mission.

He prepped to crash and burn.

Fumbling down the buttons of his shirt, she kissed and nipped her way along his collarbone. Her hands continued their frantic path down to his shorts, unsnapping, unzipping, freeing him, robbing him of the option to stop.

Her dress swirled around them, shielding her caressing hand. Not that he could have seen anything other than the back of his eyelids as his head thudded against the tree. His fingers knotted in the thin straps along her hips. "Lori, do you know where we're headed?"

"Yes! I've known since you spread the blanket on the ground. No backing out this time."

Her moist heat pressing against him fired straight through, leaving Gray grateful for the support of the sturdy oak behind his back. This woman fascinated the hell out of him and flipped his world all at the same time. And he would lay claim to her again in seconds. If only for this night.

His fingers glided a teasing stroke along the satiny outside, before twisting in the tiny strings along her hips. He tugged the strings, needing everything that scrap of satin caressed. "If you expect these panties to live to see another day, maybe you'd better—"

"Break it. Now!" She slid her heat along his thigh.

He snapped the strings along with the last remnants of his restraint.

She guided him in with a frenzied pace that still seemed agonizingly gradual to him. She sank onto him, enveloped him with incredible moist heat, Lori's heat. His hands cradling her bottom beneath her dress, he lifted, then relaxed his grip, thrusting up as she slid down. His forehead met hers as they exchanged sighs, unmoving, savoring.

He lost himself in the satiny glide of her hair against his neck. Being surrounded by her silk and softness was better than escaping to miles of blue sky.

His mind tried to tug him from the moment with irritating niggles that he should stop, clear his brain. Something wasn't right.

Impatiently she rocked against him, and he forgot how to think. He tried to slow her, needing to make it last for her, for him, because he didn't even want to think about it being over.

Which it would be soon if she didn't stop moving.

She kissed, bit, suckled his lip, immersing him in the taste of popcorn and her need. Instincts kicked in, and they reclaimed their rhythm with ease, moving, touching, encouraging the other toward the shattering end they both wanted. Needed.

He heard her breath quicken, felt the tiny tremors shake through her, early clenches he knew predicted her nearing release. And he knew something else about her. Lori was loud, something he adored about her and wished he could enjoy, but scavenged enough reason to know now wasn't the time or place.

With only a second to spare, Gray clamped his mouth over hers, swallowing her scream as she arched, once, twice, again until she sagged against him. Moaning, she shuddered with aftershocks, gripping him in a satin fist of heat.

He thrust deep. Tension built, tightened, burned, then exploded free. A shout swelled behind his clenched teeth, and he pulsed within her, his face nestled in the vulnerable curve of her neck. Her hair draped around them as he let his hoarse cry slide free. In a downward spiral straight for earth at mach speed, Grayson surrendered.

He had decimated her. Completely leveled her defenses. Physically, Lori couldn't move so much as her pinky after the intense release Gray had given her.

Emotionally she wasn't much better off.

She could only sprawl on the blanket and stare up at a star. One star. Thirty minutes ago she hadn't known Polaris from Betelgeuse. Now she would never again stand under a night sky without thinking of Gray looking at that same sky while he dreamed of bringing his father home.

She hadn't stood a chance of resisting him.

Gray lay on his side, his hands massaging over her shoulders, gentling along her breasts. Her body throbbed with a tender, beautiful after ache. Those deft doctor-pilot hands soothed, finding just the places to make her eyes loll closed in lazy pleasure. "Is this why you brought me here?"

"No." His fingers skimmed the tender underside of her breast, tracing up to her jaw. "Maybe."

"Fair enough." She shivered, then arched her neck to allow him fuller access. "It's certainly why I came with you."

He cupped her face. "That honesty is about to get you rolled up in this blanket with me."

"Feeling ambitious are we, flyboy?" She twisted to her side and wriggled against him. His shirt flapped open. Moonbeams caressed an irresistible expanse of chest for her to snuggle against.

"Give me another ten minutes and we can find out."

Experience with him told her it would be closer to five before they began again. The next time would be fun and playful sex that could singe the leaves right off those trees overhead.

And she wanted that, didn't she? Of course she did. Only a crazy woman would pass up one last chance for that.

First she wanted more time, more lazy caresses and stargazing. Too often, they both rushed life, type-A personalities at full tilt.

Stilling his hand with hers, she carried it to her mouth and kissed his palm before placing it on her hip. "Why did you bring me to your parents' place?"

His eyes met hers with expected straightforward honesty. "To see my family in action, day-to-day stuff, not a restaurant good-behavior gig."

He flipped to his back, arm flinging over his eyes. "Lori, I don't know how to put a family together. Not the kind a kid deserves. Not the kind you deserve."

His words hinted at more than an obsession with his job this time. Suddenly she wasn't sure she wanted to understand, because his reasons might be all the more compelling. Yet, the idea that he might see his actions as protecting her started a trembling in her knees that made her grateful to be flat on her back.

"My dad has post-traumatic stress syndrome. This was a good day for him."

"I'm so sorry." Lori fit her hand in his.

He didn't look at her, but he didn't let go. Piecing together bits of Gray's childhood along with some professional observations slid the picture into place. Some children of PTSD sufferers had difficulty forming deeper, lasting relationships, having missed out on crucial early bonding experiences with their parents.

Maybe she should have guessed earlier when he'd talked about his father coming home, but had been too distracted by the pain radiating from Gray. It had reached to her across that blanket more effectively than a grappling hook. Still did.

"We didn't understand for a long time, years even. He wasn't violent or terrified. He functioned at work. But at home, he just…wasn't there."

"How awful for all of you." She didn't have to imagine what his childhood had been like. Her caseload with Social Services had offered ample background material to draw from, to stir an ache for the confused little boy Gray must have been. The strong, stubborn man he was now. Understanding helped—and hurt as their problems rooted deeper. "He didn't ever get much help processing it all, did he?"

Gray peeked from under his arm. "That obvious, huh?"

"Some of the signs are still there." She paused, then dared to push him further, never having been one to back off a tough subject before she met Gray. "The signs are there in all of you when you're together."

"Putting that training to work I see."

"I should have seen it earlier."

He twirled a lock of her hair around his finger. "How could you? We never got close enough before."

"No, we didn't."

"We had other things on our mind."

His smile kicked in, and past experience told her he'd

slipped away from her again, shielding himself with a smile.

"Things like making-up sex. Morning sex."

She gave him the smile he needed. "After-dinner sex."

"Welcome-home sex."

Their eyes met, and his last homecoming—the one that had prompted her to walk out on him—slid right between them like a slippery rogue ice cube. Gray's smile faded. He tunneled his hand deeper into her hair, looping it around his wrist until she couldn't look anywhere but into his eyes.

"Lori, I missed you so damned much during that England deployment." His grip tightened, almost painfully. "For years I'd razzed the guys who called home to their wives instead of going out. I was in England, for crying out loud, and the most sight-seeing I managed was from inside those red telephone booths. Then I found myself skipping out on a trip to a pub because I wanted to call you. Hell, I had to call you."

She caressed his bristly face. "Those calls meant a lot to me."

"I know."

He untwined her hair with slow, sensual deliberation, trailing the strands down his arm and through his fingers. "The minute the plane landed in Charleston, I blew off debrief with a lame excuse and met you at my place that night like we'd planned."

They'd been so hot for each other, only to discover Lori had forgotten her pill the morning before. Gray had insisted it wasn't worth the risk, and neither of them had back-up birth control. They'd sprinted for his car in a tangle of arms, legs and laughter ready to scout out an all night supermarket, and he'd found…

Gray winced against her. "You had planted flowers."

"Flowers?"

"Yeah. Don't you remember? While I was gone, you planted those yellow and purplish little flowers in pots in front of my apartment. I missed them when I ran inside in the dark. Other things on my mind at that moment. But when we stepped back out and the porch light zeroed right in on those homey flowers..."

Lori couldn't decide whether to cry or slug him. She'd attached so many hopes to those flowers, certain that if she worked hard enough, made his home life perfect enough he would stay. And she'd only sent him running. "Imagine that. The mighty warrior downed by a flat of pansies."

"Pitiful."

The rest unfolded with a clarity that had eluded her for a year. "So you asked me to move in with you, knowing full well I wanted a ring. You knew I would bolt." Lori had turned him down flat, and he'd stormed out. She'd called a cab and left before he returned. "Do you ever wonder what would have happened if you'd had an extra condom lying around and hadn't found those flowers until the next morning?"

The drifting wind carried his dark laugh over her. "More than once. One condom, and things might—"

A condom.

Lori jackknifed up and looked down into Gray's horror-struck eyes. How could she have forgotten? The rumpled quilt mocked her with memories of their uninhibited love-making.

Unprotected lovemaking.

Icy whispers from a year ago teased over her. The lack of a single condom had once again launched her life into chaos. And this time she couldn't run away.

Chapter 15

No condom. Gray looked up into Lori's horror-struck eyes.

How could he have been so reckless? He even carried one in his wallet that he'd bought after his and Lori's near miss a week ago. Other than that brief, almost encounter with her, he had never lost control. Never. He thrived on control and structure, one of the aspects he liked and needed most in his job.

An hour with Lori had him losing sight of that, and it scared the hell out of him.

She drew her knees to her chest, her dress shrouding her legs. "So much for our talk."

He stared at Lori, a normal occurrence for him, and couldn't help but notice how totally alone she looked. How strange, since he usually thought of her as so competent, in charge, strong.

The moonlight caressing her face, she flipped her whiskey-brown hair over her shoulder. Her dress flowed around her gentle curves without a wrinkle to hint at the wild abandon she'd indulged in only moments before. Lori rarely lost her cool. Except for those moments when her incredible legs had been wrapped around his waist and—

Don't go there, pal. He zipped his pants and reminded himself to start thinking with his brain again. There could be very real—tiny, living consequences from their slip.

He knew she could succeed no matter what life brought her way. But she damn well wouldn't be facing it alone if she was carrying his child. "I'll make it right. Whatever happens, I don't walk out on my responsibilities."

"Be still my heart." Sarcasm dripped from her words like the Spanish moss draping the branches overhead.

"Lori, damn it, stop being flip." The humid night air wrapped around him with claustrophobic weight. He forced himself to breathe. "This is important, and you're not helping."

"Sorry. I know that was difficult for you."

He listened for more sarcasm, hearing nothing but determination.

Tread warily, pal. Land mines ahead. He wasn't going to get anywhere with her now and could too easily make things worse. "Let's save this talk for later. Better to wait rather than to say things we'll both regret only to find out we never needed to say them at all."

"Of course. Why even consider marriage unless I'm pregnant?"

A reasonable stance. Why then did her every word stab at him as if he'd fallen short of the mark?

"I'm sorry for losing contr—"

"Did it ever dawn on you that maybe you're not calling the shots this time?"

He paused buttoning his shirt. "What does that mean?"

"I was the one who crawled across that blanket. I wanted you. Granted, I wasn't thinking straight or I would have remembered about birth control. My brain gets scrambled around you."

Her words fizzled as the air crackled between them. How incredible to think he could move the imperturbable Lori.

For an insane moment he wanted to be exactly what she needed, and that absurd notion warred with his deep-seated need to defend. Protect. Protect her. "Lori—"

"Stop! I knew what I was doing, and I'm the one taking responsibility. No need to worry about being tied down. Go fly your planes, Major." She scrambled to her feet, shaking the wrinkles out of her dress while she slipped on her shoes. "It's been fun, as always. But I've got a child to check on."

She darted into the woods before he could untangle his brain.

Child? The word so close on the heels of their discussion had him wondering how she could already know.... Then he remembered Magda.

He knew full well Lori wouldn't be giving up Magda at the evidentiary hearing. And a single, pregnant foster mother wouldn't go over well with the courts.

She would have to marry him.

The air grew heavier, then sparse, not unlike the rapid decompression the day before. He pressed his hands against the ground, the bed of pine needles giving slightly beneath the force.

It was bad enough he'd let Lori down. Adding that impish little kid into the mess left him wanting to ram his fist into the tree trunk, a dangerous thought for a man who made his living with his hands. But Lori frequently had him thinking dangerous thoughts.

And what about a child they may have made? Images of Lori swelling with his baby, giving birth into his waiting hands, stirred a protectiveness so fierce it astounded him. He'd attended deliveries in training and had found the experience—simply awesome. Replacing the mother with an image of Lori was beyond anything he could imagine.

He had placed his foot squarely on a mammoth land

mine, blowing to pieces all his plans to keep it simple and leave town.

Gray stood and yanked up the blanket. A scrap of red satin fluttered to the ground. Memories of his and Lori's total lack of control rolled back over him like a tank. Would it always be that way between them?

He jammed the panties into his pocket and sprinted after her. He caught up with her just as she came back out his parents' door with Magda in her arms, the child an excellent chaperone and armor. Lori called her farewell and thanks to Gray's mother and patently avoided him. She wouldn't even look at him.

Instinct told him it would be a long, quiet ride back to her place. Experience from the past year told him that the silence could reach past dropping her off.

The thought of losing her again panicked him almost as much as the idea of marriage.

How far would he go to keep her?

Could she be pregnant? Lori drummed her fingers against the box of crayons on the kitchen table. She was late enough for it to be a possibility. Although she'd never been regular, and stress had been beyond normal the past two weeks.

No rationale could reason away a totally irrational wish for it to be true. She wanted Gray's baby inside her.

Had she subconsciously risked pregnancy to keep a part of Gray with her? She honestly didn't think so. That didn't stop her from cherishing a tiny dream face just as she cherished the little face across the table from her.

A CD of kiddie tunes chirped in the background, ''Row, Row, Row Your Boat'' repeating. Magda bobbed her head in time while concentrating on an ABC coloring book. Lori picked up a blue crayon and forced herself to color the picture beside Magda's.

Blue. Like Grayson's apartment. His old apartment. What would his new one in Washington look like?

She flung aside the crayon and selected a pink one.

Pink, for another little girl in her life.

That crayon snapped in her fingers.

Lori carefully chose a green crayon and began filling in the capital *T.* A towering tree waited beneath the letter, a big oak packed with memories of when she might have made that baby.

She sighed. With her luck, Magda would be coloring "stars" for the *S* on the other page.

Lori dared a look.

S for soap.

Thank goodness.

She checked her watch for the tenth time. Another two minutes and her home-pregnancy test would be complete. Meanwhile she needed to focus on having fun with the child she already had, a child as dear to her as any she might carry below her heart for nine months. No matter how the test turned out, Lori wouldn't be giving up Magda. She wanted to be Magda's legal mother. The paperwork had already been filed.

"Tree." Lori pointed to her *T* page. "Tree."

"Twee," Magda repeated.

"Good girl, Magda! Good girl." She gathered her close, smiling down at Magda's precious, healthy face. Lori folded two fingers, leaving her pinky, pointer and thumb extended. "I love you."

Magda repeated the gesture, if not the words, without hesitation. Lori hugged her tighter. She didn't know whether to attribute the sting of tears to pregnancy or PMS. Either way, her throat clogged, and she wanted to share this moment with Gray so much it hurt.

Picking away at Lori's already crumbling defenses, the CD shifted to "Old MacDonald."

With the unerring timing of a child, Magda looked around the kitchen. "Doc?"

The lone word sucker punched Lori. She stroked Magda's mussed hair back. "Sorry, Magda. Doc's not here."

Why hadn't he called before leaving? Of course she'd told him she would contact him if she had "news" when he'd dropped her off after the day at his parents' house. But she'd been scared then, not by the thought of pregnancy, but by how much making love to Gray had shaken her.

Why hadn't she made the first move to phone him even once the past week? She told herself it was because she wanted definite news when they spoke—one way or the other.

A prideful part of her insisted she needed him to come to her this time in spite of what she'd said.

Lori checked her watch again, eyeing the sweep of the second hand as it ticked away the last…two seconds.

She bolted from her chair to the bathroom. The little indicator stick rested on the edge of the marble vanity. Lori shuffled forward.

A single diagonal line glared back at her. *Negative.*

She squeezed her eyes shut as if that would change the results. It didn't. Dreams of impish little boys and dimple-cheeked little girls slipped farther away, leaving behind a hollow disappointment that had nothing to do with PMS.

Lori flung the test into the trash and reminded herself she had Magda and couldn't love that little girl any more if she was her own child. But that failed pregnancy test severed the last tie to Gray.

She returned to the kitchen and found Magda intent on dragging out all the pots and pans. Lori passed her a wooden spoon—the one Gray had used as a microphone when he'd sung "Old MacDonald." Of its own volition, her mouth curved into a smile at the memory.

Should she call him or wait for the definite sign when she started…or finally received a positive test? Lori fingered the phone on the wall and considered calling his parents for his new number. Of course, she had his cell phone number, too. She lifted the receiver.

Damn him, if he wanted to know, he would call her.

She slammed it on the cradle.

Ring. The phone vibrated under her hand.

Lori startled back a step, then yanked it off the wall, uncaring if she sounded too eager. She had been waiting by the phone after all, and since he'd finally been the one to call she didn't care if he knew.

"Hello." Her voice sounded breathless and eager even to her own ears.

"Lori, this is Barbara."

Her attorney? With the evidentiary hearing a week away, they weren't scheduled to check in for another few days. Why would she call now? Foreboding gripped Lori by the throat. "Yes, Barbara, what can I do for you?"

"Lori, I hate to tell you this. But we've got a problem."

"What's the problem with this house, Major Clark?"

Gray stared back at the matronly real estate agent, a stack of house listing printouts gripped in his hand. "I'm not sure."

He circled the empty family room, searching for some flaw. They'd started with apartments, and he'd quickly known that wouldn't work for him anymore, not enough room and strangely too generic.

He'd asked the agent to pull house listings, having since plowed through about forty. The last had too small a backyard. The one before was located on a busy street. Another didn't have hardwood floors like Lori preferred.

And that was just it.

Every house he looked at fell short of what Lori and Magda needed. Of course, he wasn't sure he measured up any better than the houses. But if she was carrying his kid, then they would just have to make the best of it.

Husband. Father. He forced himself to think the words and not overlay images of his own childhood.

Each day that Lori didn't call increased the probability she could be pregnant. What kind of parents would they make with so much unresolved mess starting them off with two strikes? Their last parting hadn't been any better than the one a year ago.

He'd waited around in Charleston an extra few days to give her time to cool down, but no luck. She hadn't called. Two weeks had passed since she'd walked out of his life again, and he wasn't having any more luck getting her out of his system than last time.

Gray looked around the room, through the windows. It was a good house. A great family home, with sidewalks and a cul-de-sac for Magda to ride her Big Wheel. He could already envision Lori and Magda in the airy sunroom with the dollhouse and Barbies scattered around. The yard stretched for half an acre, with a gentle slope for sledding in the winter, flower beds in the summer.

And there was a deep, inviting hot tub in the master bath for after the kids went to sleep.

He couldn't stop the irrational hope that she was pregnant. Then neither of them would have to make a decision. *Yeah, real honorable, pal. Force the woman to marry you.*

God, he missed her even more than the past year.

Gray sifted the through stack of house listings in his hand. What a waste of time when he didn't know if he would be putting a family in one or not. Whether he and Lori had any future or not. The papers crumpled in his fist.

Time to find out.

He started to reach for his cell phone in his back pocket. His hand stalled midreach. Some things were better said in person, when she couldn't hang up on him or hide her eyes.

He'd made a mistake in not going after her a year ago and talking it out. He wouldn't make the same one now.

A half hour to stop by the hotel to pack and he would be gone. And he would be bringing his service dress uniform, because if Lori was pregnant, they would be in front of a judge by morning.

Whether they ended up in front of a preacher or not, they would resolve this face-to-face.

Gray folded the listing for the current house into quarters and slid it in his pocket. He passed the rest of the stack to the sales agent. "I'll get back to you on this one later. I've got a plane to catch."

"Time to get a blood test."

"What?" A blood test? For a marriage license? Lori couldn't believe that's all Dr. Charming had to say after two endless weeks of silence.

Lori grabbed her doorknob for support and looked for a shotgun at Gray's back, because he certainly couldn't have said what she thought, of his own free will. There wasn't a rifle in sight, just a determined thrust to his stubborn jaw as he brushed past into her living room.

"Come on. Find your shoes. Purse. Whatever." He snagged a Raggedy Ann doll from the floor just before he stepped on it and placed it gently across a cradle. "We're going to the clinic to get a blood test."

Her anger sparked and ignited. She spun away from him to keep from indulging in a totally unproductive shouting match.

She stared at that babydoll in the cradle and couldn't stop thinking of it resting in Gray's hands, how natural it looked. She gave herself a moment to bundle her tattered nerves while kneeling to scoop up three stray Cheerios from the rug. "If that's your idea of a proposal, it needs a little polishing, Major."

Gray's gaze followed her as she stood, his eyes resting

on those three little *O*s in her palm. "To see if you're pregnant."

"Oh." A surprise wave of sadness threatened to fold her knees.

She should have understood his meaning straight off, and probably would have if she hadn't been so distracted. Magda's approaching evidentiary hearing added more stress to Lori's already taut nerves. Glitches in the paperwork had her scrambling during what should have been a smooth transition to place Magda in her foster care long-term, adoption pending. "I'm not. Pregnant, I mean. I'm not. I'm sure now."

His eyes closed. A long, slow swallow slid down his throat before he stared at her again.

Lori stifled a twinge of irritation. Of course he was relieved. Why wouldn't he be? But some crazy part of her brain insisted she saw a hint of disappointment on his face.

Gray's eyes opened, and he pinned her with a laser stare. "How long have you known?"

"A few days. I, uh, spotted for a while and wasn't sure." She winced at discussing specifics, but reminded herself he was a doctor. "But now I'm done and I'm sure."

Anger snapped in his eyes, the green glittering like jewels tossed in a fire. "It might have been nice if you would have shared that with me."

"I thought you'd left."

"They have phones in Washington."

"Yes, they do, and you could have picked up one of those phones anytime—" Her temper disintegrated. "You're not in Washington."

"No." He stepped toward her. Closer. "I'm not."

No. He wasn't. He was standing right in front of her, tall and real after she had missed him two years' worth in those two weeks. "Why?"

"House hunting can wait. You know how I feel about

shopping, anyway." He stuffed his hands in his pockets. "And I needed to know, so I flew back."

Lori clenched her fists by her sides, determined not to let her hands fall on his chest. Even in civilian clothes, he turned her heart to mush. The khakis and green polo couldn't disguise his military bearing. More than the haircut, his walk, very stance, proclaimed his warrior spirit, and he could too easily mesmerize her.

She tore her gaze away and scooped toys off the floor with a frantic pace—Barbies, coloring books, a bucket of crayons all landed in a wicker basket.

"Where's Magda?" He followed her restless path.

"With Julia." Lori pitched a toy bottle onto the haphazard heap.

Her call to Julia, in hopes of finding out about Gray, had rekindled their friendship. It felt good having a friend to count on for help, especially now. Gray had taught her that, about making friends. If only she could learn how to keep them.

"Lori. Lori! Will you look at me, please?" He grasped her arm and eased her to her feet. "I've come a helluva long way to see you. We're not going to replay our mistake from last year by both being too hardheaded to talk."

Each rise and fall of his chest brought him closer for a tantalizing second. She held herself still. No way was she going to throw herself at him, no matter how hot he looked in those khakis.

Slowly, deliberately, he raised his hand, his fingers sliding under her braid to cup her head. She couldn't move, could barely breathe. "Gray? Why didn't you just call instead of flying all this way?"

"I wish I knew. I only know I just can't stay away."

He palmed her head, his eyes filled with a confusion so unlike her normally confident man she almost didn't recognize him. She couldn't have stopped herself from speaking if she tried. She didn't try very hard at all. "I missed you, too."

His mouth crashed down on hers.

All good intentions flew out the window as she surrendered to his kiss. She'd ached for him so damned much.

Tongues dancing, dipping, tasting, Lori locked her arms around him. Gray backed her down the hall, feet tangling on their way to her room. Her knees hooked on her mattress and she fell onto her bed, Gray's body a solid, delicious weight pressing her into the eiderdown comforter.

Their hands peeled away clothing with frantic need, his shoes thudding to the floor, Lori kicking away her light linen pants. His starched khakis rasped against her tender thighs.

Somewhere between kisses, her hands worked his pants off and down his powerful legs. Her lips tore free only long enough to whip his shirt overhead. She flung it aside and reclaimed his mouth for another deep, moist kiss.

Gray opened her silk shirt to uncover more silk. He charted a path down her jaw, her shoulder. Her breath hooked somewhere short of her throat, her breasts tightening in anticipation just before his mouth closed over her.

Damp and warm silk clung to her skin with each tugging draw of his mouth. Her back bowed against him, impatient need taut within her.

"Lori." He breathed her name over the moist fabric. "Just a second, hon."

Gray rolled off her, her hands following him, scratching a light trail down his back. He glanced over his shoulder. "Hold that thought."

Scooping his pants from the floor, he tugged his wallet free and withdrew a single packet. He turned to her, flipping the condom between his fingers. An apology lit his eyes. "I just think—"

"Wait." She scooted from beneath him to reach into her bedside table drawer and pulled free a box. She refused to remember other arguments about birth control and children. The past could stay out of her bedroom for the moment. She had other plans for Gray. Lori scored her nails down his chest, raking gently lower.

A growl rumbling in Gray's throat, he pulled the box from her hands and tossed it on the bedside table along with his lone offering. ''Slow down, hon. No rushing this time.''

Would it be their last time? Lori shoved away the icy thought.

Snagging the bottle of lotion from beside her lamp, he turned, tossing the bottle from hand to hand. Every inch of Lori's body tingled in anticipation. No doubt they were falling into an old habit of escaping problems through sex, but at the moment she just didn't care.

The bottle held high, he drizzled a stream into his open palm. His eyes gleamed as he rubbed his hands together, warming the lotion, warming her with his gaze.

He lifted her foot, cradling it like an antique china cup from her knickknack shelf. Strong fingers worked over her skin. Smooth lotion and callused hands rubbed a dichotomy of sensations along her nerves. Immersed in his touch and the scent of peaches, she could only close her eyes and moan.

Gray worked up her toes, along the top of her foot. ''Metatarsal.''

Lori's eyes snapped open. ''What?''

Someone needed to tell him his language of love was sorely lacking.

He raised her foot to his mouth and kissed along her ankle reverently. ''Tarsal. Special. Because it's yours.''

She melted, totally and completely. Forget language. His hands spoke sonnets. His mouth kissed poetry.

''Fibula. Slim and perfect.'' His thumbs worked up her calf with tender reverence. Those doctor hands were so adept in nuances of the human body, and she reaped the full benefit of his training.

His mouth found her knee, working from front to back, tearing a low moan from her throat. An echoing groan rumbled in his throat. "Patella. So sensitive."

She totally agreed.

His fingers massaged a trek of homage up her thigh, higher, closer. "Femur and soft, creamy-white skin."

Lori slid her lazy lids open. "Pelvis?"

She knew that one and was past ready for him to find it.

Gray shook his head and cupped her waist. With slow deliberation, he rolled her to her stomach, her braid whipping to the side. His palm anchored her to the bed. Not that she could have moved her languid limbs.

She saw him reach for the bottle again just before she felt the cool trickle of lotion along her neck. Icy cold on fiery hot skin made her squirm. Tantalizingly the lotion trailed down her spine, pooling in the small of her waist, before continuing lower over her buttocks.

He lowered himself to rest on her back, the breadth of his chest covering her shoulders. His arousal nestled in the lotion at the small of her back. Gray blew against her neck, breathed in her ear. "Vertebrae."

The slow glide of his body against hers worked the lotion into her skin. Silky warmth and Gray against her left Lori writhing beneath him.

"Gray," she moaned.

"Want me to stop?"

"No!"

"What do you want?"

"To finish this damn science lesson."

His laugh breezed over her sensitive neck just before he rolled away.

She flipped to her side and watched him tear open the packet and sheath himself. He flung aside the wrapper and turned back to her. His knuckles grazed across her cheek, before he gathered her to his chest. "I'm sorry, hon, so damned sorry I can't give you that baby you want."

"Shhh." Couldn't they return to another lesson in *Gray's Anatomy?* At least then she didn't have to think about the outside world. "Don't talk about it now."

His finger fell to her mouth, outlining the tender pad of her bottom lip. "I tried, though, with Magda. I tried to give you the child you always wanted." His lips teased over the top of her head. "And I was right. You're so beautiful with her. You should have a houseful of them."

He stared down at her with eyes full of regret, his words filtering into her muddled brain.

Magda.

He'd wanted her to have a child of her own to love, and in the only way he could, he'd given her one.

Tears burned hot behind her eyes. Heaven help her, she tumbled the rest of the way in love with the beautiful, earnest, gorgeously flawed man over her. Not a very far tumble, after all, since she'd been teetering on the edge of loving him ever since the day she'd seen him plucking shrapnel from his leg, maybe even before that. This final nudge, however, might as well have been miles wide. There was no turning back.

Lori looped her arms around his neck, her back arching into him. His forehead falling to hers, he stared in her eyes and thrust inside her. He filled her body as he had filled her heart. Totally. Fully.

She moved with him endlessly until her body throbbed, vibrated with release, and all the while she wondered if she could ever fill his life as completely.

Chapter 16

"When do you leave for Washington?" Lori snuggled against Gray's bare side and avoided looking into his eyes. Which scared her more? What she might see in his, or what he might find in hers?

He worked the twines of her braid free, one plait at a time. "I've delayed as long as I can. I have to report by Monday. Without fail."

She stifled the disappointment. For a crazy moment at the door, she hadn't been able to squelch a thought that he meant to stay. Of course, that wasn't possible. Not showing up for work could land him in jail for being AWOL.

Lori stroked her foot along his calf, both of them smooth and slicked from their body massage. Then her foot rasped over his healing shrapnel wounds.

Oh, God. How was she going to let him go?

Loving Gray was different this time, because she knew him better. How would she ever get over him? She'd barely survived last time.

Part of her wondered what would happen if she stuck it

out, worked a little harder. Maybe she could endure past his hang-ups on family. After all, she'd studied about families dealing with post-traumatic stress syndrome.

Lori forced herself to stop. She wanted to be his wife, not his counselor.

She didn't regret stealing these last moments for herself, but she couldn't allow herself to weaken. She wanted a life with children and roots, a family who wasn't afraid to share their feelings and lavish love on one another.

Gray spread her hair like a blanket over her breasts. "Come with me to Washington."

He'd said it so offhandedly Lori thought she must have misheard. "What?"

He propped on one elbow, the lemon-yellow comforter pooling around his waist, and looked straight into her eyes this time. "Pack up. Move in with me in Washington."

Did this man live to confuse her? "Are you trying to send me running for the door like last time? Because if you don't want to have sex again, you can just say so. No need to go to such extremes to make me boot you out of my bed."

"No!" His arms locked around her as if she might run anyway. "I—" he swallowed heavily "—I want you to move in with me. I found this great house with a sunroom and a big yard. Lori, the past two weeks without you have been hell. It's time we both quit fighting it and give in."

Not exactly the most romantic declaration she'd ever heard, but he seemed to mean it. She considered it. How could she not? Then she looked deeper into his eyes.

He regarded her so warily, she couldn't tell which he feared more, her saying yes or no.

Why couldn't he have asked with his clothes on, damn him? She held strong all the same, and for good measure kept her eyes firmly planted on his face. "I have a job here. I'm building ties, putting down roots."

"Come anyway."

If he didn't understand she couldn't spend the rest of her life constantly on the move, he would never be able to give her what she needed. She wanted to build a stable home for herself, for her children, for the daughter she already had.

Still she yearned to go with him, to be with him. "I can't go."

"Because of your job."

"Because of Magda. I'm going to keep her, no matter how many courts and piles of paperwork I have to plow through. She's my daughter." Her words rolled free in an out-of-control tumble, not too different from her life at the moment. "Even if I could settle for your offer, I can't live with you. The courts will never go for that."

Gray eased off his elbow onto a pillow. His chest rose and fell deeply, twice. "Okay. Good point." Another deep breath later he continued, "So let's do it."

"Do what?"

"Get…you know." He shrugged. "Let's do it."

Lori sat up, scooting as far away from him and temptation as she could without falling off the bed. "Geez, Gray! You can't even say the word and you expect me to marry you? What about love? You know, some women expect that when a guy proposes. Silly me, I happen to be one of them."

Even though he didn't answer, Lori decided to take the biggest risk of her life. Relinquishing control didn't come easily for her, but she couldn't spend the rest of her life wondering what would have happened if she'd tried. She placed her hand on his heart as she offered him hers. "I love you, Gray. But I need for you to love me, too, or it will never work."

He blinked. Nothing more. *The jerk simply blinked.*

Lori yanked the covers off him. "Get out."

"No." He whipped the blanket off her and threw it on the floor. "I'm not going until we talk about this."

The stubborn look in his eyes told her well enough he wasn't budging his gorgeous butt from her bed until he got his way. Never in a million years would she have imagined she would run away from marrying Gray.

Lori swung her feet to the floor. She yanked her clothes on with vicious tugs before whipping her hair into a simple ponytail. "Fine, I'll go. I'm already late picking up Magda."

"Wait." Gray left the bed, stepping over the comforter pooled in the middle of the floor. "Give me three minutes to get dressed and I'll go with you."

"You're not invited." She spun for the door.

He grabbed her arm. "Okay, Lori. You want to hear the words? Fine. I have feelings for you. Feelings for you that won't turn me loose. And believe me I've tried." He drew in another one of those deep breaths as if bracing for combat. "I guess maybe you call that love."

She jerked her arm free. Did he have to trample all her dreams? Why not bomb her Barbie house while he was at it? Pain made her lash out. "Oh, wow! You're on a roll tonight, Major." She hitched her hand on her hip in her best aviator stud stance. "'Let's get…you know,' followed by 'I guess maybe I love you.'"

"Lori, damn it, will you just listen?"

Her hands slid off her hips, her anger sliding away, as well, to be replaced by a bittersweet ache. "You just don't get it, do you Gray? This is forever we're talking about. Everything. No guesses or maybes or temporary live-ins. You have to be sure."

At least he didn't blink this time, just stared back at her with solemn eyes. She had to hand it to him. For a man who made a habit of managing life with his charm and a smile, he was laying it on the line for her. His offering touched her, even tempted her, but it would never be enough to satisfy the longing in her heart.

Lori kissed him gently, then ducked out the door into

the hall, a much safer place to be than in the same room with naked Gray and his "maybe love."

She made it all the way to the front door before he caught her. She would have likely made it outside if she hadn't paused to grab her purse hanging off the coat tree. But a woman needed her keys, right? It wasn't that she was delaying to give him a chance to catch her.

And then he was there. Beside her. Naked and unrelenting. His hand fell to rest against the door.

"I'm leaving, Gray."

"Go ahead." His hand, pressed against the solid oak, defied her threat. He could keep her trapped inside, and they both knew it.

She'd run a year ago fully expecting him to follow, had even known she would likely cave to his conditional offerings in the end. But the past weeks had changed her, and she couldn't settle for less than all of him this time. She'd flat-out exhausted her ideas on how to win his unconditional love.

She couldn't spend the rest of her life cringing every time that caged look crept back into his eyes. Her love for him deserved a better end than that. She tried to tell herself remembering Grayson gloriously nude and smelling of peaches wasn't too shabby a swan song for their relationship.

"Let me go." Her eyes stung in spite of her best effort to make a dignified exit. "Please, Gray, just let me go."

He brushed away her tear and caressed it between two fingers.

His hand dropped from the door.

She stole one last look at him as he towered over her, moving neither toward or away. The message in his eyes was clear. *Stay.*

And the choice was hers. No choice really. "Please don't be here when I get back."

The door snapped shut behind her.

Gray stood in her entryway, the echo of the door mingling in his mind with a single word.

Stay.

Had he said it aloud? He'd meant to. The fact that he couldn't even speak the word said enough about why Lori needed to walk away.

His every instinct screamed, *Bail out! Bail out! Bail out!*

She didn't want him. He'd even offered her the ring she expected, and still she'd walked. He'd given her all he could. Just like when he'd been growing up trying to piece his family back together, it wasn't enough.

They should be in the car together on their way to pick up Magda. Instead he stood bare-butt naked, smelling like some fruit farm.

Gray padded down the hall back to Lori's room, kicked aside the comforter and scooped up his clothes. What did he intend to do about the mess he'd made of their lives? Inaction wasn't even an option for him.

The way he saw it, he had two choices. Leave for Washington now. Tear up that house listing. Forget about her once and for all so she could find the love she needed.

That answer soured in his mouth.

Or he could track down Lori. He could fall on his sword and beg her to accept whatever he could give her. Even though he knew he would eventually break her beautiful heart.

Neither answer offered him much hope.

The next day Gray strode across the parking lot at his parents' condo. He wasn't sure what had drawn him there. He scratched his chest, freeing a fresh drift of peaches two showers hadn't been able to wash away. His room on base had been damned quiet, giving him too much time to think and offering up not even a single answer.

Nearing the front door, he saw his mom's car wasn't in its spot.

His father's car was parked in clear sight.

Gray turned to leave…then remembered all the nights his dad had taught him about the stars. Gray's feet slowed as he thought of his night with Lori under those same stars. For the first time in too long, he'd enjoyed the memories of learning to navigate from his dad—without the bitter sting that followed.

He pivoted on his heel. He might as well stop in and say hi before he left. Things couldn't get much worse.

After three unanswered rings, Gray swept around to the back of the condo. He almost gave up, deciding his dad must be off on a walk, when he happened to look through the mesh webbing on the screened-in porch.

He found his father, sitting, staring out over the water. Gray loped up the three steps and shoved open the screen door. "Hey, old man."

His father straightened. "Hi, son. I thought you left for Washington."

"I did." Gray sprawled in the porch swing. "I came back to tie up business here."

"Something to do with Lori?"

Regret stabbed him, followed by a blanketing sense of failure. Damn it, he'd met his every goal in life. Except one. Lori. "That's over, Dad."

His father nodded slowly, his gaze staying fixed on the water. "Hmm."

A grunt from his dad. The usual response.

Gray hooked his arms along the back of the swing. His dad's chattiness at the family picnic must have been a fluke, or maybe he'd made an extra effort because Lori had been there. Whatever the reason, Gray was disappointed—for his mother's sake.

The older man folded his hands over his barrel chest. "I've been seeing this doctor out at the VA Hospital."

Slowing the swing, Gray recalled all the times his mother had asked him to visit recently. Had she needed his professional advice, and he'd blown her off, too preoccupied by the mess he'd made with Lori? Guilt was becoming a familiar companion these days. "Have you been sick?"

"Not the way you mean. Not that kind of doctor."

Gray planted both feet on the ground and stopped the swing. After all these years, his father was finally seeking help? Hell, acknowledging there was even a problem? Gray scrambled for something to say and came up dry. Instead he waited, opting to take his cue from his dad.

His father scratched a hand along his salt-and-pepper hair, still trimmed to military regulation even ten years after retirement. "We've been talking about those days in the camp. Getting some things straight in my head. If it were up to me, I'd just let it all lie. But your mother needs this. So I go. Sometimes we go together."

Those were more words than his father had strung together in as long as Gray could remember. The talkative bent at the family party hadn't been a fluke. "That's good, Dad. Real good."

"So your mother says. And I have to admit...it helps." He stared out over the water, silent for one of those long stretches habitual since his POW days. Without looking away, he cleared his throat. "Back in 'Nam, there was this box they put us in."

Gray winced at the conversational leap, his mind catching up even though his stomach still lurched as if he'd pitched off the swing.

His father's brows knit together. "In some ways the box was good, because they left you alone as long as you were in there. Then it got hot. And you needed some distraction. I came home in my mind."

Gray tried to relax his fists. He knew all about the box, a crate about the size of a dog carrier, but without a window.

His time in survival training had included a stint in a mock POW camp. How many days he'd spent there, he'd never known. He'd had no watch, and most of the time was spent with loudspeakers blaring away any hope of sleep. He'd been marched through a hellish regimen meant to prepare flyers for possible capture.

Definitely hell, and he'd had the reassurance that he would be leaving soon. Hours spent in the box had given him too much time to think about what his father had been through, a torture beyond any the instructors could have doled out.

Gray studied his father. What could he say, though, *Hey, Dad, I pulled a weekend stint in one of those, so I understand your pain?* He let his father talk.

"When I came home in my head, you and I sat out under that tree, and I taught you about the stars. Sometimes we pitched a ball around." His eyes fogged with a distant look, as if seeing long-ago days. "Other times I told you things you needed to know, things a father should tell his son. I may have been in that box, but I couldn't stop being your dad."

The words slammed on top of so many memories of waiting for his father to come home, the years after when he'd felt he lost his dad altogether. How strange to get his old man back right before a move cross country. "Dad, it means a—"

His father held up a hand. "Funny thing was, once I got home, I didn't do all those things with you like I'd planned. I was still stuck in that box, more so than when I was back over there." He turned to face Gray. "Son, you've put yourself in a box."

"What?" When had this become about him? Not three seconds ago they were discussing his father.

"Just because you're in that box doesn't mean you can stop loving Lori and that little girl."

Their eyes met and Gray looked, really looked, and found his father for the first time in nearly thirty years. His eyes were clear, sharp. Familiar. And too wise.

His father blinked, shifted away, scrubbing a hand along his bristly face, a five-o'clock shadow speckling even at ten in the morning. He cleared his throat, the gruff old man back in place. "A couple of sessions and I'm turning into some damn Sigmund Freud." He stood and stretched as if they'd done no more than pass a leisurely chat about ball scores. "Time for my afternoon walk. Been good talking to you, son."

His father lumbered down the steps, retracing his regular path along the water.

Gray's gaze slid away and down to his hands clasped loosely between his knees. He'd faced combat, flown countless missions in hazardous conditions without a qualm, yet his hands trembled at thoughts of commitment. Not some live-in offer or pathetic proposal no woman worth her salt would accept. But a real commitment.

Could his old man have been right? Had Gray put himself in a box? Lori couldn't reject his love if he never offered it. She couldn't turn away from him as his father had done.

His father had been one hundred percent correct.

Churning his father's words around in his mind, Gray welcomed a flash of gratitude toward his dad after so many years of bitterness. Too often Gray had only seen the tension between them from his mother's side.

Today he'd stood with his father, as parent and child, as a fellow serviceman.

Now it was time to stand with Lori. No more running.

Denying he loved Lori didn't make it any less real. And he'd let her slip away again.

Gray yanked his cell phone from his back pocket and punched in Lori's number. He wouldn't actually propose over the phone, but he could start the wheels rolling with an apology, followed by—

"Hello," a voice that definitely wasn't Lori answered.

Had he dialed the wrong number? "Hello?"

"Gray? Hi. This is Julia."

"Julia?" Damn, he felt like a parrot. "Could I speak to Lori?"

"She's not here. I'm baby-sitting Magda."

Gray stifled a useless punch of disappointment. He would see her soon. He wasn't letting her get away this time. "Where is she?"

The phone crackled in the silence.

"Julia?"

"She's up at the courthouse. Today's the hearing date for Magda's custody."

"Oh, well I'm sure she'll be glad to have the official paperwork all tied up."

"Didn't she tell you? The couple that backed out on taking Magda changed their mind. They want her."

A roar of denial echoed in Gray's brain. He couldn't have heard right. Lori was Magda's mother. How dare anyone threaten that?

"Listen, Gray, I've got to go. Magda's trying to pour her own juice. I'll have Lori call you. Okay? Bye."

The humming phone weighed in his hand like a brick of guilt. His family needed him, and he wasn't there for them. He and Lori may not have said formal vows, but that woman was still his wife, the only woman he'd ever loved. Lori might not be pregnant with his baby, but she still carried his daughter in her arms.

Sharing a last name didn't make a family. Seeing Lori and Magda together should have taught him that. In his heart, Lori and Magda were already his family. He just needed to wage the fight of his life to win them back.

Battle mind-set in place as surely as if he'd slipped on his combat gear, Gray punched in another phone number.

Time to call in the reinforcements.

Chapter 17

Lori sat in the courtroom and prayed. Hard. She stared at the scales of justice behind the judge's bench and prayed the balance would tip her way. Lori swiped her sweaty palms along her linen skirt—again.

She'd presented her case, offered references, cited her training and psychologist's reports, but it still might not be enough. She lacked the one thing that the other petitioner for custody didn't.

A spouse.

And just her luck, she'd drawn Judge Tradd, a hard-liner, hotshot young judge, infamous for her decisions in favor of more traditional placements. Lori could only hope her countersuit petition to adopt would relay her serious intent to be a mother to Magda. Forever.

Lori's head throbbed. Crying her eyes out all night over losing Gray, possibly losing Magda as well, hadn't helped.

The husband and wife in turn droned on in their rebuttal about their Barbie dollhouse perfect world, complete with a little brother or sister on the way. Lori wanted to grab the guy by his Ralph Lauren tie and shake him until his shiny, capped teeth rattled.

Where had they been when Magda had needed them weeks ago? They hadn't been putting stickers on a Big Wheel. No bandanna waited in that man's pocket for a shorn little head. The woman hadn't held that same tiny head and bathed Magda's brow while she'd been sick.

But in the eyes of the court they were a real family. And Lori wasn't.

Should she have accepted Gray's offer, for Magda's sake? Lori shoved aside the absurd notion. Magda deserved the best home life, not parents in a sham marriage destined to fail.

Lori had always prided herself on managing. She could handle anything. Except this. She needed help, yet had set up her life with very little in the way of a personal support system. Through her friendship with Julia, she felt she'd made a step in the right direction, but it could be too little too late for Magda.

Please, God. She hoped Magda wouldn't pay the price for someone else's mistakes. Lori started praying again as the judge listened to final arguments from the attorneys.

Why didn't some guard or bailiff quiet those people in the hall? The paneled walls bounced every grating noise Lori's way.

Commotion from the hall swelled, like the throbbing in her head, increased like the frown on the judge's face. Lori shot a look over her shoulder just as the door cracked open enough for the bailiff to poke his head in.

"Judge, we've got a situation out here."

Judge Tradd waved her hands, robes fluttering like bat wings. "Then handle it."

"Well, Judge, I'd like to, but they're mighty insistent. This guy says—"

The door swung wide. The bailiff pivoted as if to stop another adult. Instead, a child shot past. Julia knelt, shooing the squealing girl forward. "Run, Magda. Go to Mama, baby."

Lori rose from her wooden chair ready to catch Magda sprinting down the center aisle full-tilt.

"Yori!" Magda tripped over her trailing shoe lace and fell into Lori's arms.

Worry pushed through her headache. Something must be wrong for Julia to have let Magda sneak past in violation of the law. Lori gathered up Magda, inhaling the precious scent of baby shampoo, and stood. She paused halfway.

Silhouetted in the doorway stood Gray.

Sounds dwindled around her—the dim din of protest from the other attorney, gasps from the couple, a call for order from the judge. Lori ignored it all as she finished rising, staring at the man filling the door and her heart.

Gray.

Not just her regular heart-stopping Gray in a flight suit. He wore his service dress blues. Silver wings with a star gleamed above ribbons stacked down the left side of his jacket. Wheel cap tucked under his arm, Gray strode into the courtroom.

And he wasn't alone. Filing behind him with military precision trailed Bronco, Lance and Julia, the squadron commander, Tag and his family.

Gray's parents.

They all slid into the rows behind Lori, like a wall of support, with Gray standing citadel beside them in the aisle. Lori pulled Magda closer and reminded herself to breathe.

Judge Tradd raised a silencing hand. "I assume you have a reason for breaking more than a few laws designed to protect the integrity of my court."

"Yes, Your Honor. May I approach the bench?"

The judge fingered her gavel. "This is highly irregular, but proceed."

Gray strode to the swinging bar and pushed through, the gleaming wood swishing shut behind him. He shot a quick glance Lori's way, along with a reassuring flash of his heart-stopping smile, before he turned his attention to the judge. "We're here to offer family support for Lori."

Lori tucked Magda under her chin and struggled not to bawl like a baby, not a very dignified impression to make on the judge. But Gray's coming overwhelmed her. He'd gathered all these people, these friends, for her. Even after she'd thrown his proposal back in his face and left him, again, he'd done this beautiful thing. He'd brought the family she'd always wanted.

The judge nudged aside her gavel. "I thought Ms. Rutledge didn't have any family other than parents who reside primarily overseas."

Lori winced. Apparently, that had been yet another blot against her, but suddenly, miraculously, she didn't have to face it all alone. Gratitude choked her. Gray was here for her, pleading her case, battling for her. Lori had made it her mission in life to fight for others. No one had ever fought for her.

Until Gray. Towering, blindingly handsome Gray, and she couldn't soak up his words fast enough.

"Blood relatives, yes. But with all due respect, Your Honor, isn't this whole hearing about building a family where there isn't a biological connection?"

"Yes, of course."

"Then we're here as Lori's family as well as friends."

"And you are?"

"Major Grayson Clark, United States Air Force. I'm a friend of Lori's. I was also the chief flight surgeon on the mission that evacuated the orphans from Sentavo."

The couple's attorney began to stand, but Judge Tradd waved him down before he could speak. "Overruled. My interest is piqued. Irregular though it may be, I feel it's in the best interest of the child for me to ask a few questions." She turned back to order Gray to take the stand and be sworn in, before she continued, "So you've spent time with Ms. Rutledge and Magda."

"Yes, Your Honor, we all have. We've been to picnics, to family gatherings, in her home. We've all watched Lori and Magda together."

"What makes Ms. Rutledge the better choice than this couple?"

"I was with Lori when Magda was airlifted out of Sentavo. You wouldn't have recognized Magda then with her ragged dress, thin arms, and big frightened eyes. Lori picked her up and held her just like any mother gathering up a kid of her own. It would be a crime to separate them now. Magda lost one mother. Don't take another from her."

"I understand her mother died well over a year ago. What makes you think she remembers?"

"She told me."

"But she doesn't speak English."

Gray looked away for a scant second, before he braced his shoulders into a military stance again. "She showed me while we were, uh, playing with her Barbies."

A muffled laugh sounded behind Lori, and she turned to find Bronco coughing through his grin. The crowd radiated support with smiles and nods to bolster Lori. They really had come for her as well as Gray. Securing her hold around Magda, Lori twisted back to listen to the judge.

"So while you were role playing with Barbies she…did what?"

"Acted out her parents' death. Most likely it was in a bombing air raid."

Magda squirmed, and Lori jostled, whispering, "Shhhh, settle down sweetie. Just hang on."

Magda lurched forward, straining from Lori's arms over the rail. "Doc! Doc!"

With a total lack of regard for procedure, Gray shot from the witness stand, his cap thudding to the floor. He charged forward, hands extended just as Magda pitched into his arms.

Gray's gaze collided with Lori's over Magda's head—met, held, comforted. One bottle-green eye winked, before Gray hitched Magda on his hip and turned to face the judge without returning to the stand.

The judge fingered her brass-tipped gavel as her gaze homed in on Gray and Magda. "What exactly is your relationship with Magda that you've spent so much time with her since the airlift operation?"

"I love her." He smoothed a hand over her cap of tousled curls, the small child cradled to his uniformed chest. "Just as much as I love Lori, her mother."

Lori grabbed the edge of the table. He couldn't have said what she thought, and if he did, had he meant it? Or was this just another attempt to help her win Magda, give her a child?

Either way, the beauty of his words blossomed into a joy and hope within her far more beautiful than any bed of pansies.

"Ms. Rutledge didn't mention a fiancé."

"That's because I haven't been smart enough to figure out how to get this incredible woman to take me on permanently." He hitched Magda higher on his hip and began swaying from side to side, like any parent calming a restless child. Quilted watermelons along Magda's jumper offered a tender contrast to Gray's military crispness. "But let me make it clear, whether she marries me or not, ever, Lori is still the best mother Magda could have. Lori knows more about building a family than anyone. Believe me, Your Honor, there's nothing this woman can't handle. And no one will ever love that little girl as much as she does."

"Well, Major Clark, or is it Dr. Clark?"

"Either will do."

"Major Clark, your testimony has been enlightening, if a bit unorthodox." The judge turned to Lori. "Ms. Rutledge, I'm not going to ask you to respond to his rather unique proposal. Your bid for custody is that of a single parent. It would be unfair to either of you, and especially this child, to exert undue pressure on your decision on how to respond."

"Yes, Your Honor." Lucky for her, since Lori wasn't sure she could push words through her closing throat.

The judge nodded to Lori's attorney. "Any questions for Major Clark?"

Barbara dropped her pencil on her legal pad. "I think he covered everything quite well on his own, Your Honor."

Judge Tradd quirked a brow at the couple's attorney. "Cross-examination?"

With a poorly disguised wince, the attorney replied, "No questions. As Ms. Rutledge is a single parent, we find his testimony irrelevant."

"So noted." The judge shoved aside a folder of papers. "I believe I have enough evidence before me to render a decision. I'm prepared to rule from the bench." The judge shuffled aside a sheaf of papers before closing a folder. "The basis of the law requires that I rule in the best interest of the child, not in the interest of those contesting custody or adoption. I hereby assign said minor to the foster care of Lori Rutledge with adoption proceedings pending." She rapped her gavel. "Court is adjourned."

Before Lori could clear her throat or her thoughts, the crowd engulfed her. Friends and family, they surrounded her with support, words of encouragement.

And love.

She wasn't going to lose Magda, and she had these wonderful people to thank. Gray and his—their—friends had given her more than any family ever had. She'd been so fixated on a silly little dream house she'd almost missed the real thing. A family wasn't about the house or the place. It was about the people.

One person in particular.

Lori surged forward. "Gray—"

"No. Lori, stop." He passed Magda back to her, their eyes locking over the girl's whispery curls. "Don't say anything now. Not while you're feeling grateful or riding some emotional wave. We'll talk later." Gray shot a pointed look over his shoulder at Bronco, who was leaning not too subtly toward them. "And without an audience."

Lori stared into Gray's eyes as she gathered Magda close, hoping he'd meant what he'd said earlier. She needed him, and that was a strange feeling for a woman who'd prided herself on managing anything life threw her way.

More than anything, she needed for his words to have been real.

Gray stood on the balcony outside Magda's room, stars winking encouragement overhead. A night breeze stirred the muggy humidity, yet offered little relief for the sweat beading his brow.

Slowly he unfastened his service coat. His gaze traveled the length of the balcony, past Magda's room, then to Lori's further down…

He jerked his eyes and his thoughts right back. Talk first. Hopefully making love after. But no way would he let them fall into their old trap of using sex to avoid difficult conversations.

Lori's voice drifted from Magda's room through the open French doors as she tucked her daughter into bed for the night.

Her daughter. Gray smiled.

Even if Judge Tradd had decided in favor of the fickle-minded couple, Gray had no doubts that Lori could have won Magda in the long run once she'd had a chance to gather more testimony. But now she didn't have to.

Magda's caseworker had told them later the judge had admitted to being swayed by Gray's grandstanding. His hurried calls and a quick change into his uniform had helped. And helping Lori felt damned good.

Except she didn't need him anymore, not really. Lori rarely needed anyone.

But did she still *want* him in her life?

He wanted her in his, with a fierceness that made the past year's frustration seem like a cake walk. He rehearsed his proposal for the fiftieth time, swiping away the perspiration on his brow. He shrugged out of his uniform coat, the silver wings glinting in the overhead light.

Gray ran his fingers over the ribbons, then up to his wings. He'd flown a lot of hours and worked hard for that star over them. Damned hard. He'd once thought those pilot wings meant everything to him.

Now he knew better.

His world was in the room beside him. Lori and Magda. If he had to give up those wings to keep them, then he would do it. Nothing was worth risking losing them again.

So easily he could envision a lifetime of nights like this. Except he would be reading the bedtime story with Lori, singing Magda a song.

Gray draped his jacket over the balcony railing, smoothing out the wrinkles with one slow sweep, then pivoted to face his future.

Lori stood framed in the French doors, one silky shirttail hanging loose from her skirt. Sticky, chocolate fingerprints dotted her shoulder. Wisps of hair escaped her braid, caressing her face.

Mussed, maternal, and so unbelievably beautiful she stole his breath. He knew without question, she always would.

Lori stared at Gray, the porch light cascading down his coal-black hair, glimmering in his bottle green eyes. Eyes that met hers with resolution, determination and—dare she hope—love.

She pulled Magda's doors closed behind her and joined

him by the wooden rail. An ocean breeze ruffled the muggy air along with his close-shorn hair. He tugged his tie free, smoothing it over his jacket before he loosened the top two buttons on his shirt. "Mind if we sit?"

"Sounds great. It's been a long day."

He ignored the rocker and lowered himself to the planked floor. His leather shoes squeaked as he sat with his back against the house. He opened his arms to her and waited. "Please."

Slowly Lori sat between his knees, the warmth of the boards nothing in comparison to the heat of Gray's thighs on either side of her. Sitting straight and stiff in his arms seemed ridiculous after all they'd shared.

After all he'd said.

She relaxed against his chest, his starched shirt rasping against her silk. Had he meant it in the courtroom? A last fragment of insecurity whispered, trying to shake her with doubts that he'd only spoken to help her keep Magda.

This was about so much more than Magda.

He raised his arm beside Lori's face and pointed, the scent of dry cleaner starch oddly arousing. "That grouping of stars there. Cassiopeia. They always rise in the east, set in the west, without fail anywhere in the Northern Hemisphere. No matter what porch we sit on, we'll be able to see them."

"We?" She held herself still, didn't dare turn.

He answered without hesitation. "You, me, Magda...any other kids we add to the mix."

Wary expectancy tingled over her. He'd mentioned marriage before, and again in the courtroom when she'd been in danger of losing Magda.

This was different. Real, somehow. "Is that a proposal?"

His chuckle rumbled in her ear, against her back. "Still not quite there, am I, hon?"

"You're getting closer."

He turned her sideways. Streetlamps and the moon cast

mellow beams across his face as he stared down into her eyes. "Close isn't good enough. It has to be right. You said so yourself, and you're the smartest woman I've ever met."

If she'd been smarter, she could have saved them both so much heartache by figuring it out the first go-round. But then they never would have met Magda, the precious child who had brought them back together.

"Please come with me. I know your job's important, so I checked. There's a northwest branch of the NGO in Tacoma." He cradled Lori to his chest. "I can't do anything about the Air Force right now. I owe them—"

"Gray, I understand—"

"No." He gave her a gentle squeeze. "Listen. I owe them four more years for financing part of med school." His chest rose and fell deeply behind her. "But when my time's up, if this isn't working for you, I'll get out."

Lori twisted to see him, hope blossoming into full bloom. "You would do that? For me?"

She would do that for him, but hadn't expected he would do the same for her.

He answered without hesitation. "Yes. You mean more to me than anything else. I can't lose you again."

Peace settled within her as she leaned back against the man who'd given her the only thing she'd ever truly wanted. His whole heart. Of course she couldn't let him give up the military, but she'd needed to hear his willingness to do it for her all the same.

"Thank you, Gray, but I could never ask you to do that." She heard herself echoing Angela's words, finally understanding a depth of love she'd never felt before. "It's too much a part of who you are. A man I love so very much."

He clasped her braid, wrapped its length around his arm and cupped her head close to his thudding heart. "Thank you. But know the offer stands."

Lori nodded against his chest, savoring a whiff of bay rum and the scratch of starch against her cheek. She'd tried so hard to make things work between them. Finally she realized what she had to do to earn Gray's love.

Nothing.

It was already hers, but she'd been too blinded by insecurities to see it. Love wasn't like a house or piece of land to be bought, but had to be freely given—and received.

She'd wanted Gray to fit her cookie-cutter image of what a husband should be, down to dictating the way he should propose, and hadn't recognized the gift of his unique love.

Something she intended to change.

Lori relaxed into the warm security of his chest, her head nestled under his chin. "Marry me."

The muscles cording his chest contracted against her. "What?"

They had never held back with words before, and she didn't intend to start now. "Will you marry me?"

"Wait!" He gripped her shoulders, turning her to face him. "I'm supposed to say that. I've been practicing all day."

"You have?"

A slow smile spread over his face, stirring a shiver so like the first time he'd cast his best bad-boy grin her way.

"Oh, yeah, hon, because I am not going to mess it up again." He shoved to his feet, his arm extended for her.

Lori laced her fingers with his and stood. "Okay, flyboy, give it your best shot."

Their hands clasped between them, Gray looked into her eyes. "Please be my wife. Let me be Magda's father. Let me give you more babies so we can grow old together and watch their babies grow. Lori, honey, I love you like crazy and if you don't answer soon I'm gonna die here. What do you say?"

Late-night shadows couldn't hide the determined thrust of his jaw or the ring of resolution in his voice. He wasn't going to leave her if she didn't plant perfect pansies.

Her stubborn man had decided what he wanted, and he

wanted her. Forever. And she looked forward to every single day. "Where are those stars again?"

He draped an arm over her shoulder to point, his breath playing through her hair. "Right there. Cassiopeia. Just to the left of the moon."

"And we'll see those same stars in Washington?"

"We?"

She allowed her fingers the pleasure of caressing his bristly jaw, a delight and right that would be hers for the rest of her life. "Yes."

"Yes? Yes, what?"

"Yes, I'll go to Washington with you. Yes, I'll marry you and give you all the babies you want. And yes, we'll be Magda's parents. Grow old together. All of it." She arched onto her toes, breathed her answer across his mouth. "Yes."

He took her answer and her lips in the same possessive sweep, giving, receiving, loving her. Her arms looped around his neck, surely the safest place to be as her limbs hummed with the musicality of his kiss. No doubt the man was a stylist with that mouth of his.

Gray scooped her into his arms, kissing her as he walked the length of the balcony to the porch doors leading to Lori's room.

Tossing him her best wicked smile, she twisted the doorknob. "Wanna play wounded Allied pilot and saucy French nurse? I'll let you be the pilot this time."

Gray nudged Lori's bedroom door open with his foot, his beautiful smile free of shadows, full of constancy and playful promise. "And I'll show you how to see those stars with your eyes closed."

Epilogue

"I can't believe you talked me into this!" Lori puffed through the next contraction. "I'm never going stargazing with you again!"

"Push, Lori! Push!" Gray straddled the chair at the foot of the birthing bed, hands poised and ready to guide their child into the world. He wasn't Lori's OB, but the presiding doctor stood by the IV. Nerve-wracking as hell, incredible beyond belief, Gray wouldn't have it any other way. He had "caught" their other two babies, a miracle he would repeat in seconds. "Just one more push and we'll have our baby."

"We? *We?*" Lori barked between puffing breaths. "I don't see *us* birthing a Buick!"

"Just hang on, hon. You're doing great. The baby's crowned and ready. One more minute and *you'll* be done." Gray gave himself a mental thunk on the head for letting the *we* reference slip. Hadn't he learned anything from her first two deliveries? But worrying about Lori battered his defenses more than a little.

God, she was a trooper. This labor had been short but intense. She'd sworn like a crew dog during transition, and she looked ready to fling a few more curses his way.

Then she deflated back on the pillow with the end of her contraction, exhaustion stamped along the gentle curves of her face. "I wanna stop for a while." Lori gripped a nurse's hand while turning pleading eyes on Gray. "Can't we go home and finish tomorrow? I've already done this twice. Isn't it your turn yet, flyboy?"

"Next go-round, I'll see what I can do." Gray eyed the fetal monitor. Good strong heartbeat for the baby. The other line monitoring contractions inched upward, already predicting an end to Lori's brief respite. "Break's over, hon. A ten count and you're done. Come on. Bear down. One. Two. Three. Four. Good job. Almost there. Five. Six. Seven—"

He palmed the head, a rush of love already firing up his arm. Thank heaven for professional instincts. "Hold on while I turn the shoulders…"

The baby shot forward, already wailing, into Gray's waiting hands and straight into his heart. "It's a boy! We have another little boy, and oh, God, Lori, he's wrinkled, red, and scrunched but so damned perfect."

The tiny, damp body squirmed in Gray's hands and in some distant part of his mind he knew he should be evaluating. But he simply stared mesmerized until his vision blurred.

"Gray?"

His wife's voice broke through, freed a blink and a tear that Gray shrugged his shoulder to swipe away. "Yeah, hon?"

"I want to see him. Hold him."

Her whiskey warm voice drifted over Gray. Six years of marriage hadn't diluted the potency at all, merely aged and enhanced.

"You bet. Just a minute and we'll have him cleaned up

for Mama.'' Gray made quick work of the umbilical cord and traded places with Lori's OB while the pediatrician checked and wrapped the newborn.

Wisps of hair escaped Lori's braid, caressing her damp brow. Purplish stains of weariness smudged beneath her eyes.

And she'd never been more beautiful.

Their four years in Washington had passed in a flurry of change, love, the occasional argument and more love. He still enjoyed the hell out of making-up sex.

Lori had taken a year off from work to play with Magda and teach her English. After Travis was born, Lori had cut back to half days and consulting, eventually adding John Grayson to their growing family.

The transition to military life hadn't been wrinkle free for Lori, but they'd worked together, talked, compromised and loved. His boots no longer restless, Gray welcomed the return assignment to Charleston Air Force Base to serve as Chief of Flight Medicine.

He'd missed his parents and was glad to have them close again. They spoiled their grandchildren shamelessly—giving Gray and Lori the occasional evening to themselves.

He lifted his son from the warmer, the baby now swaddled, the head of dark hair covered with a tiny cap. Gray passed their infant son to Lori as he'd done twice before with their boys and once with their daughter, Magda, who'd come to them older but every ounce as special. ''Here's your mama, little guy.''

Lori reached, happy tears already streaking her face. Cradling him in her arms, she opened the blanket to count fingers and toes. ''Oh, Gray, he's beautiful.''

''Yeah, pretty incredible.'' He stared straight at his wife. ''I love you.''

How easily the words flowed these days.

''I love you, too.''

Lori tugged Gray down by the front of his scrubs for a

kiss. Their lips met with a tenderness as powerful as passion. The baby squawked between them, and they pulled apart, laughing.

Gray sat on the edge of the bed, tucked Lori into the crook of his arm and admired all eight pounds three ounces of their latest son, a son they'd conceived on a midnight walk nine months ago. "Any thoughts yet on a name? Mom's got that charm on hold at the jewelers."

A mischievous smile played with Lori's full lips, stirring an urge in Gray he wouldn't be able to fulfill for six more weeks.

"How about Ryan? To commemorate our most recent night beneath Orion's belt?"

A smile of his own broke free along with a chuckle. "Ryan. I like it." He stroked a knuckle along his new son's baby-soft cheek. "Ryan Davis it is."

They sat wrapped in each other's arms and the moment, until Gray realized the room had been cleared and the doctor leaned against the wall flipping through a chart. A nurse poked her head in the door, "Colonel Clark, are you ready for the rest of your family?"

Family. What an awesome word. "Sure. Send them in."

The nurse stepped away, and Magda, Maggie as she now preferred, stood in the door with a brother on either side. His parents hovered in the doorway, giving the children time to meet their new brother.

Maggie's hair, longer these days, was gathered in a ponytail trailing over her shoulder like her mother. Barbies a thing of the past, Maggie now focused on basketball and boys.

She plowed forward, dragging her little brothers along. "Wow! Mom, he's so cool! He looks like Travis, don'cha think, Dad?"

"Hey!" Travis furrowed a serious little brow just like his mama's. "I don't got a funny face or a pointy head."

"Pwetty baby!" John Grayson catapulted forward, Gray

catching his middle son before he tripped over his shoelaces. This one kept them on their toes, all motion, smiles and a song on his lips before he spoke his first words.

Gray reached to pull Maggie into the circle, the child who'd brought them all together, and waved his parents in. Sometimes he thought life just couldn't get any better. And then, the next day, he found out it most certainly could.

Lori's honey-warm eyes met his as their family gathered around them, and he couldn't believe he'd ever doubted.

She gave a contented-mother's sigh. "You know that bit about never stargazing again?"

Gray gave her his best bad-boy grin. "You didn't mean a word of it."

Lori laughed that great husky laugh that still rolled right into him, dive bombing his senses.

"Not for a minute, flyboy!"

* * * * *

The Wingmen Warriors *series will continue.*
Don't miss Bronco's story,

TAKING COVER,

coming in November from
Silhouette Intimate Moments.

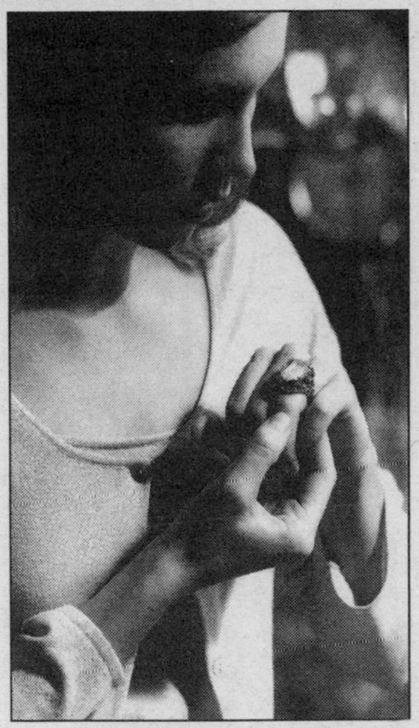

Coming from
Silhouette Books
in September 2002

All she wanted was
to turn back time....

Suddenly she could!

The Way to Yesterday

by

SHARON SALA

(Silhouette Intimate
Moments #1171)

Unbelievably, Mary Ellen O'Rourke's deepest wish had come true—her wonderful husband and beautiful baby girl were alive and well. Now, if only she could keep them that way....

But maybe she could. Because a strange encounter with an unusual ring had brought back the husband and child Mary Ellen had despaired of ever seeing again. Was this a dream? She didn't care. For she'd spent six years praying for a second chance—and she wasn't going to waste a single second of it!

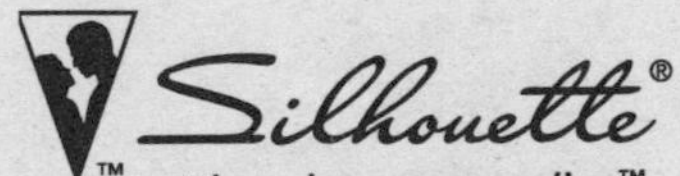

Visit Silhouette at www.eHarlequin.com SIMTWTY

JAYNE ANN KRENTZ

Sizzling attraction, strong heroes and sparkling relationships are hallmarks of *New York Times* bestselling author Jayne Ann Krentz, writing as Stephanie James!

Here are two of her classic novels

THE CHALLONER BRIDE

&

WIZARD

available in one terrific package.

Don't worry—it's well

Worth the Risk

Silhouette®

Where love comes alive™

Available in stores
September 2002

Visit Silhouette at www.eHarlequin.com

PSWTR

If you enjoyed what you just read, then we've got an offer you can't resist!

Take 2 bestselling love stories FREE!

Plus get a FREE surprise gift!

Clip this page and mail it to Silhouette Reader Service™

IN U.S.A.
3010 Walden Ave.
P.O. Box 1867
Buffalo, N.Y. 14240-1867

IN CANADA
P.O. Box 609
Fort Erie, Ontario
L2A 5X3

YES! Please send me 2 free Silhouette Intimate Moments® novels and my free surprise gift. After receiving them, if I don't wish to receive anymore, I can return the shipping statement marked cancel. If I don't cancel, I will receive 6 brand-new novels every month, before they're available in stores! In the U.S.A., bill me at the bargain price of $3.99 plus 25¢ shipping and handling per book and applicable sales tax, if any*. In Canada, bill me at the bargain price of $4.74 plus 25¢ shipping and handling per book and applicable taxes**. That's the complete price and a savings of at least 10% off the cover prices—what a great deal! I understand that accepting the 2 free books and gift places me under no obligation ever to buy any books. I can always return a shipment and cancel at any time. Even if I never buy another book from Silhouette, the 2 free books and gift are mine to keep forever.

245 SDN DNUV
345 SDN DNUW

Name (PLEASE PRINT)

Address Apt.#

City State/Prov. Zip/Postal Code

* Terms and prices subject to change without notice. Sales tax applicable in N.Y.
** Canadian residents will be charged applicable provincial taxes and GST.
All orders subject to approval. Offer limited to one per household and not valid to current Silhouette Intimate Moments® subscribers.
® are registered trademarks of Harlequin Books S.A., used under license.

INMOM02 ©1998 Harlequin Enterprises Limited

THE
COLTONS

invite you to a thrilling holiday wedding in

A Colton Family Christmas

Meet the Oklahoma Coltons—a proud, passionate clan who will risk everything for love and honor. As the two Colton dynasties reunite this Christmas, new romances are sparked by a near-tragic event!

This 3-in-1 holiday collection includes:

"The Diplomat's Daughter" by Judy Christenberry

"Take No Prisoners" by Linda Turner

"Juliet of the Night" by Carolyn Zane

And be sure to watch for **SKY FULL OF PROMISE** by Teresa Southwick this November from Silhouette Romance (#1624), the next installment in the Colton family saga.

Don't miss these unforgettable romances... available at your favorite retail outlet.

Visit Silhouette at www.eHarlequin.com

PSACFC

buy books

♥ We have your favorite books from Harlequin, Silhouette, MIRA and Steeple Hill, plus bestselling authors in Other Romances. Discover savings, find new releases and fall in love with past classics all over again!

online reads

♥ Read daily and weekly chapters from Internet-exclusive serials, and decide what should happen next in great interactive stories!

magazine

♥ Learn how to spice up your love life, play fun games and quizzes, read about celebrities, travel, beauty and so much more.

authors

♥ Select from over 300 author profiles and read interviews with your favorite bestselling authors!

community

♥ Share your passion for love, life and romance novels in our online message boards!

learn to write

♥ All the tips and tools you need to craft the perfect novel, including our special romance novel critique service.

membership

♥ FREE! Be the first to hear about all your favorite themes, authors and series and be part of exciting contests, exclusive promotions, special deals and online events.

Where love comes alive™—online...

Visit us at
www.eHarlequin.com

SINT7CH

Where royalty and romance go hand in hand...

The series finishes in

Silhouette®

Desire®

with these unforgettable love stories:

THE ROYAL TREATMENT
by Maureen Child
October 2002 (SD #1468)

TAMING THE PRINCE
by Elizabeth Bevarly
November 2002 (SD #1474)

ROYALLY PREGNANT
by Barbara McCauley
December 2002 (SD #1480)

Available at your favorite retail outlet.

Silhouette®
Where love comes alive™

Visit Silhouette at www.eHarlequin.com

SDCAG

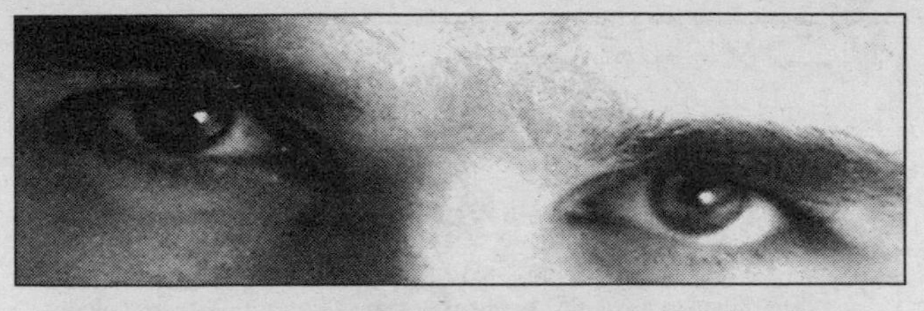

Delight yourself with four special titles from one of America's top ten romance authors...

USA Today **bestselling author**

DIANA PALMER

Four passionate and provocative stories that are Diana Palmer at her best!

Sweet Enemy

Love on Trial

Storm Over the Lake

To Love and Cherish

"Nobody tops Diana Palmer...I love her stories."

—*New York Times* bestselling author Jayne Ann Krentz

Look for these special titles in September 2002.

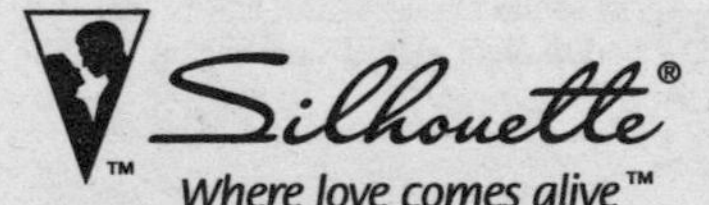

Visit Silhouette at www.eHarlequin.com

RCDP1

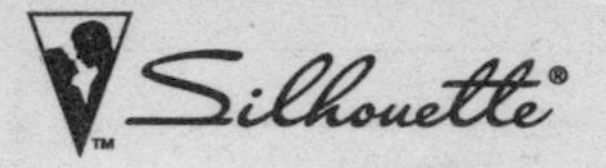

INTIMATE MOMENTS®

COMING NEXT MONTH

#1177 THE PRINCESS'S BODYGUARD—Beverly Barton
The Protectors
Rather than be forced to marry, Princess Adele of Orlantha ran away, determined to prove that her betrothed was a traitor. With her life in danger, she sought the help of Matt O'Brien, the security specialist sent to bring her home. To save her country, Adele proposed a marriage of convenience to Matt—fueled by a very inconvenient attraction….

#1178 SARAH'S KNIGHT—Mary McBride
Romancing the Crown
Sir Dominic Chiara, M.D., couldn't cure his only son, Leo. Without explanation, Leo quit speaking, and child psychologist Sarah Hunter was called to help. Dominic couldn't keep from falling for the spirited beauty, as together they found the root of Leo's problem and learned that he held the key to a royal murder—and their romance.

#1179 CROSSING THE LINE—Candace Irvin
When their chopper went down behind enemy lines, U.S. Army pilot Eve Paris and Special Forces captain Rick Bishop worked together to escape. Their attraction was intense, but back home, their relationship crashed. Then, to save her career, Eve and Rick had to return to the crash site, but would they be able to salvage their love?

#1180 ALL A MAN CAN DO—Virginia Kantra
Trouble in Eden
Straitlaced detective Jarek Denko gave up the rough Chicago streets to be a small-town police chief and make a home for his daughter. Falling for wild reporter Tess DeLucca wasn't part of the plan. But the attraction was immediate—and then a criminal made Tess his next target. Now she and Jarek needed each other more than ever….

#1181 THE COP NEXT DOOR—Jenna Mills
After her father's death, Victoria Blake learned he had changed their identities and fled their original home. Seeking the truth, she traveled to steamy Bon Terre, Louisiana. What she found was sexy sheriff Ian Montague. Victoria wasn't sure what she feared most: losing her life to her father's enemies, or losing her heart to the secretive sheriff.

#1182 HER GALAHAD—Melissa James
When Tessa Earldon married David Oliveri, the love of her life, she knew her family disapproved, but she never imagined they would falsify charges to have him imprisoned. After years of forced separation, Tessa found David again. But before they could start their new life, they had to clear David's name and find the baby they thought they had lost.

SIMCNM0902